LETHBRIDGE STEWART

THE LAUGHING GNOME
SCARY MONSTERS

SIMON A FORWARD

CANDY JAR BOOKS · CARDIFF
2018

Scary Monsters © Simon A Forward 2018

Characters and Concepts from 'The Web of Fear'
© *Hannah Haisman & Henry Lincoln*
Lethbridge-Stewart: The Series © *Andy Frankham-Allen*
& Shaun Russell 2015, 2018
Fiona Campbell created by Gary Russell

Doctor Who is © *British Broadcasting Corporation, 1963, 2018*

Range Editor Andy Frankham-Allen
Editor: Shaun Russell
Editorial: Keren Williams
Licensed by Hannah Haisman
Cover by Richard Young & Will Brooks

Printed and bound in the UK by
CPI Anthony Rowe, Chippenham, Wiltshire

ISBN: 978-1-912535-07-1

Published by
Candy Jar Books
Mackintosh House
136 Newport Road, Cardiff, CF24 1DJ
www.candyjarbooks.co.uk

PROLOGUE

'**TERROR!**' The word screamed from the paper. A panic attack, printed in bold block capitals, between the red banner and a photograph of the airliner standing, isolated, on a Moscow runway. As though the ordeal wasn't bad enough for the passengers trapped aboard that aircraft, the newspapers appeared determined to whip the rest of the watching world into a frenzy.

A sorry business.

Brigadier Alistair Lethbridge-Stewart drummed his fingers on the front page. Then realised he was drumming along to that awful 'tune' thumping out from the jukebox. He had heard more pleasant artillery barrages. He arrested his percussion and reached for his pint glass, stationed on the nearby coaster.

He checked his watch. The minute-hand crawled to five-past-one. Old 'Duffer' Hackett wasn't late – yet. It just felt late. Time had a habit of synchronising pace with personal activity. Thus, it flew – by all accounts – when you were having fun, marched when you were working, and dragged when you were idle.

If this was the speed of retirement, then it was rather like the early days of steam. The dread of suffocating at twenty MPH.

Freddie was supposed to meet him there to discuss a teaching position. After nigh on thirty years of military service, Lethbridge-Stewart hadn't expected to trade in his cap for a mortar board, but with the UN putting him out to graze he had started to look for new pastures. Education seemed a natural enough transition, after all that's what he had originally trained for. And the position struck him as a more attractive proposition the more time he spent waiting.

Everybody else appeared to be enjoying a leisurely lunchtime. He sipped his pint, endeavouring to follow their example.

The record droned on fine without his accompaniment. Banging on about *The Call Up*, Lethbridge-Stewart had to assume it was a fairly typical anti-war anthem by average layabouts who had no understanding or experience of military affairs. It hadn't helped that the track started with a blaring siren. It had annoyed him the first time it struck up, and now it was onto its second play. It drowned out the lunchtime chatter from all but the adjacent tables in the pub, and muted the commentary from the television above the bar to an incoherent mumble. The customer responsible for the jukebox selection was perched on a stool making almost as much noise as his choice of record.

Lethbridge-Stewart didn't know whether the man was naturally loud or merely possessed one of those voices that carried.

'Set me up with another there!' The Irishman rocked his barstool forward to lean further over the bar and pushed his empty at the landlord. He settled straight back and tugged the ashtray close, lit up, and started rapping the bar with the lighter. Effectively replacing Lethbridge-Stewart on drums.

The landlord picked up the glass. 'Same glass?'

'Sure, why dirty another?'

The man spun on his stool and studied the rest of the pub through his own cigarette smoke. He clocked Lethbridge-Stewart and the paper.

'Terrible business,' he said.

Lethbridge-Stewart gave a curt nod, but said nothing. At the next table, a young brunette winced in sympathy, an indicator he was not alone in finding the man taking up his unfair share of the pub's lounge. She glanced in the direction of the lavatories, where her fella had disappeared a minute or two ago. No doubt willing him to hurry up and return.

The Irishman turned back to the bar and his drumming with the lighter. Every few beats, he'd flip it in a deft juggling move. His record was coming to a close and Lethbridge-Stewart hoped he didn't get up to pop more coins in the machine.

He stayed put, attention fixed, for now, on the TV.

'They want to send in the SAS, that's what they want to do. Princes bloody Gate didn't teach these people a damn thing, eh? Russians have got their own SAS, haven't they? *Spetsnaz*. They'll not sit quiet while these Afghans give them a bloody nose. Mark my words.'

The TV had more pictures of the Aeroflot jet. The ribbon across the bottom of the screen bore the caption MOSCOW HIJACK. The main image was practically a replica of the front-page photograph because nothing had changed in twenty-four hours.

The man was right about one thing. The Russians wouldn't allow that situation to stand too much longer.

He rechecked his watch. Like the girl on the next table, he willed his lunch date to get a move on.

'Ah, cheers!' The landlord slid the Irishman his Guinness. The man raised the glass in a toast and sent his moustache in for a quick dip. Setting the glass down, he dug in the backpack on the stool beside him. Dropped his lighter in the small pocket and dug out a wallet. He flattened a fiver to the bar and let his fingers ride it like a magic carpet. 'While I'm here, I don't suppose you could point me in the direction of any decent lodgings around these parts? Hostel, something like that? I'll not say cheap, but nothing that'll cost me an arm and a leg, you know.'

The landlord shrugged. 'I can fetch you the Yellow Pages.'

'Sure enough, if I don't find anywhere to sleep I can use it for a pillow.' The man hopped off his stool and patted his backpack. 'Watch me bag while I finish me smoke outside, will you?'

'More than welcome to smoke it in here.' At least half the other customers were already contributing to the pub's hazy atmosphere.

'Nah, I need to stretch me legs. Been cooped up on a train most of the morning. And I need the fresh air.' He laughed, easily promoting himself to the loudest thing in the room. 'Cheers. I won't be two shakes.'

He swaggered to the door, pulling the lapels of his donkey-jacket up around his neck. He half-tripped on the pub step, perhaps an effect of the afternoon drinking meeting the bright daylight outside.

Lethbridge-Stewart sipped his pint and looked at his watch again. *Come on, Freddie.* Something itched at his stomach lining. Odd case of butterflies.

He glanced at the backpack. Then to the door.

Pedestrians milled past the window, shadows in the frosted glass. Any one of them could've been the Irishman...

No. He didn't want to jump to suspicions. Still–

The bomb ripped through the lunchtime crowd.

CHAPTER ONE
Ashes to Ashes

NOVEMBER 2011.

It was a day of conflicts. Cloudless blue and bitter chills. Joan probably would have enjoyed it. She might've launched herself on one of her spontaneous bracing walks or seen it as an opportunity to attack the garden as part of her horticultural winter campaign.

The sunshine was alone in finding nothing to reflect on today. The rays found no welcome among the black suits and buttoned-up dress coats. Only the hearse and other cars parked along the cemetery driveway presented their polished bonnets and roofs as sombre mirrors.

Sir Alistair Lethbridge-Stewart had meant to mention sunglasses to Fiona, his ex-wife, but with the wheelchair and everything, just getting out of the home these days was like organising divisional manoeuvres. Ordinarily such operations would have fallen to Doris, but she had excused herself from today, not feeling she ought to intrude on a sad occasion for a family she didn't really know. His wife possessed the logistical skills of a quartermaster and knew where to find everything. Fiona, bless her, did not. So, while Fiona collected gloves, scarf, hat and a blanket for his knees, sunglasses had slipped their minds. He was, therefore, obliged to squint every time he glanced up. Fiona, stationed behind him, was probably doing the same.

5

Some others gathered around the graveside had remembered their sunglasses. As much to be alone with their thoughts as to screen out the brightness.

It was good to see the familiar faces, whether hidden behind dark glasses or under black hats, heads down as they lowered Joan Pemberton into the ground.

David, of course, and his wife – Emily, wasn't it? Their son and daughters, their spouses or partners, plus a gaggle of grandchildren. The small platoon of kids stood quietly, still as troops assembled for inspection. Even the youngest, anchored to her father's hand, only glanced shyly around, looking for cues from the grown-ups, before tipping her blonde curls forward to cover her face.

Extended family and friends formed second and third rows behind the main Pemberton clan. Alistair wondered if there weren't others who deserved a front row seat more than he, but people tended to make space for wheelchairs. Not everyone present would know his relations to the Pembertons. Blood was thicker than water, no doubt, but history was as good as blood in some cases.

From a world away, a faint peal of laughter rode the cold breeze. Some other children playing in the field past the church perhaps.

The sound felt like an intrusion, but Alistair smiled. Why shouldn't they play? Children shouldn't stop living because one old woman had died.

'Ashes to ashes, dust to dust...'

An energetic gust whisked the vicar's words away. Alistair's thoughts wandered from Joan to other funerals he had attended. The graves he'd stood and saluted over. Too many goodbyes to too many young men and women. More names than he could ever recall, although he could still see many of their faces through closed eyes. So often torn from life by violence.

Days like today brought it home. Today was about Joan, of course. But it was about Old Spence too. And other ghosts stood watch. Most of those who floated into memory now had given their lives in strange, extraordinary battles. Battles that almost blurred into a single war. Battles he carried with him because, over the years they could only be spoken of in whispers to a select few. Today belonged to Joan, but today was also part of what all those battles had been about. Lives given in secret conflicts so that others could live free and safe – hopefully happy – lives and die peacefully of natural causes.

Latter years had seen more of those sorts of funerals. History formed friendships as strong as family, but time was a duplicitous sort. Friend and foe alike.

'...Be honour and glory for ever and ever. Amen.'

The committal came to its natural close and the vicar led the gathering in a final prayer. Their small corner of the world seemed to take a long breath. Birds sang. There was that laugh again, from far away. People began to move.

Fiona reached over to rearrange the blanket on his lap. She wheeled him into the line filing past the grave.

The slow trickle of people broke apart, different branches of the family and guests congregating in small knots not far from the vehicles. Chauffeurs readied themselves beside car doors.

Fiona parked the chair in front of David and Emily. They greeted Alistair with smiles that wished they were elsewhere. Fiona stepped around him to proffer a hand. 'We're so very sorry. It was a beautiful service.'

Beautiful service.

Hahahahahaha!

Alistair winced at the unfortunate counterpoint. He wished those children would stop playing just for a minute. Then immediately felt bad for thinking such a thing.

'We're glad you could come,' Emily said, gratefully shaking Fiona's hand.

David opened his mouth to add something, but the words never made it out.

'Of course,' Fiona said.

'And how are you both?'

How was Alistair, was what they meant. He huffed faintly and fidgeted in his chair. Fit as a fiddle, he thought. An old fiddle. Positively antique, but still in tune.

'Sir Alistair? How are you, Sir?'

'Mmm?' Alistair turned. Dashed sun was in his eyes. Gripping his wheels, he manoeuvred the chair around to face the fellow looming over him. He offered up a handshake. The chap stood back to salute instead.

'Beg your pardon, Sir. I've waited thirty years to do that.' The fellow had officer written all over him – and through him. A chip off any number of old blocks Alistair could name. He couldn't place the face though. He returned the salute all the same. 'Barney Hackett, RN. Retired, of course. Freddie's son, you know.' *Ah, dear old Duffer, of course.* 'We worked together back in '81. In a manner of speaking.'

1981 was one of the hazy years. Patches of fog everywhere. Nothing alien to it. Just plain old time and amnesia. 1981? Thirty years. 'Teach at Brendon, did you?'

'No, I was still serving at the time. As were you, Sir Alistair. Lieutenant commander, I was then.'

'Ah. I see.' Alistair fell into a frown. He didn't see at all. Blasted fog. *Hahahahahaha!* That laughter from the field was getting a bit much. Alistair drew a smile across his frown like a curtain. 'Well, pleasure to see you.'

'We didn't meet before, I'm sorry to say. I just wanted to introduce myself. I only wish it were under happier circumstances. I'm a cousin of Emma's, you see. It's… a small world.'

'Indeed.'

Emma? Who the dash was Emma? Alistair glanced at David's wife. Perhaps the fellow meant Emily.

Alistair eyed the man, trying to roll back the years – and the fog – trying to picture what he would have looked like as a younger lieutenant commander. But what was the use, if they had never met? *Small world.* If only the fellow realised how small Alistair's world was nowadays.

'Well, I must go, Sir. I've my own flock to take care of.' The chap pointed with a thumb back at a woman in a broad-brimmed hat conversing with two daughters near the driveway. 'Will we see you back at the house?'

'No, I – I don't believe so.' Alistair looked around to Fiona for confirmation. She was locked in small-talk with David and Emily. Emma? 'We're expecting visitors back at… at home this afternoon.'

Home. Alistair always referred to it as *the* home. Except to strangers.

Barney Hackett nodded. He lingered a moment, littering the ground with unspoken words. Then picked his way between the headstones to rejoin his family.

1981…

Alistair's frown returned.

'Everything all right, Alistair?' Fiona leaned in to check on him.

'Mmm? Yes. Fine. Absolutely – ship-shape.' He glanced to see David and his family heading for their cars. 'Are we off then?'

'We can be.'

Hahahahahaha!

The children were still finding plenty to amuse themselves in the nearby field. Although now, away from the graveside and with the mourners dispersing, it sounded like a lone boy. What game could keep one child so entertained?

Hahahahahaha!

The laughter tugged at Alistair somehow.

'This was Joan's parish for heaven knows how many years,' Alistair remarked. 'Spencer's too, of course.'

'It's a lovely old church,' Fiona acknowledged. She pushed the chair along at a gentle strolling pace, following the gravel path along the east wall of the building.

Towards the back of the churchyard many of the gravestones nested in overgrown grass, shaded by large sycamores. Along with a stone hedge spilling over with bramble and ivy, the trees conspired to hide the field from view. Alistair listened for the laughter. It came and went with the swish of breeze through the foliage. It was definitely a solitary voice. What was more, it had matured into a sort of reedy cackle, as though rust had crept into the pipes. As though the child had aged in a few minutes of play.

'You can really feel the years,' Fiona said. 'Almost as though you don't need the numbers on the headstones. It's all there in the walls and the roof.'

Alistair thought about craning for a glimpse of the field past the trees and hedgerow. He looked instead up at the church. 'Those tiles that aren't falling off, yes.'

'All this – today – it must bring back so much. Spencer and everything.'

'Yes.' Immediately, Alistair relived a moment like it was yesterday. It provoked a shiver. 'You know, I told Joan once – shortly after Old Spence passed – that I wished it had been me instead of him.'

'I know, Alistair. You've told me. On a few occasions.'

Had he? Yes, he supposed he must've done. They were married for a good number of years in the '70s, after all, and had become friends again in the last ten years.

And in all that time, Fiona had never lost contact with Joan. 'I meant it too,' Alistair said. 'At the time.'

'I know.' Fiona patted his shoulder. 'It doesn't take anything away. From what we shared. Or the life you have with Doris.'

Alistair rested his hand over hers. A thank you. 'We say and do things and we mean them. Every word, every action. With no idea what we're losing or giving away. Exchanging one future for another.'

'Just as well the universe doesn't listen. It's water under the bridge. We can't go back and change the flow. The universe knows you meant it. I'm sure Joan did. But I'm equally sure she would never begrudge you the life you had since. It was Spencer who set you on that path.'

'It was. The military part, at least. And more besides.'

The chair jolted. The right wheel bumped against some obstruction or other. Some larger stone that had found its way onto the gravel, no doubt.

'Sorry!' Fiona hurried around to inspect the damage. She crouched to lift the offending obstacle out of the way. She grimaced. 'Well, if that isn't a life lesson for us all.'

'Excuse me?'

'Good people steering us along the right paths. Ugly blighters doing their best to derail us.' Smiling, she held up her find.

A gnome.

'Ugly' was a fair observation. It was as much gargoyle as gnome. Clad in a carved jacket with oversized buttons and a pointy hat that drooped to his right shoulder, its features appeared smushed all out of shape by a sculptor's heavy thumbs. A lazy eye, one heavy lid falling over it like a roll of dough, cheeks puffed into mounds, big inflated clownish mouth to accommodate a massive imagined laugh rising from the depths of its pot belly. Unruly rows of teeth like subsiding headstones. The gnome might have boasted lurid colours at one point but, in its current condition, it was fashioned only in rough stone with a light patchwork coat of moss and lichen. It appeared happy for all that. Excessively so.

HAHAHAHAHAHAHAHA!

Alistair glanced to the field. But the laughter was right with him, bouncing around in his ears. At the same time it seemed to hail from down the length of a tunnel. A tunnel that opened in the gnome's gaping, mocking mouth. Or in the blank stone pupil of its single open eye.

'Strange little fellow.'

Fiona searched the nearest headstones. 'Wonder where he's strayed from?'

Alistair teased the gnome from Fiona's hand and turned the figure upside down. The base was faintly etched with odd circular symbols, but otherwise smooth and flat, no sign of any fractures. 'Doesn't look to have broken off from anywhere.'

'He might've stood on any of these graves. People leave all sorts of things. Maybe the owner was fond of garden gnomes.'

'Garden gnomes are usually more colourful, aren't they?'

'Maybe his paint has come off. Yours would too, left out in all weathers for who knows how long.'

'True enough.'

HAHAHAHAHAHAHAHAHA!

'What the devil?'

'What is it, Alistair?'

Couldn't she hear it? Alistair pressed fingertips to his ear, wondering if he was developing a touch of tinnitus. 'Oh – nothing.' Alistair shrugged, as though shaking off a dream. 'I – I thought I saw a mark on the base, thought it might be a signature. These old eyes getting the better of me.'

'We should find out where he belongs. I'll take a look around, see if there are any more like him anywhere.'

'Good idea.'

Fiona backed away onto the grass, taking care where she stepped between the graves and peering up at the church roof, probably scanning for gargoyles roosting around the spire.

Yes, thought Alistair, *little chap does look more like a gargoyle than a gnome.*

He had some experience with gargoyles. He turned the figure in his hands again, making sure the blighter didn't have wings sprouting from its back.

Movement caught his eye. Back along the path, a woman emerged from the porch and began affixing papers to the church notice board. She appeared to be humming to herself through a serene sort of smile. Whatever tune was on her mind, the breeze stole it away.

HAHAHAHAHAHAHAHAHAHAHA!

'Oh,' Alistair said. 'There. That must be the verger. I'll go and ask her.'

Fiona didn't answer. She had wandered away, already disappearing around the back of the church.

Alistair dropped the gnome in his lap. He steered his chair around, preparing to push for the church entrance. The gnome rested in the blanket, happy as a sailor in a hammock, winking up at him.

HAHAHAHAHAHAHAHAHAHAHAHAHA!

The laughter rang in his ears. Alistair gripped the wheel-rims. But the strength left his arms.

HAHAHAHAHAHAHAHAHAHAHAHAHAHAHA!

The laughter tugged at him again. Dragging his eyes down and down. The gnome's mouth seemed to stretch open like an enormous cavern. Alistair felt himself drawn in and in, between the stone teeth.

Into the black...

CHAPTER TWO
Changes

HEADRUSH. *Like being catapulted into orbit, punishing G-force slammed Alistair into the back of his own skull. At the apogee, his thoughts churned in a dark freefall. Before he plunged, down and down, memories tearing past like oncoming traffic. Collisions jarred, but most memories ripped on through him like ghosts.*

Sea monster looms over the Thames riverbank. Whoosh! Silver colossus tramples a Land Rover. Whoosh! Dinosaurs. Claws. Tentacles. Grinning plastic dummies. Yellow car. Blue Box. Yeti. Giant Easter eggs. Alien plants. His dead brother. Riding the rapids of his life, the more violent splashes of colour drowning the quieter, treasured moments. The birth of Conall. Bill and Anne's wedding. The birth of Kate.

All the while the gnome laughed.

Alistair fell and fell.

He jerked awake as though hitting the ground in a dream.

The hard back of a chair shored up his shoulder blades. Paper lay under his right hand. Music and murmurs in his ears. The clink of glasses and more laughter. Not the gnome this time. Only people. One voice louder than the others.

His fingers drummed to an awful tune. Alistair glanced down.

It was the wrong hand. The skin was firm and smooth, veins and bones buried beneath the surface

14

where they belonged. Moles and more than a few wrinkles had gone AWOL. The fingers arrested their drumming and the hand went to the pint glass on the coaster nearby. Unveiling the newspaper front page in full.

TERROR. The photograph of the aircraft on a runway. The date at the top: 1st July, 1981.

Not here. No. Not back here.

A fifty-two-year-old Brigadier Lethbridge-Stewart, dark hair, only a hint of grey in his moustache, looked back at him from the mirror behind the bar. Old thoughts examined the world through younger eyes. How? How could he be sitting here? The taste of ale soaking his tongue, the smell of cigarette smoke in his nose. Memories of the cemetery, a warm blue sky, Joan buried only minutes ago. Getting ready for the funeral, forgetting his sunglasses. Everything. It was all there, intact, in his head. A future lived through and remembered when he was here in the past? It didn't make sense.

Everything was vivid. More vivid than memory. Some things could be remembered like yesterday. This was today.

An Irish accent cut through the background chatter.

A woman with Maureen O'Hara hair. A khaki longcoat draped over the backpack occupying the barstool beside her. She ordered a fresh pint of the good stuff from the landlord. Enquired about lodgings in the neighbourhood.

Wrong, thought Alistair. *This is all wrong.*

Stop her! He fired the thought at himself. Launched himself from the chair. But his legs refused to budge. His body stayed seated. There was the impulse to move, but no response.

Do something! he urged.

The woman hopped from her stool, pulled on her

coat, strolled outside and was gone.

The bomb ripped through the lunchtime crowd.

The blast hurled Alistair from his chair, smashed a table under him and slammed him to the floor. Face down in a world of dust and smoke and ash.

All noise hailed from some great depths, as though everything was drowning in a leaden ocean. Muffled screams and cries surfaced, reaching him through the blood and ringing in his ears.

Alistair lifted himself onto his hands and knees, but even that low altitude cost him an attack of vertigo.

He heard a dull crash of falling masonry. He rolled onto his back and threw up a guarding arm. Through a cratered ceiling he looked up at a wheeling sky.

A raw screech pierced his muted senses and he searched the reeling space to his right. Against a backdrop of splintered furniture and flailing, moaning figures, a girl knelt, screaming into her hand. She peeled her hand from her face and stared, blindly, from a mask of streaming blood and tears. Alistair had the vaguest notion he knew her. Her body convulsed with the force of her screams, even as Alistair lay in a strange not-quite-silent movie.

He fought to lift himself again. Pain seared through his midriff. He strained to inspect the wound. His hand hovered above his stomach and landed in a soaked patch of pullover. Blood or beer? He raised his hand and it came up red. His head swam some more, this time borne on a wave of nausea. His insides burned, and he shivered with a sudden cold.

Somewhere, glass rained on floorboards. A loud crack broke overhead.

The rest of the ceiling fractured away and tumbled in like a melting glacier. It crashed down and buried him.

Bright light stabbed at his eyes.

Alistair threw a hand up to shield his vision. His head swam with the effort and his arm dropped back by his side. Onto rough blanket. His fingers curled, stroking the unexpected texture.

The room was filled with voices: the hubbub of too many conversations in a public space, but tinged with a sombre undercurrent. Whimpers and sobs mingled with the general murmur.

'Ah,' said a voice from many rooms away. 'How's our patient?'

A face floated into view, suggesting the speaker had been nearer than he'd sounded. A rumble still lay trapped in his ears.

He lifted his hand slowly, fingertips testing his cheek and temple. No tackiness. Somebody had done a thorough clean-up job. His hand shot to his midriff, feeling for the worst news. He touched wool. No blood, no bandages. He wasn't even tucked up in bed, merely laid out atop a blanket on a basic camp bed.

He trusted there was no permanent damage. There couldn't be, could there? He was still *himself*.

Memories of the funeral, of Fiona, the gnome, of years that hadn't yet happened – all intact.

So strange to be living this unremembered past. Foreign, like a stranger's life. And yet coldly familiar. An out of body experience inside your own head.

'Pupils are responsive. And more besides,' joked the doctor, just as he shut the pen-torch off with a click and stowed it in his breast pocket. Under the white coat he wore a uniform jacket. Army. He stood back, allowing the other figure command of Alistair's bedside.

'If you'll excuse me, Sir Frederick,' the doctor began.
Sir Frederick? Freddie?

'Of course, of course. Other patients.'

Alistair blinked to banish the afterimage left by the doctor's torch and concentrated to mould familiar

17

features from the blur hovering by his bed. Thin brown hair and a fringe that refused to stay tidy, sideburns surrendering to advancing grey. Full, well-groomed moustache styled on Lord Kitchener and a stern brow that would have looked at home on the recruitment posters. Bags under the eyes. A slight puff to the jowls and a touch of blush to the cheeks, a hint of the hearty merlots and cabernet sauvignons that he enjoyed so much showing through an otherwise thick skin.

Definitely Freddie.

Memory flashed up a portrait: Freddie's son at the cemetery. Did Alistair's being here change the future he remembered?

'Go easy on him,' the doctor advised, as he withdrew. 'He's made of sterner stuff than most, but he's still in shock.'

'It's an interview, not an interrogation. Not even that. A cosy chat, that's all.'

Freddie pulled a chair close and parked himself in it. He coughed, making a bit of an asthmatic song and dance of sitting down.

'Duffer?' Alistair pushed himself upright, fighting dizziness and a rush of memories: tumbling visions of a pub interior, shattering furniture and windows, the taste of ash and dust on his tongue, bodies in motion and others eerily still.

'Steady there, old boy.'

'I'm all right.' Churning thoughts freeze-framed on a girl, brown hair matted and streaked with blood. She cried her throat raw, tears carved tracks through a mask of dust and deep cuts. Alistair closed his eyes, trying to shut the image down. To Freddie it probably looked like a wince of pain. Not so far from the truth.

The brunette's image lodged there in his mind like a poorly-swallowed tablet in his throat. Suddenly Alistair remembered: she was the girl from the next table, the one who'd been waiting on her boyfriend. Alistair wondered if her fella had ever made it back from the gents? He searched the room, rather enjoying the improved mobility of being in his younger body once again.

His bed was one of about twenty cots under a high ceiling, ornamented with peeling paintwork, touches of crumbling plaster. Scuffed floorboards and a stage at one end. Town Hall, perhaps? Patients occupied every bed. Others sat shaking, hugging each other and themselves in a row of chairs against the far wall. Still others were laid out on mattresses on the floor. Those who scanned the room did so with distant and empty looks, as though isolated in individual cells and seeing something other than their surroundings.

He couldn't locate the girl.

His view of some patients was blocked by attendant nurses and medics buzzing from bed to bed. Army personnel. Soldiers guarded the doors. At one bed, two officers sat interviewing a patient. At the very next cot along, a young man with straggly hair and a corduroy jacket appeared deep in discussion with another of the victims, while sketching away in a large A3 pad.

'You're late,' Alistair reproached Freddie.

'Very. For which I count myself fortunate.'

'Well, we can postpone talking about that teaching position.' He swung his legs off the bed. A delayed wave of dizziness struck, but it felt manageable, as long as the regularity and intensity continued to fade. 'There's work to be done.'

'A great deal. But nothing you need trouble yourself over, Alistair.'

'We have to catch her.'

'Her?' Freddie frowned.

'Yes, *her*. If you'll give me a minute I can provide a description.' Alistair nodded in the direction of the man with the pad. 'Is that your police sketch artist? Get him

19

over here.'

'That doesn't tie with what we know. Eye witness accounts uniformly report a man. Descriptions vary in small details, but our artist has already worked up three or four sketches. We already have a fair picture of our man.'

'I don't care what it ties with. I know what I saw.'

Alistair tested his legs. There was a degree of wobble. Pain sliced at his stomach like the slash of a knife. He clasped a hand to the offending area, but again couldn't understand the lack of bandaging. He glanced around the room. There were no bandaged wounds to be seen anywhere.

'Even so, Alistair. I'm not just talking about eye-witness accounts from today. There was Sunderland. Leeds. Coventry, too. This is not an isolated incident.'

Sunderland? Coventry? Alistair dredged his memory. Of course, memory was a confused mess right now. But he dimly recalled news reports from this time. The mood of a nation buoyed by anticipation for a royal wedding turned sour by a short wave of terror attacks. The first struck a police station, hadn't it? And incidents abroad: Afghanistan, the Moscow hijack – and hadn't there been strikes in Europe? America too – not including the unconnected attempt on the President's life. And some bounder taking pot-shots at the Pope. All of it so long ago for him and, what was more, so damned elusive for reasons he couldn't pinpoint. Naturally he couldn't share any of that with Freddie.

'Do tell me you've kept up with the news, Alistair.'

'Mmm? Yes. Sorry. Miles away.'

Alistair imagined Freddie would attribute his momentary inattention to post-traumatic stress.

'Listen, old boy, perhaps you had best lie back down. Take your time and allow yourself some proper rest. You're not long off retirement. May as well take this as an opportunity to make an early start.'

'Nonsense.' Alistair stood. His head complained of wooziness, but otherwise he felt steady enough. Which, if nothing else, saved him from looking a complete fool in front of Freddie. 'I'll be fine. It's not my first explosion.'

Freddie bushed up his moustache like a cat with its hackles raised.

'If you're going to insist that you're fit, Brigadier, then I must insist you come with me. There's something you need to see.'

It was a short walk.

Out of the main hall, through a small foyer with a reception kiosk, they exited through a set of double doors and passed two more soldiers standing guard on the steps. Then along a paved path to the street. Alistair glanced at the sign proudly displayed by the low wall: Maidenwood Community Centre.

He wondered if this walk was going to bring him closer to any greater truth. Or truths, plural. There was the mystery of the bomb and the terrorist – man or woman. Then there was his internal – or temporal – mystery…

Freddie fired him looks with every other step, apparently anxious to ensure he was keeping up.

Behind a feigned smile, Alistair occupied himself with a recce: behind them, a pair of Land Rovers parked at angles across the street, the improvised gateway manned by a dozen soldiers. Two more Land Rovers formed a similar blockade at the far end of the road.

No traffic or pedestrians allowed through, the neighbourhood appeared deserted. Nor were there any twitching curtains or signs of life from the houses they passed. The street possessed a quiet he hadn't seen since London and the death of Princess Diana. Odd to remember that, since now he was here in the same year she was to marry Prince Charles.

A large canvas-covered truck was parked in the middle of the street. The roof of the pub was visible above its canopy, but Alistair couldn't make out any gaping holes in the tiles.

Troops stood guard while others offloaded packages from the truck's cargo bed. A number of men ran cables from within a small sandbag nest, past the front of the truck.

'What is this? What's going on?'

Alistair rechecked the street. Where were the ambulances? The police? Come to that, why hadn't he woken in hospital? He cursed himself for being so slow to ask the right questions.

He didn't know whether he was dazed from the blast or from his – what would he call it? Transportation? His arrival here courtesy of the gnome, anyway. He had no clue why he was here, whether the universe was trying to tell him something. Perhaps because it seemed such a blank chapter in his memory. Perhaps life had some great lesson to teach. Only two things were certain: it wasn't Christmas and he wasn't Jimmy Stewart.

With an effort, he filed that question away. The gnome, he supposed, would have to wait a lot longer. Perhaps decades. There were more pressing questions. Questions of now.

'We sent them home,' Freddie said. Answering one of Alistair's unvoiced questions. 'The emergency services. This is our baby now.' He extended an arm, encouraging Alistair to slow as they reached the truck.

'Excuse me, sirs. Coming through.' A soldier passed, unspooling cable.

Alistair frowned. The lads appeared to be trailing wires into the pub in preparation for a controlled detonation. If there was a second, unexploded device on site, Freddie would hardly be walking him towards it...

22

'You had best brace yourself, Brigadier

'For what?'

'A shock.'

'Well, I think I've had my daily ration of those.' What could be worse than a bomb?

Freddie guided Alistair around the rear of the truck and stopped them in full view of the pub. The building stood intact and utterly unscathed. Glass in every window. *The Old Fusilier* sign hung above the entrance, as still as the deserted streets. Not so much as a scratch on the paintwork.

Impossible.

CHAPTER THREE
Take a Look at the Lawman…

JULY 1981. SHEMYATOVO AIRPORT, MOSCOW.

The stairs were lowered. The door open. One target was framed in the doorway, face smothered in balaclava, machine-pistol in hand, his other arm holding a passenger as a shield. A woman, of course.

Major Grigoriy Bugayev parked the service truck at the base of the steps. In his mirror, the fuel truck veered gently to a stop under the airliner's wing.

He visualised the Il-86 interior: *Twin aisles, three-three-three seating configuration, tapering to three banks of double seats towards the rear. Three-hundred-and-fifty passengers. A lot of background in a space not even six metres wide.*

He clambered out. Presented empty hands to the gunman. Turned to show off his plain overalls and flat pockets. Then slowly reached inside the truck's cab and collected the large box from the passenger seat.

Under the wing, his troops hopped off the back of the refuelling tanker and crept in under the fuselage. Safely out of sight.

Bugayev carried the box up the stairs. Nice and slow. The gunman waved his machine-pistol and tightened his hold on the woman. The woman stiffened, so terrified she cried, but no sound emerged. A second target lurked inside the vestibule. He clocked the muzzle of an AK jutting above the man's shoulder.

Six gunmen. One spent a lot of time in the flight deck.

Interviews with the two released hostages had confirmed that much, along with descriptions of armaments carried. *Two with automatic handguns, two with machine-pistols, two with assault rifles. Any explosives? Uncertain.*

Bugayev climbed the stairs. Wondering when they would tell him to set the box down. They wouldn't want to venture out too far. They would have spotted the snipers on the hangar rooftops and on Shemyatovo Airport's traffic control tower. Bugayev had made sure of that. Another step. Another. Target One shouted and pointed his machine-pistol at the top step. Bugayev stole one more step. He lowered the box. Slid a hand inside, through the open back. Closed fingers around the grip of the Makarov automatic, secreted amongst the food packages.

Unwilling to risk the snipers, the gunman pushed his hostage forward, ordering her to collect the delivery. Below, Bugayev knew his troops would be in position.

The woman reached for the box. Bugayev pulled the pistol and let the box fall. He yanked the woman's arm and shoved her down the steps behind him.

Target One wasted precious breath in a yell.

Bugayev fired. Closed the distance as the target dropped. Swung to cover Target Two. The terrorist bolted for the interior staircase.

Up those stairs: first-class cabin, three economy sections aft of that, separated by wardrobes and cabin crew accommodations. A lot of aircraft for four gunmen to control.

Bugayev fired. Clipped his man above the knee. Target Two pitched forward, smacked his face on the stairs. Bugayev closed, put a second bullet in the man's back. Grushkin and the rest of the men hustled up the external steps two-abreast and burst into the vestibule. Bugayev was confident they had caught the woman and parcelled her off to safety. Fierce shouts and frightened cries hailed down from the passenger cabin. Bugayev snatched the flashbang from the back of his belt and tossed it above. He waited on the bang then followed the grenade upstairs.

Target Three staggered, blinking at him from the top of the stairs.

Bugayev shot twice. One: centre forehead. Target Three toppled backwards. Bugayev's second shot punctured the aircraft's ceiling. Damn. Bugayev crested the stairs, stepped over the corpse, sweeping gun left-right, pressed on through first-class. Port aisle. Close on his heels, Grushkin and three others broke left and stormed the flight deck. Target Four announced his presence with wild AK fire. Bugayev's men answered with restrained precision.

Bugayev advanced into the next section.

'Heads down! Hands on heads!' he ordered the passengers. 'Heads down! Hands on heads!'

Target Five was in the aisle, to the rear of the section. He backed up and made a clumsy grab for the nearest passenger, fighting to tug her out of her seat. Bugayev put two rounds in his chest. His human shield fell back into her seat, screaming and crying and covering her head in her arms as she stared at the downed gunman close to her feet. Bugayev moved on through. Popped the clip and snapped another in place.

'Heads down! Hands on your heads! Heads down! Hands on your heads!'

His men joined the chorus as they followed. Passengers screamed and ducked and covered their heads. Bugayev hit the middle section.

Target Six popped up in the far aisle. Sent a machine-pistol burst in his direction. Bullets blew padding from a seat headrest inches from a passenger. Bugayev pressed a shoulder to the nearby wardrobe. 'Heads down! Heads down!' He answered with two clean shots. Centre forehead, centre chest.

Target Six crashed back onto the passengers behind him. They screamed. Wrestled the dead weight off and pitched him into the aisle.

'Stay down! Hands on heads!'

Bugayev swept on through.

Six gunmen. So said the two released hostages. Time to make sure.

'Heads down! Hands on heads!'

His men continued the sweep behind him. Bugayev reached the tail section, where the cabin tapered towards the row of WCs. He kicked doors in, one by one.

'Clear! All clear!'

'Clear!' Grushkin answered. Troops echoed the call.

Bugayev turned and marched back to meet his men. Coming up the starboard aisle, he stopped at the first dead body.

Target Six.

Wrong.

He looked down on the corpse of a civilian. Bullet wounds exactly where he'd placed them, but in a brown-haired man in a beige suit. No balaclava. He scanned for the rifle. No sign. A strange cold seized him. He sprinted back through the plane, checking each of the dead targets in turn. Some of his men were there before him, stalled like dumbfounded pedestrians around the site of traffic accidents.

Target Five, same story. Target Three, same story. On the flight deck, Target Four, same story.

Behind him, throughout the plane, passengers screamed. Bugayev ordered his men to shepherd them out of there, guiding them past the dead. The sight of the bodies set them off afresh.

Who were the terrorists now?

Alistair steadied himself on the truck's tailgate. The young brunette screamed in his head. Her eyes bulged with terror above the bloody hand she clamped over her face. Blood and screams escaped through her screening fingers. She knelt in broken glass and splinters, shredding her throat with raw, terrible sound.

'All right, old boy?'

'Fine. I'll be fine.' As a term of endearment, 'old boy' was probably more warranted now than ever. Alistair straightened. If the building was still standing, then he ought to manage it without too much trouble.

For the umpteenth time he tested his midriff. Again, beneath the pullover he was tender to the touch. But the twinge was like the memory of an old war wound. Like some shrapnel he might've caught in Korea, not some grievous injury he had sustained – what? – mere hours ago.

Freddie tugged at Alistair's arm. 'Come on. You had best see the whole picture.'

Alistair sleepwalked into the pub.

For an establishment that was supposed to have been levelled, it was on the busy side. Troops secured charges to walls and to shelves behind the bar. Alistair registered their activity, but fixated on everything that was static. He drifted through it in a walking dream.

Flashes of the aftermath – ash, splinters, screams, the crash of masonry, the ringing in his ears – the blood-faced woman – jarred with everything he saw. He faltered, almost stumbled. He touched the backs of chairs, slid fingers across a table. All the furniture was in place. Not a speck of dust or rubble. He looked up. No craters in the ceiling. Nothing more than hairline cracks in the plaster that were a part of the building's character and age. The TV above the bar had been turned off. The jukebox was lit up, but thankfully silent. Alistair was grateful for that at least.

He flicked a glass, listened to the chime. It was half-full of ale.

28

Alistair moved between tables. He froze. There was his pint, unfinished. The newspaper too. None of it the worse for wear.

TERROR. The grainy photo of the grounded aircraft.

How strange: news of elsewhere rendered his immediate surroundings more real. The reality came with a chill.

And there before him was the barstool that the terrorist - *he* or *she* - had occupied. Alistair saw both, superimposed on the same stool: the loud Irishman; the redhead. A pint of Guinness, pristine black with a slender crown of white, rested on the bar towel in front of the stool. A nearby ashtray housed a family of dead cigarettes. The backpack perched on the adjacent stool.

Alistair lost all sight of Freddie. The soldiers went about their business somewhere on the periphery. He approached the abandoned backpack, half-expecting it to go off. Half-expecting a warning shout from Freddie. Warily, he reached out and unzipped the main pocket.

He peered inside the sack. A slow rummage turned up books - two copies of a London A-Z, a telephone directory, chunky paperbacks - six rolled-up towels, three chunky sweaters. He switched to a search of the smaller back pocket. He found two packs of cigarettes - empty, a handful of loose change. He fished out a silver lighter. *The* silver lighter. He remembered it, clear as day.

He turned it over. An inscription adorned one side. Initials: B. F. H.

'BFH,' Alistair read aloud. A clue? Their terrorist couldn't have been that careless, could he? She?

'What's that, old boy? Let me see.'

Freddie pounced from nowhere and snatched the lighter. He flipped it over and over, scrutinised the inscription three or four times.

Alistair shook off his sleepwalk. 'You okay, Duffer? You look like you've seen a ghost.'

'Eh?' Freddie pocketed the lighter. He flexed his mouth, making his moustache bristle again. 'I think we've all seen ghosts. That's the essence of what's going on here. The pub. As you can see, perfectly unharmed.'

Alistair eyed the troops setting charges. 'It is for now. Freddie…What aren't you telling me?'

'A great deal, Alistair, old boy.' He drew Alistair aside. 'This much of the show, I needed you to see. Tough old sort like yourself, I was sure you could take it. It'll require some adjustment, that's all. But I needed you to know, this is all in hand. It's unfortunate you got caught up in it, but we can't change that now. All we can do is govern how we proceed. And it's all in hand.'

'Come on, Freddie. I was here. The bomb…' Alistair eyed the backpack.

Freddie gave Alistair's shoulder a sympathetic pat. 'Did you see a bomb in there? There was no bomb.'

No bomb. Not even normal luggage, in fact. Where were the toiletries? The personal items? Alistair sensed a cold dizziness returning. Ash, splinters, screams, ringing in his ears. That girl who would surely haunt him the rest of his days. Even now, a warm trickle of blood coursed down the side of his face. Pain bit deep in his stomach. He touched his cheek. Nothing there.

He was fine. And that was wrong.

All so very wrong.

Clarity.

Bugayev sat on the edge of the couch, locked in a staring contest with the empty shot glass on the coffee table. A bottle of Stolichnaya stood close by. Unopened. Nice to have a couch. All the comforts of home. First of its class in service, as a command centre the An-124 was unsurpassed. When Bugayev first introduced the men to their new mobile accommodations he had joked that this was their very own Air Force One. Today was not a day for jokes.

Bugayev snatched up the bottle, twisted the cap like he was wringing its neck and poured. He filled the glass to the danger point: serious threat of major spillage if he attempted to lift it and knock it back. Especially if he did it fast.

A clear liquid bullet to the back of the throat. That had to be why they called them shots.

Shots.

Bugayev replayed every discharge of his pistol. Reviewed the inside of the Aeroflot Ilyushin-86 airliner along 9.35 centimetres of gun barrel. He saw a sharp portrait of every balaclava-clad target. Gear, expressions – as much as could be seen. One: mouth open, yelling, bullet in the head. Two: face down on the stairs. Three: stunned, top of the stairs, headshot. Four: not his kill, but he could picture it. Five: economy section, grabbing a passenger for cover. Six: took out a seat, headshot, chestshot, down. All down. Job done. Every bullet found its target. All but one. A single stray round into the airliner's ceiling. No mistakes. Bodies hit the deck with heads in balaclavas.

Six civilians dead. No balaclavas. No guns.

Why? The burning question.

There was rare clarity in vodka. Purity. You couldn't hope to fish for answers in clearer waters. Not that you'd expect the fish to bite. Answers weren't what drinkers went searching for. The cleansing of wounds. Loss of control. Abrogation of responsibility. Absolution. Bugayev wanted none of the above. The kind of clarity he wanted was not to be found in a glass.

He raised the glass. And turned it. Slow, like a planet revolving on its axis. He watched for the slightest wobble, any microscopic tilt. The liquid surface trembled minutely, as though expecting – or hoping – to be spilled. Fluid wanted to follow its natural course.

Bugayev had believed his own moves to be a matter of physics. Rehearsed and rehearsed and rehearsed, until it was second nature. Duplicate Ilyushin aircraft, identical internal layout. Dummy passengers. Balaclava-clad comrades playing terrorists, dotted about in different positions every time. Varied obstacles with each practice run – steward trolley, stray luggage, fallen bodies, all the way to the tail. Every imaginable variation of the scenario. Everything, but the conclusion they were handed.

Voices erupted outside: Grushkin laying down the law to unwanted visitors. A knock shook the door. Bugayev set the glass down. The only moisture on the table was attributable to condensation.

'Come.'

Grushkin opened the door, keeping the gap narrow as he entered. He pushed the door shut. Saluted. Bugayev waved the salute down. No need for ceremony between them.

'Mikhail...?'

'Two *gentlemen* from Lubyanka to see you, sir.' Grushkin's special introduction made it plain that these were the kind of gentlemen, in his opinion, often found deposited on pavements by dogs. Bugayev reserved judgement, but he was under no illusions: he would have to take care where he stepped.

'Show them in. Wait...'

Grushkin hadn't budged. Bugayev wanted to ask about the passenger interviews, but a dozen other questions crowded in at once.

Grushkin nodded towards the vodka. 'You, ah, wish me to hide that for you, sir?' The trace of a sly smile suggested he knew the ideal hiding place.

Bugayev couldn't help but smile in return. No act of bravery or self-sacrifice was too great for Grushkin. 'It can stay.' Bugayev stood, smoothing his uniform. 'You know, Mikhail, the difference between being a drinker and being a drunk is in the *reason* we drink. It seems to me our reasons for doing many of the things we do have been corrupted.'

'You are not to blame. We have completed interviews with a third of the passengers so far. I do not believe the story will alter with the remaining two-thirds. Six gunmen. Precisely the six we put down.'

Bugayev grimaced. 'So, what changed?'

'The gunmen? I don't know.' Grushkin shrugged, obviously uncomfortable with the gesture. 'You... You remember Baikal?'

'Hmm? Oh, the target reverted to its natural form on death.' Bugayev weighed the memory of that mission against events on the plane. 'Yes, I don't think that's what we're dealing with here. The deceased weren't aliens. They were ordinary civilians. All of them on the passenger manifest. Unconnected, unrelated.'

'It is a mystery. We will figure it out, sir. We figure them all out.'

'One way or another.' Bugayev stationed himself behind his desk, but remained standing. 'Sift through *every* item of luggage. Anything remotely out of the ordinary, anything slightly out of place, bag it and set it aside. Meanwhile, you had best show in my guests.'

'Sir.'

Grushkin exited, then briefly reappeared to usher in the guests. He ducked out again, leaving the two plainclothes visitors waiting for a salute or an offer of a seat. Bugayev gave them none of the above. He knew the pair. Sivakov, with the frost-bitten hair and face like a stoneware frying pan, Yubkin, with the scalp smooth and grey as slate and chin like a trowel. Thorns in his side on one previous mission. He hoped they weren't going to double that record.

Of course, they saw the vodka. And simmered like a

couple of Catholic priests who'd found him hitting the sacramental wine.

'Processing the aftermath?' Yubkin asked. He had a way of flexing a smile like a pair of scissors. He held fast to a briefcase, gloved thumb caressing the handle.

'Not in the way you think.' Bugayev didn't care to explain himself. 'Help yourselves, if you like. How can I help you?'

'We are here to help you,' Sivakov said. Even their olive branches had thorns.

'Help me do what exactly?'

'Catch the individuals responsible.'

'That shouldn't be too difficult. I have a feeling two of them just walked into my office.'

Sivakov reddened like a steaming lobster. 'Consider retracting that statement.'

'What statement? This isn't an official proceeding. As far as I can see, you are here to furnish me with information. Information you have withheld up until now. Information which might have made a difference on board that airliner. Am I warm? If I am anything like warm, that makes you complicit.'

'Take care, *Major*. You have been passing up promotions for years now. How much longer do you suppose you can postpone climbing that ladder? We can accelerate your ascent very easily.' Sivakov pretended to cast an interested gaze over the office, as though he could make the furniture disappear with a click of his fingers. An anti-genie.

Every promotion offer that came his way, Bugayev had converted into resources for his unit. So far.

'Two or three more rungs and you will be behind a desk,' Sivakov continued. 'Permanently. No more active field duties. A dog confined to his kennel.'

'Wolf. I think you mean wolf,' Bugayev corrected.

'Very good. We do not want you too domesticated.'

'Indeed,' Yubkin added. 'You will be off the leash for this one.' He popped his briefcase. Produced a folder and tossed it onto the coffee table. It landed with a light slap at the opposite end to the vodka, avoiding the minor hazard of condensation. 'Take a look. You will find some of what you're looking for.'

Bugayev walked around his desk and retrieved the reading matter. He began flicking from page to page, but settled into a more absorbing read.

'And then pack,' Yubkin continued. 'Go hunt what we are looking for.'

'The artefacts, we would like recovered,' Sivakov explained. 'The individuals…Well, those are your terrorists.'

Bugayev nodded. Things weren't exactly crystal, but they were becoming uncomfortably sharper.

CHAPTER FOUR
Absolut Beginners

JANUARY, 1943. BERESTECHKO, UKRAINE.

Vasily woke into a nightmare. No. Other boys had nightmares.

He darted from foxhole to foxhole in a field of rubble. Bullets cracked the winter air, chasing him like wasps. He clambered up a rocky slope and stood on the backbone of a broken building. A German dive-bomber, crooked-winged, screamed down at him. A fat bomb tumbled from its belly.

The explosion whipped up snow and fire and brimstone, and tore through Vasily like wind through a ghost.

He crash-landed into a pit, face-down onto a hard mattress. Something snapped. The mattress shifted. It wore a big grey coat and a Nazi helmet. Black fingers curled around the trigger of a machine-gun. Vasily rolled off the body. The dead face was black and purple and bleached with frost. Some of the features had been bitten away.

Vasily woke in his bed. He tugged the blanket up over his head and curled into a ball. And he refused to cry out. Mama was in her bedroom, one thin wall away.

He prayed. He prayed Papa would never come back. No man should ever come back from such a place. Alive or dead.

NOVEMBER, 1956. BUDAPEST.

The giant head of Stalin rolled on its side in an urban No Man's Land. The decapitated statue, on its plinth, raised a fist in defiance.

Vasily stared across the city square at a wall of angry faces. Three hundred or more, jostling to hurl their anger at him. Standing shoulder to shoulder with his comrades, he held his Kalashnikov across his chest. His mind searched past the front row, floating through the crowd like a ghost, oblivious to the crush, but with their suffocating rage all around. Quick-moving hands stuffed rags into bottles. Other hands hefted bricks. Two men clutched pistols, aimed down, half-hidden by coat-sleeves.

Vasily broke ranks and strode towards the enemy.

'Rabbit!'

'Rabbit! What are you doing?'

Rabbit, his comrades called him. They had dubbed him Rabbit's Foot soon after they arrived in the city. That first patrol, leading a T-34 down a street under a bridge. *RUSZKIKHAZA!* daubed on a grocery shop window. Vasily had seen past the white-painted words, into the store, where a dozen men armed with Molotovs waited in ambush. Vasily had warned his lieutenant. He had taken some convincing. But he halted the tank and ordered the patrol to storm the shop. Killed the Hungarians, but Dobrynin had taken a bad burn from a Molotov. One tank shell through the shop window would have been easier. Would have saved Dobrynin the pain. But the tank commander refused to waste shells on a hunch.

Still, his comrades called him their lucky charm. Warnings would not suffice this time.

'Rabbit! Come back!'

'Rabbit!'

His commanding officer joined in, barking rabidly: 'Soldier! Get back in line! Get back in line this instant!'

Vasily levelled his rifle and fired into the crowd. Cut down three men. Anger fled. Replaced by terror. The front row pushed backwards, mob turning to stampede. Vasily fired again. The crowd answered with screams and shouts. Terror and fury together. Molotovs and bricks and other missiles sailed from their midst. Behind him, Vasily heard his lieutenant call the order to open fire.

'Rabbit!' his comrades yelled, urging him to rejoin them.

Rabbit's Foot. They didn't understand. In order to be lucky, the rabbit had to bleed. Had to die. Had to stop being a rabbit. Vasily told them that at the court martial. They sentenced him, not for killing, but for killing before he was told to do so.

'A rabbit is prey,' he said. 'I am a predator.'

*

1963. SOMEWHERE IN THE USSR.

'This? This is what we have to work with?'

'They are intended as weapons. Weapons are meant to be dangerous.'

'Some of these strike me as too dangerous.'

Vasily dug at a knot, excavating the wooden table with a fingernail. He eavesdropped on the conversation in the corridor. He wondered when they would come and talk to him, instead of about him.

Every day they would march him to this cell. They put two guards in the corridor, right outside. Vasily wondered if they accorded his neighbours the same 'courtesy'. He fancied meeting them – his fellow inmates. Subjects. But no, his guards always told him, 'You are not here to make friends, Vasily.' And they laughed, as though the idea of Vasily making friends was a good joke. The better joke was that they were dogs themselves and did not realise it. More, they did not understand that before you became a dog's master, you should befriend the animal. And never show it you were afraid.

Sit, they told him. Stay. Like a good dog. Then they retreated to their posts outside the door. Waiting for their master to come and begin today's experiment. And Vasily played the good dog. Chain a dog in your yard, you could watch it fret and hear it whimper. Watch it jump to attention, barking or snarling at every passing stranger or squirrel. Driven mad by the things it couldn't see, beyond the fence. And by the passage of empty hours. All that solitary time, which was supposed to mean nothing to it because it was only a dumb beast.

Maybe it was, but for a man, every second ticking by cost something. No clock was needed to count them.

Vasily knew how to be a good dog and disobey at the same time. They could not see where he strayed, seated there at this table.

He gazed at the wall. Clinical whitewashed brick conspired with the unshaded bulb to create an almost hostile glare. Its unfriendliness was nothing to Vasily. The hospital décor invested the miserable underground bunker with more brightness than it deserved. But bright white or shadows served equally well as a canvas when trying to picture the world past those walls.

Vasily roamed. Free, but not far.

In the next cell: a young man, with hair that had never met scissors or comb, huddled over his table. He scrawled in a notebook, shielding his writings with one hand like a student zealously protecting his test answers. A poet and a revolutionary, Vasily was surprised the guards had allowed him the privilege of notebook and pen. Vasily flashed to a document bearing the budding Dostoyevsky's photograph. Tsarsko, was the name.

Vasily wandered onwards. Scouting other cells.

A tender teenager. Irena, her document supplied the name. A shrinking violet, plain with a drab brown pony tail. She met the walls of her cell with darting eyes, like a frightened bird separated from her flock. Three cells on, another man. Wispy straw-coloured hair already cobwebbed with threads of white, despite no particular age in the face. Vasily *recognised* him. Ekel, said his official documentation. But there was another name – The Creeper – alongside a remembered black-and-white newspaper photo: a courtroom, a lot of angry, grieving families – and that face. That high forehead and hungry eyes, the mouth that naturally defaulted to that same snarl. Next, a dusk-faced Turkmen with a precision-trimmed goatee. Name: Abdulin. Sulking, chin resting on folded arms. His right hand was curled into a fist, as though he believed he was holding something. A weapon? A throat? Vasily could not see inside the man's skull. Then there was Valentina. Platinum blonde, a product of too much bleach and make-up and not enough food, she sat too upright, like a starved queen on her throne. Blue frost in her eyes enticed Vasily. She would be one to watch.

There were others in different cells, different blocks. Some would fall by the wayside. This was a school as much as a prison, and not everyone would pass their exams. Vasily would, of course. He would play the good dog. Good behaviour would earn him privileges. He would serve the experiments, but those experiments served him. Training him to become top dog.

It would only be a matter of time before he contacted the other dogs in their kennels. He would get to know them. He would make friends with them.

1964.

Rabbits again. It amused Vasily that it had to be rabbits.

This time they were to be fried. Electricity.

Vasily floated above the cages lined up on the bench-top. Followed the wires from the cages to the switch where the laboratory technician had a hand on the master switch embedded in the tiled wall. Vasily tasted the creatures' fear before the technician threw the switch.

The animals had witnessed the procedure before, many times. It always ended with one of their number cooked. They were primed. Associations born of a few simple steps and an unmistakeable smell in the air. They *knew*. Vasily used that. Tapped into the fear and threw switches of his own. Inside their pathetic brains.

He watched the animals writhe. And listened. There was no current in the wires. The animals died all the same.

'Well?' said the officer seated across the table from him.

Vasily nodded. In his mind, he watched the last rabbit twitch and expire. 'Tell me,' he said. 'Why do you have me kill them?'

'What?' The officer looked up from his clipboard.

'Why kill them? I know the answer, I believe. I am curious, that is all, whether you understand. Why do you not have one of your laboratory technicians cuddle the bunnies? Pet them? Feed them carrots? Then have me make them see those nice things.'

'You ask strange questions. I do not devise the experiments.'

Vasily smiled. Only following orders. Interested in some truths, no care for some others. He kept his truth to himself. It was one he'd known since he was a boy.

Cruelty – horror – was easier to see than kindness.

'At least tell me you are going to cook them.' Vasily laughed. 'We could all have stew tonight.'

The officer stood and took his leave, without another word. The staff always wanted to keep conversations short.

1967.

The officer slid a photograph across the table. Vasily interpreted the officer's expression as a death warrant.

'May I ask why you want this man dead?'

Vasily studied the picture. A little fuzzy around the edges from a long-distance zoom, the subject appeared engrossed in conversation with two other men seated around an al fresco café table. The man appeared inoffensive enough.

'What's this?' said the officer. 'You've developed a conscience, Vasily?'

'Have I said I won't do it? I'll do it.'

The officer sighed. 'They killed one of ours. In an East Berlin hospital. We believe in fair exchange.'

Vasily reckoned neither the officer nor the 'we' of whom he spoke believed in anything of the sort. 'Consider it done. Now shut up and let me concentrate.'

The officer scowled. Vasily went to work.

He studied the photograph. Saw the man. Imagined himself descending into the photograph, travelling every line of that face. Then, gradually, *saw* the man. *Now.* Walking. A scene resolved around him.

Sunny street. Shoppers and traffic. City breeze. The beep of a car horn. A phantom face bled through the painting like a rebellious watermark. Pretty, young, black. Not the first time her face had invaded his visions, but her name still refused to come to him. He concentrated. Banished her. Then returned to his walking.

Walking. Walking.

Pedestrians brushing past. A hasty apology in German as a woman brushed too close. The city was full of impatience. Walking. Walking. There, along the street, the perfect opportunity. A Porsche, roof crested with lights and doors emblazoned with *POLIZEI.*

Vasily slipped inside, between the officers' shoulders, watching the target through the patrol car's windscreen. He added a detail or two to the picture. Artistic touches. A gun in the target's hand. The target raising his arm.

The police car swerved and screeched to a halt. The officers bailed out. They pulled sidearms and shouted the requisite warnings. The target froze and raised his hands, frightened, confused, pleading. Vasily's version swung his gun in a threatening arc. The police officers kept their firearms trained on the armed lunatic. The target begged and proclaimed his innocence. Vasily's version aimed the gun at the police officers.

The officers yelled their warnings again. And again. Gave the criminal every chance to surrender. Then they killed the target for Vasily.

Everything according to the book.

*

41

1971.

There were days when Vasily idled and drifted beyond his cell, beyond the walls of the facility. Across the seas, around the globe. Why not? He searched out places, people. Not targets. Travelling for its own sake. Then there were days when the world led his mind elsewhere, like a child with something of tremendous interest to show its parent...

Today it led him down into a tunnel or a tomb. Chambers of sand and shadow. Under a New Mexico mesa, two women read pictograms in torchlight.

For an instant, he saw her again: the black woman, sketching furiously in a pad. She faded, as always, but it seemed he could hear her pencil scratching at the paper somewhere close by.

Then there it was, something moving in the rooms below.

It was a skeletal demon. Like some prehistoric archaeopteryx stripped of feather and flesh. A dragon – or a giant bird of prey – spreading wings of pearlescent bone. A graceful, majestic dead thing – and yet so alive. More alive than anything he had ever seen. A skull sculpted like no creature he had ever seen, in books or in dreams. Eyeless, but seeing. How could a thing with no surface possess so much beneath? Soul was its marrow. It rose from shadow and carried him high above the world.

He was powerful. A god.

It rose, and it swept him high on wings of bone. And it spoke to him.

Vasily, it said.

1981. MOSCOW.

The kettle shrilled. There was a knock at the door.

Vasily glanced down the hall. He went to the stove. Hand wrapped in a tea towel, he picked up the kettle and poured the tea into the pot. The visitor knocked again. He twirled the tea strainer, giving it a hearty stir. He leaned over the pot, inhaling the steam. Then trapped it in with the lid.

The knock became a hammering.

Vasily picked up the bread knife. Gripping the loaf, fixing it in place, he sawed through the crust down to the bread board. A few loose crumbs flew free and fell into the grooves at the edge of the board. He carried the pot and the fresh slice of bread to the table. Set the pot down beside the waiting cup and dropped the slice onto the plate. He pulled up a chair and sat. Lifted the lid of the butter dish and dug into the stick of butter with the knife. Spread his butter with forceful strokes.

A fist pounded at his front door. Someone angry called his full name. Twice.

Vasily poured his cup and let it sit. He lifted his bread and sniffed the crust. Inhaled the light dusting of flour. He took a bite.

Someone smashed in his front door.

As he chewed, he pulled the heavy Tokarev from his belt and set it on the table. He washed down the taste of butter and bread with a mouthful of tea. No milk. He watched the men storm into his apartment. He carried on chomping, between slurps of tea.

They rushed about him. Their captain loitered in the doorway and surveyed the kitchen. He moved to the stove, passed a hand over the kettle, testing the heat. He peered around, staring through Vasily. He prowled to the pantry door and kicked that open, looked over the shelves. Then he did the rounds, yanking open drawers and cupboards, rummaging through every square foot of storage. They wouldn't find anything. Vasily had packed last night.

His bags were stowed in the corner, beside the refrigerator. Vasily projected a laundry rack in the same spot, something they would see without feeling the need to search too closely.

He enjoyed two more bites of bread and washed them down with two long mouthfuls of tea. He rose. Tucked his pistol back in his belt. Fetched his bags. He moved slow. Calm. He walked down the hall, side-stepping briefly into the living room to avoid one trooper. Then proceeded to the front door.

He left the KGB to their search. He had a plane to hijack. And a train to catch.

CHAPTER FIVE
We Are the Dead

JULY 1981.

Alistair exited the pub into another world. An otherwise ordinary street that refused to stop spinning. Freddie tugged him aside, clearing the doorway for the soldiers who trotted past to the sandbag nest.

'We had best make our retreat. I get the impression the lads are almost ready.'

Alistair allowed himself to be led back along the street. Inside the sandbag nest, the demolition team wired up an old-school plunger detonator. Rather like old times, but for the fact he wasn't calling the shots. The last of the soldiers hastened from the pub and joined their squad mates behind cover. Freddie let go of Alistair's arm. They strolled on almost side by side. Not quite in step.

'What exactly is happening here?'

'Crisis management. You know the drill.'

'I'm not sure I understand in this instance.'

Again, Freddie could attribute his slowness to having his brain knocked about. Whether the attack had actually occurred or not, Freddie appeared to be treating him as though he were a victim of *something*.

'Second device found. Controlled detonation,' Freddie explained, warming to the role of storyteller. 'Those back at the community centre will be needing an explanation for the second explosion. Evacuees and victims. When they're allowed to return to their homes they'll need to know two things. Item one: that their neighbourhood is safe. Item two: that reality matches their perceptions. We need something for the news cameras as well.'

'What? This is... What? Window dressing? You can't be serious.'

'Oh, come now, Brigadier. You've sanctioned bigger lies than this. Swept so many monsters and God-knows-what under the carpet; the ground beneath your feet must be terribly uneasy to stand on.'

Alistair thought about his wheelchair waiting for him in 2011, then barred his friend's path. 'I'm well aware of my part in every incident. But I'm not a hundred percent clear on what exactly is being swept under the carpet here.'

'Terrorism. That's all you need to know. We know what we're doing. It's not our first rodeo, as the Americans would say. Sunderland, Leeds, Coventry. As I said. You have been keeping up with the news from your Swiss ivory tower?'

'You're saying this is the same woman?'

'*Again,* all our eye-witness accounts say a man. An Irishman. None of the usual groups claim responsibility. We suspect a lone wolf. Rogue paramilitary. Working his way south. God knows where he'll strike next.'

Whatever the man was – illusion or memory playing tricks – he had been *too* Irish. Like he'd been advertising his nationality. A performance.

A diesel engine growled into life. The military truck rumbled away down the side street. Alistair took in what was probably his last view of *The Old Fusilier*.

'This isn't UNIT business,' Freddie said.

'So, whose business is it exactly?'

'*National* interest. It should be abundantly clear, this was no ordinary attack. We can be grateful there were no deaths. But make no mistake: there are victims. We have seen this before. You are made of sterner stuff, old boy, but I'd have to be a fool to miss how shaken you are, seeing this pub still standing. Doesn't tally, does it?'

Very little did.

'Most of those people back at the community centre, the sight of this would break them.'

'So, you're bending reality to fit their truth?' Alistair asked.

'We can't say what the truth is yet, but I can advise you this much: leave well alone. When the doctor has given you the all-clear, take yourself home, get plenty of rest and start thinking about that teaching post. I'll be happy to come talk it over with you. I'll try to be more prompt next time.'

'Fine. But I might stay locally. Tell me, do you happen to know of any hostels in the area?'

'Hostels? Come off it, old boy, we can do better than that. Put you up in a four-star at the very least.'

'Never mind, I'll find my own way.

'Go and see the doctor first. That's an order.'

'Oh, I intend to.'

The explosion shook the street. The pub caved in under a cloud of dust and rubble. A shockwave blew through Alistair like a gale.

He never knew déjà vu could be so violent.

The dead lay covered. For all the good that did. Bagged and arranged in a neat row along one wall, they shared hangar space with the practice plane. The internal layout had been a perfect match. Perhaps the only aspect that hadn't turned out to be a lie.

Now these six lay before Bugayev. The hardest of truths.

He could have ordered the remains located elsewhere, but they were evidence, and this was where evidence belonged for now. He made a mental note of each name-tag. They had all been IDed via their passports. None had family or companions aboard the flight. All lone travellers. Bugayev made a silent vow to each.

He crossed the hangar, under the plane, to the jumble sale on the far side. Tarpaulin and trestle tables, all the luggage set out. Bags, backpacks, suitcases, coats, jackets, sweaters, belongings disinterred from overhead compartments and below-deck stores. Thirty of his best troops sorting and sifting through everything like keen-eyed customers hunting out bargains.

'Sir,' Grushkin said with a salute. His gaze flitted to the hangar door.

'Our guests have departed,' Bugayev informed him. He had seen the pair off his command centre before heading here.

'Did they tell us anything useful?'

'Names and photo IDs for the six suspects. Quite a comprehensive file on each. Whether it proves useful or not, that's up to us now.'

Grushkin's arched brow quickly folded into a frown. He was not usually so open a book. Bugayev studied the industrious activity around the tarps and tables. A platoon of highly-trained soldiers cataloguing and setting out items for the two snipers-turned-photographers who buzzed from display to display. A waste of skills, but these were the men he trusted. The fact that the KGB hadn't muscled in on the investigation with their personnel was surprising. Suspicious, even.

'What about our efforts?' he asked. 'Have they turned up anything?'

'Ah,' said Grushkin. He retrieved a single plastic evidence bag from the table behind him. He dangled it in front of Bugayev. 'So far there is this. Useful? I can't say, sir. But it fit the search parameters: "anything out of the ordinary".'

Bugayev lifted the bottom of the bag a degree or two for closer scrutiny. Inside, a trinket; a crude flanged cylinder, the size of a tuna can, three gnarled stumps projecting from one side like fingers cut short at the knuckle. A single moulding best described as organic, it had the fluid sheen and depth of a strangely deformed pearl. Useful? He couldn't say either. But his gut said it had served a purpose.

'Where was it found?'

'In the coat pocket of passenger one-one-nine.' Grushkin nodded towards the makeshift morgue. Bugayev knew the number and the name that accompanied it. 'Kovalev. The coat was located in the overhead compartment above his seat. Does it tell us anything?'

'Plenty.' Bugayev beckoned Grushkin a pace or three aside, clearing room for the men attending the table. 'What does it look like to you?'

'A bone. Specifically, a vertebra. But the composition...'

'The composition we can worry about later. In fact, let's set aside what it was and concentrate on what it is now. What it means to the various players in this scenario.'

Wolf, Bugayev had insisted to those KGB representatives. His thoughts were a pack, chasing down answers.

'According to our guests, we are dealing not with terrorists but with thieves. That is one of the treasures with which the thieves have supposedly absconded.' Two or three photographs in the KGB dossier had depicted similar artefacts. 'To our Lubyanka comrades it's stolen goods. For the thieves, I don't know. Yet. But it served some purpose, over and above its value. Part of the mechanics of the situation we experienced here.'

'What did we experience? Some sort of mass hallucination?'

48

'Collective illusion? Six deceased. Six fugitives. That can't be a coincidence. They wanted us to believe it was them. Or rather, they wanted the KGB to believe it was them.'

'Diversion. Decoy.'

Bugayev nodded. Grushkin was on the scent with him. 'Tie us up here while they make their getaway. By road,' Bugayev said. 'Or train.'

'Twenty-four hours. They could be anywhere.'

'Not quite anywhere, Grushkin. When you're fleeing the KGB, it's best to leave the Soviet Union. By the shortest route possible.'

'West? They intend to defect?'

'Perhaps. The West would welcome such recruits. But I'm not sure these people wish to trade one master for another.'

'We have no idea of the range over which they can exert their powers. We should alert the Border Guards. It may not be too late.'

Bugayev smiled. He took the evidence bag from his friend, tossed it and caught it in his palm. 'That net is already cast.'

Putting out the call had been his first step after seeing off the KGB. Bugayev strolled away towards the hangar doorway.

'Leave half the men here on luggage detail,' he ordered over his shoulder. 'The rest, have them assembled on Air Force One. Ready for wheels up at a moment's notice.'

'Sir.'

He wanted to be in the air, ready to pounce on the first promising lead. Bugayev cast a farewell eye over the row of six body bags.

Efficiency was the least he owed them.

Alistair played the dutiful soldier. It wasn't often in his

life that the role was an act. But Freddie had obliged him to play games.

Back at the Maidenwood centre, he presented himself to the doctor. The exam amounted to little more than a prod, a blood-pressure test and a few simple questions to ensure he was *compos mentis*. Freddie, meanwhile, took to the stage, making an announcement about the second explosion everybody had heard. Not a natural showman, but he sold the story well enough. Many of the faces appeared visibly shaken – doubtless the blast had rattled the windows and brought a fresh wave of traumatic memories for all concerned. Freddie's explanation was a sugar pill, but an uneasy calm settled over the room once he was finished. Illusion or reality, civilians should never have to face such nightmares. Alistair counted himself fortunate: there were benefits to being no stranger to violence.

Awarded the all-clear, Alistair thanked the doctor. Watching and waiting for Freddie to depart, he went for a roam between the beds and mattresses, searching for one face in particular.

He finally found her. Features frail, lips tightly pinched together and eyes on the point of tears, but perfectly clean of blood and uninjured. Her beau sat with her, brushing the long brown hair from her face. She barely registered the caresses. But it was something to see her safe, if not altogether sound.

Alistair wandered out to reception, keeping a wary eye out for Freddie. By the look of things, the old boy had gone. Alistair found the fellow he was after and collared him just as he was on his way to the front door.

'You there. I need to borrow you.'

The sketch artist turned. 'Sir?'

'I need you to do a sketch for me. You've not taken my description of the suspect yet.'

The chap patted the large pad tucked under one arm.

'Oh, that's all right, got what we need. Sir Frederick reckoned a dozen would suffice.'

'All the same, I insist.' He flashed his UNIT ID.

'Um. Okay. Sir. Um.'

Alistair gestured to a nearby open doorway. An administrative office. Empty. 'Shall we?'

Soon they were each settled into a chair, the artist opening his pad over his knee, pencil at the ready.

Alistair cast his mind back. Like casting a net and not knowing quite what he was going to trawl. Two versions of one incident shared the same cloudy waters. He dismissed the image of the Irishman.

A portrait swam to the surface.

'She had red hair.'

'She?'

'Yes. She. The most incredible red, really. Long, wavy. Rounded face. Like an egg, I suppose you might say. Eggshell complexion too. Pale. Fine eyebrows, very dark – almost like they were drawn with charcoal.' He raised a hand to his mouth. 'A full pout, big, blood-red. Eyes quite far apart, not especially deep-set, but – I don't know, the way she looked at you... It was like she saw everything from a distance. Like a cat, you know, the way those animals seem to know more than you could ever know, but what she saw she was – haunted by it. Yes, that was it, a haunted look. Nose...' How the devil did one describe a nose? 'Uniform width from the bridge down. Not much curve to it. In profile, I mean.' The artist nodded, still scratching away with his pencil. 'Small nostrils.' Alistair shrugged.

The artist turned his pad, presenting the page for Alistair's inspection.

'Good gracious. Did you read my mind, man?'

'Ha. Nothing like that, sir. Just a talent. So, can we call that a print?'

'Um, cheekbones less pronounced. Fuller in the face.

51

Otherwise, spot on.'

The artist applied quick finishing touches. Yes. That was her.

'I'll take that if I may.'

The receptionist pushed the sketch back across the counter. 'Sorry, guv. Can't help you.'

Alistair sighed and folded the paper. The page had been through a lot of hands that afternoon and was looking as worn and tired as he felt. He had pounded a great deal of pavement to get nowhere. He wouldn't admit it normally, but he missed Google.

Good old-fashioned detective work was tough on the resolve as well as the shoe leather. Still, he had a few more addresses to check out before he was done. The theory remained sound.

As part of her act, his suspect had enquired about lodgings. Reasoning that the most effective lies were seasoned with the truth, there was a chance she had installed herself at a hostel or B&B in the area. The items in the backpack suggested padding, but if she had been working her way southwards, Alistair wagered that she would have genuine luggage and need of a place to stay. Perhaps not too close to the pub, but possibly within the same postcode. He had included all the local budget bed and breakfasts in his search. This was the fourth hostel.

He wondered if he should have borrowed one of the sketches of the Irishman as well. To cover all his bases. Why did he have both memories sitting side by side in his head? Of course, there were, in a sense, two of him in there too. Did his future self inhabiting his past self's body interfere with the illusion somehow? Was his presence here altering the past? He understood that to be bad. But it wasn't as though he was in any position to do anything about it. He had enough on his plate without fretting over timelines and what have you.

A cough stalled him on his way to the door.

A scruffy figure slouched at the base of the stairs. Barefoot, hands in pockets, hair and beard apparently in a race to reach the floor. He extricated a hand from his jeans pocket long enough to favour Alistair with a wave.

'Got a fag, mate?'

'I'm afraid not.' Alistair continued towards the door, then reconsidered. 'Excuse me, perhaps you can help. Have you been a resident here long?'

'Eh?'

'Have you stayed here long?'

'Long enough. What can I do you for?'

'I'm looking for someone. Wondering if she might have stayed here.'

Alistair handed over the sketch.

'Oh yeah.' The fellow nodded immediately. A bolt of something – fear or anticipation? – pierced Alistair's chest. 'Romola, said her name was. Gypsy blood, I shouldn't wonder.'

'Did she have a surname?'

'Assume so. Didn't share it with me though.'

'What else can you tell me about her?'

'Not much.' The gentleman scratched himself inside his jeans' pocket. 'Wasn't much into sharing. Was a bit tight with her personal space too, if you know what I mean.'

'I'm not sure I do.'

'Well, you know. Didn't want anybody crowding her. I made small-talk, she kept it smaller. Mind, I was only trying to cadge some baccy. Maybe she twigged to that, didn't care for spongers.'

'Quite possibly. Did she mention where she might be heading after this?' This was a person with a plan. The 'bomb' had been part of that and, as far as Alistair could gauge, it had gone well. So far, she had been given no cause to veer from her plan. As such, it was exceedingly unlikely she would divulge anything of it to this individual.

'Not really, man.'

Alistair accepted the paper, folded and tucked it away.

'But,' said the hippy.

'But...?'

'Like I said, I tried to cadge some baccy. No joy.' He dug at the back of his head, grinned. 'So, I – you know – waited until she hit the showers. Had a bit of a poke around in her pack.'

'I see...' Alistair said, doing his best not to judge.

'Well, she had tickets. For Europe.'

'Europe? Where in Europe?'

'All over, man. One of those travel everywhere rail tickets. You know? I was going to take a sabbatical before college. Take the tour. See the sights. Paris. Berlin. Rome. Venice. Venice, man!'

If let loose across the continent, there was no telling the damage the woman could do. Even if the damage amounted to purely mental trauma, Alistair shuddered to think what effect that might have on a widespread scale.

'Did she have brochures? Any indication as to her choice of destinations?'

'Nothing like that. She had a ticket for the hovercraft. Dover to... France, someplace.'

'Boulogne.'

'Sure. That's all I can tell you.'

'Did you happen to notice the date?'

The gentleman shrugged. 'Today?'

There was still some of the day left. But Alistair had the sinking feeling he was already too late.

54

CHAPTER SIX
Jean Genie

JULY 1981. *GARE DU NORD*, PARIS.

Alerted by the PA, Alistair tucked his newspaper under his arm and strode to the gate. He checked his watch. The 17:27 from *Boulogne-Sur-Mer Ville* was pulling in at platform twelve, right according to schedule. You had to credit the French for the punctuality of their rail services.

He watched the SNCF locomotive slow through the last hundred yards.

It was a long shot. But far from the first long shot of his career. If pressed, he would maintain he wasn't a gambling man, regardless of the risks that came with the territory. This strategy had involved more than its fair share of calculation. To say nothing of a deal of hasty organisation and effort.

Carriage doors opened and passengers spilled onto the platform, converging in a stream. He scanned the bobbing faces.

She had to be among them – *Romola,* if that was her real name. Even if there was a fight yet to be fought, he had to have won this race.

Timetables didn't lie. Albeit, they made promises the world couldn't always keep. Assuming she had hightailed it to Waterloo directly after the blast, she would have had a choice of two trains to Dover, either of which would deliver her in time for the last hovercraft of the evening, for an arrival in Boulogne at 5pm. Taking Paris as her most likely destination from there, she would then face a two-and-a-half-hour ride on this train. No Channel Tunnel in 1981. Any substantial delays or hitches would play to his advantage.

Meanwhile, he had managed a five o'clock flight, followed by a dash for a taxi and a forty-minute ride from Orly. This was a hare and tortoise affair.

He had cut things finer in the past.

'Come on, come on,' he muttered.

The vanguard of the crowd milled through the gate. Alistair cut a course through to the other side. Along the platform, a father stooped and spread his arms to capture two children in his embrace, revealing the final knot of stragglers to disembark.

There she was: a splash of red hair, khaki longcoat, grey backpack patched with denim and topped with a blue sleeping bag. The relaxed stride of a gap-year student hitting the first stop on her tour.

Alistair slipped into the oncoming crowd and forged his way upstream, doing his best to use the taller passengers as cover while tracking his prey via glimpses. He arced behind her and closed.

Three people between them. Two. One.

He reached – and grasped her coat collar.

She stopped.

She turned her head, slow, and studied him from the partial cover of her backpack and a half-curtain of hair.

'Question is, what now, Captain?'

There was a gleam in her eye, a silky hiss in her voice. Less like cornered prey, more like a snake delighted to have him overturn her rock.

'Brigadier, actually,' he took some pleasure in correcting her. 'You recognise a military officer when you see one though?'

'I've known one or two.'

The last of the passengers had left them behind. They had that small patch of station to themselves. Alistair suffered a brief and uncomfortable vision of Trevor Howard and Celia Johnson.

'What now, Miss, is I arrest you. Come quietly and you may count yourself fortunate. Believe me, it's only the fact that nobody was actually killed that this option is on the table.'

'Funny.' The gleam in her eyes turned to icicles. 'There's something different about you. But despite your lofty vantage point, despite everything you've seen, you're so sure of yourself. So sure of your senses.'

The tall, slender woman in the white hat spun free from his hold and slapped his arm. '*Lâche-moi! Lâche-moi!*' She retreated, staring, then searched for help. She backed away until she broke into a run. The coat-tails of her pink mac flapped behind her.

Of course! Stupid.

Alistair scanned the crowds and the many faces turning to follow the fleeing woman. Before long they would be looking his way, possibly racing to a phone box to report an assault.

Alistair put distance between himself and the scene of the crime. He scanned the platforms, the kiosks, the queues at the ticket office. Everywhere.

There! Red hair, khaki longcoat, denim-patched backpack. Hastening into the river of people flowing through the main station exit.

He chucked his newspaper aside and ran after his true target.

Turned out, he was the hare who had arrived here first then fallen asleep. But his rival, she was no tortoise.

CHOP, UKRAINE.

The aerial view of the railyard could have been

mistaken for the scene of a major accident.

A riot of flashing red and blue vehicles surrounding the train – ambulances, police, fire trucks, military – cluttering every space between the tracks and even parked across the rails here and there where they weren't occupied by rolling stock. Men swarmed the length of the train and guarded every gap between vehicles.

Bugayev counted four BTRs: their spotlights added fierce illumination to the railyard's floodlights. One of the spotlights swung aloft, catching the helicopter, then directed its beam left to a relatively clear patch outside the perimeter of vehicles. The Mi-24 obediently homed in on the selected landing spot and descended.

Wheels touched ground and Bugayev hopped out. Grushkin and six of his troops followed in close order. They cut as straight a course as possible between all the vehicles and manpower. The train coaches were jacked up between blue posts, the operation to change bogies perhaps halfway completed. Dogs led their handlers along the train, the animals sniffing the undercarriage for hidden ordinance.

Bugayev awarded the Border Guards points for diligence. The task now was to find out if the fugitives had left him anything by way of a scent.

He searched out the officer in charge, finding a Border Guard colonel locked in discussion with a small circle of police and troops. The colonel broke away from his little pow-wow and presented his best salute. Basic message: *this mess is all yours now, you are most welcome.* Good. No jurisdictional arguments and a fair assurance of co-operation.

'Colonel Vovk.' The man stepped aside to afford Bugayev a clear view of everything he was doing to control the scene and manage the operation. Bugayev threw him an approving nod.

'Major Bugayev. Give me a capsule summary.'

Vovk considered, like a man recalling a shopping list. 'So. As far as we can estimate, a fire broke out in Coach D, roughly forty minutes into the gauge change. The blaze spread quickly to adjacent carriages. We have patients being contained and treated on board for mental trauma. But no burns. Although people swear to being caught in the blaze. It is—'

'Strange,' Bugayev supplied the word for him. 'Don't concern yourself over the credibility, Colonel. We're going to need to search those coaches.'

'There is also no fire damage.'

'That's not what we're looking for.'

'Very well. And you're going to want to speak to this man.' Vovk gestured to a young man in SZhD uniform, beckoned him forward from the small knot of Border Guards and police. 'Nenashev. Train conductor. He reports passengers missing according to the manifest. And… well, you had best hear from him.'

The conductor approached like a man on trial.

'Let me guess,' said Bugayev. 'Six passengers?'

Despite his obvious nerves, the lad summoned a firm answer. 'Five, sir.' Then the firmness evaporated. 'As well as a… That is, an item from the baggage car.'

'What item?'

'A corpse, sir.'

Bugayev gestured to the train. 'Show us.'

Alistair burst from the station into the bustle and lights of a warm Paris evening. The surge of passengers separated into trickles: towards the bus stop, hailing taxis, or joining the general flow of pedestrians in either direction.

His first thought: *Hopeless.*

Then he spotted her: moving briskly among a small group passing a long café front. Two of her civilian escorts peeled off to examine the menu posted by the entrance.

Alistair launched into a sprint. He cut past a woman coming the other way and had to vault the small pup trailing her on a lead. His jump provoked ferocious yapping, but the woman tugged the savage pet on its way. He sidestepped more oncoming pedestrians, dodged around the café's al fresco furniture – and nearly ran into another set of tables and chairs he was sure hadn't been there before. Illusion or no, he avoided them.

She was a few yards ahead, striding calmly.

Too calmly. He clamped a hand on her backpack, pulling at one of the straps securing the sleeping bag.

The fellow turned, and Alistair's heart sank.

'Dash it all, I'm sorry. *Pardonnezmoi.*'

The fellow had no backpack. He had a beret, a clipped silver beard and an angry tirade of French to hurl at Alistair.

Backing off, attempting to calm the man with raised hands, Alistair searched up and down the pavement. There at the curbside! The denim-patched backpack. She hauled it off her shoulders, stowed it in the back of a taxi. Then climbed in after it.

Alistair ran to the curb, flagging a cab as the target vehicle pulled away.

Aboard the baggage car, the conductor showed Bugayev and Grushkin the open cage. He stood back, inviting them inside.

Amid the stacked trunks and cases and the bicycles propped against the larger pieces of luggage, the standout exhibit was the coffin. A simply-ornamented pine box, the lid was off and leaning upright against one of the bicycles. Bugayev noted the cushioned interior and the pillow, plus a rumpled blanket. The deceased had been made comfortable. And warm.

Grushkin gave a wry grimace. 'Are we sure they

weren't transporting their master home to Transylvania?' He lifted the padlock on the cage door to show the cut. 'They broke their dead friend out.'

The poor conductor stood looking lost and troubled, as though afraid the transportation of the undead was a genuine possibility. 'According to the manifest, the deceased was Hungarian. An uncle. They were shipping him home to be buried in Budapest.'

Bugayev waved him onward. 'Show us the compartment.'

'It's empty, sir.'

'Still, let's see it.'

'Of course.'

The conductor led the way through the train. They only had to pass through a single carriage, suggesting their fugitives had wanted to be close to their dead relative. Bugayev glanced in on every compartment.

'Were these occupied?'

'Most, yes. All passengers from this coach have been relocated to the dining car, sir. They... cannot face the site of the blaze. As you see, sir, there is no sign of fire, but they believe it. I saw the flames myself when I came to answer the alarm and evacuate the passengers. I...' He swallowed audibly. 'I saw some people on fire, sir.' Several of the compartment windows were missing their curtains. Torn down and thrown over burn victims, no doubt, in the fight to extinguish non-existent flames. 'I cannot imagine what it must feel like. To remember, but to see this. Not a single scorch mark.'

Bugayev knew full well how experience and reality might refuse to add up.

The conductor halted at the third compartment from the end. Again, he tucked himself to one side and pointed within.

'This one.'

Bugayev ushered Grushkin in ahead. He took in the

seats, the overhead racks, tiny fold-down table affixed under the window. Grushkin set about pulling the seats apart. He drew his combat knife and opened a gash in the upholstery.

'And the alarm went off at – what? – sixteen-hundred-hours?'

A near-two-hour flight time from Shemyatovo to Stryi airbase, then another forty-minute chopper had delivered him and his team there. He wanted a precise snapshot of the enemy's travel timetable running parallel.

'Around then, sir. Sorry we cannot be any more exact. Different passengers noticed the flames at different times, and then the panic. It was... chaotic.'

'Naturally.' Bugayev patted the man on the upper arm.

Almost five hours ago. Just as he and his men were processing the aftermath of their assault on the plane. No coincidence. The fugitives would have realised their diversion game was up at that point. So, time to disembark. The blaze? It fit their modus operandi. Another distraction. To cover for breaking their sleeping partner out of storage. Why the coffin? Their powers of illusion probably required concentration. And possibly isolation. A coffin was the perfect way to transport a friend who had to lie down and shut out the world.

'Here,' said Grushkin, rising from his excavations. Held between finger and thumb, he presented Bugayev with his find: a second pearlescent bone. Slender and long, knobbed at either end, like a metacarpal or metatarsal.

Some dead thing appeared to be leaving pieces of its skeleton everywhere.

Bugayev bagged and pocketed the evidence. Done there. He led the way back along the carriage. They ran into Colonel Vovk, standing outside like a headstone in uniform.

62

'Something for me?' Bugayev asked.

Vovk nodded. 'Abandoned SZhD bus ten kilometres west of the border. And a body inside.'

Bugayev thanked him and heard out the details. Death appeared to be a theme.

Alistair was caught in some insane motor-racing variant of the 'shell game'. Sat up front in his taxi, he strained to keep his eyes on the target vehicle – shuffling from lane to lane – now a half-dozen cars ahead.

His driver shouted and swore profusely, thumping the horn. Alistair half-regretted waving a fistful of francs under the man's nose as incentive. He might have purchased too much eagerness. At the slightest scent of a gap, his driver slammed his foot on the accelerator and willed his car through, risking wing mirrors and the permanent enmity of his fellow Parisian drivers.

Alistair was securely belted in, but with each violent burst of speed he felt liable to be crushed into his seat, or hurled through the windscreen into roaring traffic.

Still, they were gaining. Perhaps his suspect hadn't been quite so generous to her chauffeur. Another jolt of acceleration and they cut in front of another car. A belligerent horn blared from behind. Alistair's driver responded in kind, with volume fit to bring down the walls of Jericho. The target switched lanes again.

'They're taking a right,' Alistair warned.

His driver waved at him to relax. He spun the wheel over, obliging every car in the adjacent lane to brake and sending the taxi screeching around the bend. Unobstructed space opened between them and their prey. Alistair's driver stamped the pedal like he was planting his footprint in a Hollywood Stuntman Walk of Fame.

The bonnet gobbled up clear road.

Alistair's driver whooped like he was piloting one of those X-fighters in Con's *Star Wars* nonsense. Then his eyes bulged, excitement killed outright. They were playing chicken with a lorry. His driver threw the taxi into a hard swerve. Alistair grabbed the dash. They climbed the pavement, scraping shopfronts. The driver sent them back towards the road. Not soon or far enough. The taxi skidded into the back of a parked Peugeot.

Credit to his driver, he braked hard enough to soak up the worst of the smash. Alistair shook off the daze. There was no receding lorry in the mirror – of course there wasn't. The driver glanced everywhere, baffled and furious. Alistair tossed him the money and climbed out.

He ran in front of a motor-scooter.

Which braked less than a yard short of ironing him to the tarmac. The rider and his pillion-passenger girlfriend threw their arms up and looked from him to the crashed taxi and back again.

Their reactions convinced him they – and their transport – were real. Which persuaded him he wasn't done yet.

NE HUNGARY.

Traffic rumbled by, waved on by a cordon of Hungarian police. Every driver wanted to slow to take in the sideshow. Flat open fields that would never have drawn attention were suddenly a major tourist attraction because of the bus tipped at a drunken angle in the roadside ditch, and the military helicopter nesting in the grass beyond like a giant dragonfly. The sight of a handful of armed troops encouraged the drivers to accelerate away as soon as they passed the site of the incident.

Bugayev boarded the bus, Grushkin close behind. They worked their way up the inclined central aisle to the corpse slumped in a seat, head against the window. Dried blood streaked from a holed forehead, over the chin and inside his collar. War paint for a man who probably hadn't been given the opportunity to put up a fight.

The deceased wore oil-stained overalls, but not SZhD. This wasn't a railway man. Staff at Chop had verified the missing bus from their yard but, as far as they knew, all the station crew were present or accounted for. The hijackers hadn't felt the need to kidnap a driver. No, these fugitives were a close-knit group. A family who didn't need or want outsiders tagging along.

'No identification. Seven-sixty-two calibre wound,' said Grushkin, reiterating what they'd been told by the Hungarians. 'Border post reports no sight of this vehicle making the crossing.'

'No. They wouldn't,' Bugayev said. 'This bus could pass for anything with these fugitives working their head magic. Still, it's impractical and perhaps takes effort to maintain the illusion for a lengthy cross-country drive. Best guess: they switched vehicles. Ditched the bus, hailed the driver of a vehicle that took their fancy. The overalls suggest a utility vehicle of some type, from a garage maybe.' Bugayev knew when he was straying into guesswork and didn't like it. 'Something large enough to accommodate six.'

'Slender lead. And if they made it to Budapest they might switch again.'

Bugayev concurred with Grushkin's assessment. 'This trail is cold.' He gestured at the corpse. 'Colder than him.'

'What's our next step?'

'Time to come at this from another angle.'

'What other angle?'

Bugayev fished in his pocket and dangled the pair of evidence bags. 'These. I happen to know a lady who might know a thing or two about strange bones.'

'You do, sir?

Bugayev smiled, enjoying the rare chance to surprise his friend. 'And I know a man who should know where we can find her.'

Target reacquired.

Alistair didn't feel much like Steve McQueen on the lilac-coloured scooter, but he threaded his way through traffic, nipped between the tightest gaps in his mission to catch up.

Every lane slowed. Finally, some luck. Seven or eight cars ahead, her taxi stopped at the lights. In pole position.

Alistair threaded a route down the narrow channel between cars. His elbow clipped a wing mirror. No damage done.

Ahead, the taxi door swung open. His suspect jumped out, dragging her backpack after her. She wrestled it onto her shoulders as she ran across the street. Her taxi driver was out of his vehicle and shaking a fist. Alistair kept an eye on her as he sped to intercept.

She made it to the traffic island and dipped out of sight down the subway steps. *Alexandre Dumas* Metro.

Alistair zipped across to the pavement and leaped off the scooter. The bike toppled behind him and he dashed for the steps.

Into the Paris underground.

NW HUNGARY.

Vasily climbed into the passenger seat and rapped the dash to snap Valentina to attention. He waved for her to get the van moving, dug into the carrier bag and began distributing provisions to his comrades in the back. Bread, cold meats, cheese, bottled water and the few unwanted tomatoes that the supermarket had left at the end of their day.

Abdulin, Tsarsko, Irena, Ekel. Everyone grabbed a share and tucked in greedily.

'Don't I get to eat?' Valentina demanded. Her hands rested on the wheel, but the van remained idle. The beams illuminated the few other vehicles dotted about the store car park. Cars that no doubt belonged to the staff who had all looked very ready to head home. 'It has already been a long drive. I'm hungry too. And we could all use a rest.'

Ekel more than all of them. Huddled by the van's rear doors, he sank his teeth into a torn hunk of loaf like Nosferatu feeding on the body of Christ.

Long before the drive, all those hours in the coffin had taken their toll. He had been the best one – the only one really – for the job. Such a detailed and complex scenario benefited from a divided mind, a mind that could run in multiple directions at once. He needed the peace and separation from the world that came with confinement, but given the right environment he was the strongest of them. The cost was high though, and he looked far from the strongest now.

Once on the road through Hungary, Vasily had not wanted to stop. Stopped they had in Budapest, but only to leave the city a small gift. They had discussed grabbing a bite to eat at a restaurant – Valentina's suggestion; the woman had lost none of her refined appetites from the life she had left behind – but Vasily had insisted they press on. Because of the *Spetsnaz* on their trail. And because, for Vasily, that city was full of fallen statues and angry mobs.

He was half-tempted to hand Valentina a chunk of bread to rival Ekel's, and a wedge of cheese just to watch her attempt to tackle it with fingers that longed for cutlery and a palate that missed caviar.

'Drive,' he ordered.

She hissed like a cat. But she released the handbrake and started them rolling.

Vasily twisted the cap on a water bottle and took a long gulp. He thirsted for something stronger. But a clear head was needed. They would switch vehicles again once into Austria. And if they reached Vienna before eleven, he would search for an open restaurant for Valentina – with a bar for him. Schnitzels all round.

He raised a silent toast to their success. It would be a long and difficult night, waiting on word from their American cousins without a decent meal in their stomachs, and with an unhappy Valentina in the van with them.

Another race through a river of people. Alistair's world was a blur of faces and luggage and voices and a steady stampede echoing loudly along white-bricked tunnels. He scoured the crowds all the way, fearful of more decoys.

The tunnel branched. He hovered, having to dance to keep out of everyone's way. No choice but to toss an imaginary coin. He sprinted for the stairwell to the Eastbound platform.

There! A wash of red hair, the large denim-patched backpack with the blue sleeping bag. Carried along in the main current of people turning at the bottom of the stairs. Alistair battled his way down the steps, annoying Parisians with his pushy haste. He burst onto the platform.

Where a boxy green train waited. Doors wide. The narrow strip of platform afforded no hiding places. His target hopped onto the third carriage along. The carriage door in front of him was an open invitation. He glanced up the train. She was there in the window. Daring him.

But she was also further up the platform. Perched on a yellow seat, her backpack resting between her boots. And she was there: down the platform, perusing the Metro map on the wall. And there! Glimpsed through the carriage windows, standing on the Westbound platform. And there! Settling on a banquette inside the carriage right before his eyes.

He sprang for the train. The doors slid shut in his face. The train pulled away, dragging his prey out of reach. One by one, the decoys winked out of existence, blown away in the draft of the departing train.

Leaving Alistair immobilised, while his mind raced along the coloured lines of what he remembered of the Metro map, picking out likely stops, possible changes and probable destinations. *Gare de Lyon* was near. Perhaps she was heading east.

But all the thoughts ultimately crashed into one. The same one that had struck him on first breaking out into the Paris evening air.

Hopeless.

CHAPTER SEVEN
Young Americans

1959. LOS ANGELES, CA.

Salt. That ought to do the trick. Salt and elbow grease.

Bonnie went to the kitchen and ran a bowl of warm water. Twisted the cap off the salt shaker and poured. Grabbed a cloth, carried the bowl into the living room and scrubbed. Worked that sucker into the rug.

Seemed like after a while she was just working in more red. She wrung out her cloth for the fiftieth time, thinking there had to be more blood than water in the bowl now. She'd washed the patch out to a ham pink, but managed to spread it around some.

Alvin stared up at her, all accusing like. *That's some sloppy work,* his eyes seemed to say. *Not good enough.* Nothing new there.

'That's the best it's gonna be,' she told him. 'Nothin' you can do about it.

She got off her knees. Picked up the poker, gave it a wipe and placed it in the stand. She smoothed her apron and walked to the hall. Sat on the chair they kept next to the phone table. She took a deep breath. Dabbed her eyes.

Then called the police.

If her boy came down from his bedroom with all the noise or if they carried him through the living room, she didn't want him seeing so much blood, that was all.

'Please, Lord,' she muttered, with barely the strength to say it aloud, 'make sure they take care of my boy.'

1963. SOMEWHERE IN THE UNITED STATES.

Bryant watched her through the glass. That was some

serious art-student hoodoo vibe the young woman had going on in there. The Shepherd joined him at the window. Bryant made some room.

'A new addition to the flock,' Seth said. He muttered a random string of numbers.

For that verbal tic, Bryant had considered dubbing him the Accountant, once upon a time. That, and he had the look of a greasy mathematician, with his spectacles and more hair cream than hair, rolled-up shirt sleeves and neck-tie knotted tight as a noose. Like a sweaty NASA engineer watching a situation go south in mission control, with his job and the lives of several astronauts on the line. Given such a hypothetical, Bryant would've warned the astronauts not to get their hopes up. Seth was not great with people. The sort of guy parents would want to keep fifty miles from the schoolyard. Bryant's skin crawled, standing so close to the man. It rankled that he was the best fit for guiding new intake. In the line of recruitment, beggars could not be choosers.

Seth relished the role that came with his codename with the delight of a child told he would be getting apple pie for dessert. He murmured more numbers, then adjusted the sit of his glasses. He hadn't once taken his eyes off the subject. 'Who is she?'

'Her name's Bonnie.'

'And what are we calling her?'

'The Engraver. Look at her go.' Eyes down, the young woman carved dark art out of the white paper. The pencil etched black wounds, manifesting into some furious picture. It was a miracle she hadn't snapped the lead. Bryant couldn't make out the illustration from here – upside down, it looked like a portrait. 'If that pad could bleed, she would've bled it dry by now.'

'This one is going to need nurturing.'

'Knock yourself out, Shepherd.'

She was a real African beauty, with talents outside her artistic skills. Afro held in check by a broad yellow headscarf. Sad brown eyes. Hell of a figure. Bryant's gaze slid down those legs, crossed under the table. He wouldn't mind nurturing that. If he hadn't read her file.

'You disgust me, Bryant.'

Seth glowered like he was projecting heat. Bryant felt like an insect under a pair of magnifying glasses.

71

'*Director* Bryant.'

'Once you have learned to direct events as I do, I shall employ your full title.'

'Don't get smart. It's my rank. And your reminder who's in charge. So, do your job. Let her know the lay of the land and guide her into the fold.'

Bryant turned and dismissed Seth with some swift distance. The girl was a promising addition, but he prayed for the day they might find a replacement for the damned Shepherd.

The woman, Bonnie – yes, he liked that name – downed her pencil. *Nine seven two thirty-three...* Seth gestured at the unoccupied chair across the desk from her. 'May I?'

Bonnie sat back and folded her arms, but nodded. Everybody moved away and put up their defences when he visited. Seth slid onto the chair. The face, etched with heavy pencil lines, stared out from the page. The young artist flipped the pad around for Seth's appraisal.

Nine seven two thirty-three forty... Forty-eight? Don't know. No. Not right.

The portrait was of a man who would not retreat, not shrink away. It defied order. Harsh lines, weathered hollow cheeks, bald head and a face scratched with stubble. There was a piercing sourness in the eyes. And hating. Hating everything they saw. Seth quickly pushed the pad back to the young woman.

'Anyone I should know?'

'Dude's a regular Bela Lugosi, huh? I see him a lot. I think he *sees* too. You see too, right?'

Seth smiled tightly. That was the trouble with people. They said unexpected things. Upset the sequence. He had to control the dialogue. 'I understand your name is Bonnie.'

She nodded.

'How much do you understand your gift?'

'Remote-viewing? That suit – Bryant – that's what he called it.'

'Yes.' Seth mirrored her nod, happier if he kept his gaze on her and ignored the glimpse of portrait encroaching on his lenses. 'What we're about here is an extension of the CIA's Remote-Viewing programme. Every leap forward is a stepping stone. It's all about getting to the other side. But when the other side is the Soviets, well, it gets to the point where men like Bryant would like us to do more than spy. Our next step is about making things happen.'

'Moving stuff? I can't do that.' Bonnie grasped her pencil, seeking comfort. 'I just draw. My head draws, you know, and my arm just copies.'

'And you need that… The creative outlet?'

'Uh huh. I need it.' Her look dared him to try confiscating her pencil.

Yes. *Nine seven two thirty-three fourteen… This girl could be the very thing.*

"Remote-Viewing is about seeing – and hearing. But creativity could take us all further. What if we can train our candidates to do more? We can see and hear through the eyes and ears of our subjects, so perhaps – with a little extra effort, and imagination – we can influence what the target sees and hears. I have made some progress in this regard myself. It's why Bryant has appointed me to a position of seniority among the candidates.'

'You a trustee, huh?' Bonnie was unimpressed.

'Think of me as team leader. We are a team.'

'Not yet we ain't.'

Nine seven two thirty-three fourteen twelve seventy…

Creatives were difficult. Like… fire. You had to learn how to direct it, to tap its energy without it burning you.

'We will become friends,' said Seth. 'And think on this: alter perceptions and we can change what happens. Imagine your target…' He let his finger dart forth and strike the sketch pad. 'This man, for example. Say he's at a crosswalk.'

'He ain't at no crosswalk. Most of the time he's in a room. Like this.'

Seth bunched a fist. He wanted to bite his knuckles. Bonnie kept changing the script. Throwing the sequence out.

'A man. Any man,' insisted Seth. 'He looks left, he looks right. There's a car coming and the DON'T WALK is blinking. But what if he doesn't see the car and the light is telling him okay, go ahead: WALK?'

'You're talking about getting a man killed.' It wasn't the murder she was objecting to, but something else.

'No, no. Bad example.' Seth laughed. But he pictured a man sprawled in a busy street. Pedestrians running. A driver rushing from the car with the dented hood. Yes, that was part

73

of the correct sequence. That was the sort of picture they should all be sketching.

'All I am saying for the time being, is that the ability to alter perceptions is the ability to change the world. So, for a simpler example... Perhaps we manipulate a target to turn left instead of right. Or... have our target sign a document because he thinks he's signing something else. Simple matters. No killing.'

Until we graduate. All of us.

'I don't know if I can get in someone's head like that.'

'Indeed. Well, that is what we are here to find out.'

Seth relaxed, as best he could with that portrait still lying there, face-up. Bonnie would challenge everything. Perhaps throw him and everything into chaos on occasion. One didn't throw away a grenade because it was volatile. One merely decided when and where the throw would do most damage.

1967.

'Morning.'

Four years, a steady job. That was some record.

Bonnie strode the corridor like she was management. Like she had power. She did. More than she ever knew. But she also knew the difference. Her powers could reach to the far side of the world, but her power there was limited. Still, it felt good. Came the time she had given up thinking of her room as a cell, started thinking of it as her office.

And here she was, reporting for duty. Saying 'hi' to her colleagues. Class of '63. The few who'd graduated. The handful who'd made it through the programme and landed themselves a job.

There was Rufus. Skinny dude, looked like he was still at college, always chewing his lip like he was fretting over his latest assignment. Check shirt hanging open over a Hendrix t-shirt. Give the boy a shave and a haircut and some home-cooked dinners, he might start to look like a man.

Bonnie passed Florence La Beau. The woman stood in the corridor, drinking vending-machine coffee from her Styrofoam cup, dressed in her earthy colours, a regular chameleon doing her best to blend with the brown brick. She was there a lot, maintaining her solitary vigil in the corridor, like it was some ritual and the machine was her tribal totem pole. Far as Bonnie knew, she was Narragansett. If she had sacred spots they ought to be way north of there.

There went Slow Earl, shuffling off to the tank room. Sensory deprivation. Bonnie didn't need that juju. Floating in a bath would play hell with her sketch pad anyway. Slow Earl shouldn't have needed it either: he gazed at the world like he was peering through Mary-Jane's veil. He was tall enough he could've lived with his head in the clouds. Bonnie had a theory the brother only went in the tank for a lie-down on company time. He nodded and that was what passed for 'Morning' in Earl-speak.

She arrived in her office and got set up. Pad. Pencils, arranged like cutlery in a fancy restaurant. A photo of her boy. She'd had to fight Bryant for that. He'd worried it would be a distraction. But she kicked up a storm and won that round. Promised him it would be her first thought for the day and that would be it. Not a distraction, but a spur. Four years. Bryant told her nothing about what her boy was up to. A ward of state and then God knows where. Bonnie added a few years on him in the photo, pictured him blowing out birthday candles. But she never *saw* him. Truth was, she was too damned scared to try.

She opened the folder. Inside was another photo. Her target.

Hair like an oil-slick, face like the work of an upholsterer. East European. What was he? Bulgarian? Yeah, that was it.

She'd drawn him only yesterday. He'd been tucked up in bed in an East Berlin hospital. Appendix.

She peeled the photo back. Underneath was a typewritten instruction.

Eliminate.

Bonnie slapped the folder closed.

She stormed out and hunted down Seth. Found him in his office. The Shepherd had an actual office.

'You lied to me.'

Seth braced himself, running through his standard meditation. He made his face a blank page.

'No killing, you said.'

'It was not my lie, Bonnie. These are the lies I am paid to tell. That is the role of the Shepherd. To steer the flock into the fold.'

'No. That right there's the role of the sheep dog. You working for the shepherd. Langley. Refresh my memory: what they call that? The Farm. You working for Old Farmer Bryant. He whistles, you bark. The rest of us run wherever he wants us because you're *his* dog.'

Bonnie watched Seth crunch his numbers like they were bad breakfast cereal. Getting bits stuck between his teeth. Math was his prayer and he was waking up to the fact he didn't have one.

'Situations change. Everything changes,' Seth said. 'You yourself are an agent for change. Constantly. If any of us elect not to follow through on Bryant's instructions, we may change our situations. But there is no guarantee we will find our lives changed for the good.'

'Maybe we ought to think on how we can do that.'

'Maybe. What will you do?'

'Today?' Bonnie thought of the two photos. The one in the file and the framed picture standing on her desk. 'Today, I'm gonna be a good girl.'

She went back to her office and drew.

She sketched in a fury, drawing up a darkened hospital bed and a patient and a monitor going haywire. Readouts spiking. A rush of nurses and doctors fussing and flustering around the bed, doing all the wrong things for the patient because they were getting all the wrong signals. Bonnie watched the Bulgarian guy code. She drew his eyes without pupils, like they'd rolled back into his head.

Oh yeah, she had powers. Only, her power around here was limited.

Maybe one day that would change.

1971.

Bonnie was at her desk early that morning. Drawing away, and her pencil led her on a detour...

New Mexico.

Two women poking around in tunnels. A Spanish lady and a British chick, shining lights where light hadn't belonged in an age. Pictures on the walls, dust in the air, history in the stone. Then there it was, surfacing in the shadows. Never revealed itself on her page, but it was there all right. Sleeping in the scribbled darkness.

Bones without the good sense to be dead. A fossil of some winged dinosaur or a freaky giant eagle. Graceful as a swan, fierce as a dragon. Rainbow filaments threaded through every bone, colours swam in the pale surfaces. Hypnotic. Alive. So damned alive. It raised its skull of twisted horns and scimitar tusks, and fanned its skeleton wings like it meant to take off. And it did. It soared up and up, lifting her from the shadows, up and up into the night sky until she was looking down from the stars, and the world shrank away to nothing.

She was powerful. A goddess.

It rose and swept her to the heavens on wings of bone. And it spoke.

Bonnie, it said.

JULY 1981. EDMOND, OK.

Upside Down, Diana Ross. Man, she liked that record. Food in the diner sucked, but the music was cool. Bonnie rocked her head and shoulders, getting into it while her pencil went to work. Skyscrapers went up on her page. Shimmering water flashed between buildings. Plain old lead couldn't capture that sunlight. Her pencil darted across each slice of lake, turning quick scribbles into ripples.

Bonnie watched it all slide by on a cab ride. There in the window, a woman's portrait trapped in glass. Bonnie mimicked the woman's smile. Her pencil raced to record every line. She spotted a ball park. Wrigley Field. *Go Cubs.*

Bonnie looked up.

'Chicago,' she said to her friends, all jammed into the same booth. Seth and the rest, washing down their French fries with soda and coffee as they waited on her to finish. 'Woman's in Chicago.'

Ten years had been good to the woman since Bonnie had first spied her in New Mexico. Bonnie liked the look of that face. Decided her portrait was a keeper. She wrote a name in the bottom corner. Call it a title for the piece.

ANNE BISHOP.

'Very well then,' said Seth. 'Let's go get her.'

CHAPTER EIGHT
Sound & Vision

JULY 1981. CHICAGO.

Anne Bishop (née Travers) knew she was being followed. Carrying a loaded briefcase in her right hand and two ring-binders clasped to her chest, she was in no position to fight off a stalker. The briefcase could fetch someone a nasty wallop, but she would rather avoid causing the kind of scene physical violence would create.

Instead, she tried to give her pursuer the slip amid the general flood of fellow scientists spilling from the conference room into the hotel foyer. Unfortunately, her follower wasn't so easily shaken off. Much to her comprehensive lack of surprise, she was tapped on the shoulder.

She turned and dredged a smile from the depths of her fatigue. She blinked the tiredness from her eyes and hoped to goodness he didn't mistake that for an eyelash flutter.

'Professor Guterman. Forgive me, it's been a long day and I'm really not —'

'Feel free to drop the *professor*. Please, call me Ryan. But I totally understand. Hell, I only flew in from New York yesterday and I'm still feeling it. That was a terrific speech though. Nobody in that room had any idea you were dead on your feet.'

'Ah, that was a simple case of matter-to-energy

conversion. When the subject matters, I find the energy. Unfortunately, that means I now have to recharge. So, if you'll...?'

'Well, you know the best tonic for jet lag, right?' He gestured at the bulk of the crowd migrating around them towards the bar. And he winked.

Anne smiled again. If diplomacy failed, she still had her briefcase.

'By all means, knock yourself out. I am British and fragile, and I need my sleep. Good night, Professor.'

She turned and, now that the crowd had thinned, found a clear path all the way to the lifts. Of which she took full advantage.

Well, he had wanted her to drop the professor.

A gaggle. Seth decided to assign 'gaggle' as the collective noun for scientists. They moved like geese and filled the lobby with their honking. There were islands of stillness in their midst.

He rose from the lounge chair and threaded his way through the gaggle towards the pair that had just separated. Bonnie and Rufus converged along his route. As a loose trio, they stationed themselves around their target, waiting at the elevators.

Their ride arrived with a chime. Two hotel guests emerged, one nodding curtly at Mrs Bishop before crossing the still-busy lobby. She boarded and sagged against the back wall.

Seth and Bonnie filed in with her. Rufus stepped in to block the doorway. Naturally, they wanted Mrs Bishop to themselves.

Anne rode the lift alone, waiting out the clunk and whir of machinery like the clockwork of a very noisy timepiece. She ran through the pressing items on her agenda: ditch the paperwork, shower, sprawl out on the bed, call room service for something to eat, call Bill. She was sure her husband wouldn't object too much at finding himself fifth in the queue. He understood priorities.

She smiled.

Her elbow brushed against something. She jumped – not quite out of her skin – and looked left. Nothing there.

She thanked jet lag and a long first day at the conference for messing with her normally level head. Never mind. That was what the shower and sprawling were intended to sort out.

The lift chimed. The doors parted on the third floor. Two below her stop. A woman hesitated on the threshold. She peered around, inspecting the interior. She looked briefly disappointed, then stepped back.

'Oh. It's okay, I'll catch the next one,' she said.

'What? There's plenty of –'

The doors slid closed. The lift resumed its ascent.

Anne felt a sudden chill. She looked at her reflection in the polished metal. Alone and tired. She blinked and wished she had a hand free to rub her eyes. Her mind was clearly playing tricks.

That or the air conditioning was playing up.

Seth felt it, like a rash. Under his coat, a tingle where Mrs Bishop's elbow had made contact with his forearm. Such fleeting contact with a remarkable power to linger. As though skin remembered.

The enforced proximity dried and tightened his throat. He masked his discomfort. A foolish impulse, given that Mrs Bishop could not see him. In the imperfect mirror of the elevator wall, his expression was blank like an uncarved headstone. Bonnie appeared relaxed, leaning against the wall to their target's right. Rufus made an imposing barrier, standing guard directly in front of Mrs Bishop. His breath stank of Cheetos and he puffed like an elephant with a heart condition after taking the stairs.

Seth swallowed, almost choking on the sandpaper in his throat. He would help himself to a glass of water when they reached Mrs Bishop's room.

She was a British lady. They could be sure she would play the perfect hostess.

A hand clamped over Anne's mouth. She dropped her binders and her briefcase. She yelled, but her cry died in a big sweaty palm that smelled of a cheesy snack. An arm locked around her waist and pulled her back against an airship-sized stomach. She stamped her heel on her attacker's foot. She met steel toe-caps and the blow jarred her shinbone.

The dirigible guy spun her and shoved her onto the bed. He was more fat than muscle, doughy jowls and a torso founded on beer and burgers. His (incredibly appropriate) Zeppelin t-shirt reeked of sweat.

He had friends lurking behind him.

'Calm yourself, Mrs Bishop.'

It was a smooth, well-oiled American voice. The name-drop stayed her struggles. A man slithered into view, wearing glasses. He had hair like a thin coat of creosote. He smiled like a reptile. 'Calm yourself.'

He crouched to gather up her scattered papers. The door closed with a click. The quiet work of a third person she had yet to see. The man arranged the papers in a stack and tapped the edges to align the corners. He tucked them into a binder. If he was a serial killer, Anne decided, he would be the sort to arrange her innards neatly.

He rose, happy with his tidying. Gave the tiniest of nods.

The fast-food gorilla stood aside and finally she got a good look at her third visitor. A black woman, pretty and skinny, eyes that seemed heavy with sadness the way they were aimed at the floor. She wore a shoulder-bag and carried a small hold-all. She set the latter at her feet.

Anne directed her anger at the spectacled creep. 'How did you get in here?'

'We rode the elevator. With you.'

'I don't understand. Have you mastered invisibility?'

'After a fashion. But it's less a case of concealing ourselves, than influencing what you see.'

'Illusions then?'

'You be the judge. I might be holding a gun, for example.' A revolver appeared in his right hand. Then faded from existence. 'I might not. You are free to exercise your instincts. Fight or flight. Either will serve as a test. You may not know for certain that you have been shot, even if you feel the bullet tear through your innards, even if you find yourself lying on the floor bleeding out into this fine carpet.'

'So, I might die, illusion or no.' Like falling in a dream and hitting the ground, she supposed. 'All right. I get the message. But given that you can make people see what you wish them to see, what is it you want from me? You'd make the perfect bank robbers. You could stroll into Fort Knox and take anything you want.'

'The thought has crossed some of our minds.'

'Mine for sure,' said the big guy.

'Rufus imagines he would enjoy the trappings of a wealthier lifestyle, but would probably continue to shop at Wal-Mart. But wealth is not top of our wish list.'

'What then?' said Anne.

'Let us hold back on the show and tell,' he said. 'We have a wait ahead of us.'

'A wait? For what?'

'There is no sense having you visit your friend at this hour.' He presented the face of his wristwatch. 'I recommend a social call over breakfast. Which means we should wait until two. Tell me, is Señora Montilla an early riser?'

Sophia!

'Now, look here!' Anne jumped up. Nobody moved to stop her. A fact she processed as she collapsed. If the cheese-snack fumes had contained chloroform, it did nothing to anaesthetise the impact.

Rufus hauled her off the carpet and planted her back on the bed.

The spectacled man touched a finger to his lips, shushing a child. 'You have heard of phantom limb syndrome?'

Anne frowned. 'Yes, it's —'

'What you are experiencing might be considered the opposite. You are, after all, a healthy woman in full possession of her limbs. No unfortunate encounters with agricultural machinery or landmines.' The man's smile was hypnotic and a little revolting, like the movement of some of nature's slimier invertebrates. 'But belief is everything.'

His expression switched. To something she liked less than his smiles.

Pity?

She looked down. To the stumps where her legs used to be.

'Alistair? Having trouble sleeping, are we?'

'I'm in Geneva. I stopped by the office.'

The United Nations Peacekeeping Offices were deathly quiet this time of night. Major Adrienne Kramer had jumped to attention on his arrival, but Alistair had dismissed her. For one thing, he didn't want anyone else taking their unfair share of responsibility; for another, he had operated alien artillery, disintegrator guns and Hotmail, so he was damned sure he could manage an old fax machine.

'Geneva? Good lord. I thought I sent you home.'

The distance in Freddie's voice was more than geographical. He didn't sound like a man roused from sleep. He sounded like a man likely to be up a good while longer, with a lot on his mind. Alistair was about to add to his worries.

'I'm going to fax an artist's impression of our suspect to Interpol. Her picture will be all over Europe within the hour.' The portrait gazed up at him from his desk, looking none too pleased to have her face criss-crossed with folds. 'Thought I'd best keep you in the loop.'

'Loop? What loop?' Duffer began to sound more like a grizzly with his hibernation rudely cut short. 'Are you sure this is the best use of your authority?'

'Frankly, I wondered if there was anything more you wished to share with me. Now would be the time.'

'Nothing springs to mind, old boy.'

'Really, Freddie? Come on. What's the word on that lighter?'

'It's being analysed. Now listen, Brigadier, you've heard from me everything you need to know, plus another good measure between friends. But this is my loop, understand? You need to be giving this and yourself a rest. You've had a bad day. Best not go making it worse by tearing all over Europe on some wild goose chase, and quite possibly jeopardising my investigation.'

The line died with an emphatic click. Another dead end to go with his lost suspect.

Alistair set down the phone and reached for the portrait, surprised that he missed the easiness of mobile phones; being able to send photos in an instant. He began smoothing out the folds in readiness for the fax machine. But allowed himself a momentary pause to imagine those ridges as prison bars.

He was interrupted by a buzzer emanating from his waistline. He unclipped the pager from his belt and examined the tiny letterbox display.

The LCD characters spelled out RED BEAR.

The code word was a blast from the past. An even more distant past when mingled with his 2011 memories. 'Good lord.'

The hours had dragged in unpleasant silence. But Anne was glad to have her legs. Occasionally, propped up against her pillows, she caught herself patting her thighs or massaging her calves. The habit plainly amused the big guy, while the spectacled creep – Seth – watched her with a detachment that she hoped was scientific and not sociopathic.

When he stood, it was a sudden intrusive motion. Noiseless, but somehow like an alarm breaking her out of a half-sleep. The woman, Bonnie, moved from the armchair in which she'd been curled.

'Please,' said Seth, patting the end of the bed, 'make yourself comfortable here.'

Anne didn't care much for the man's concern over her comfort. She shuffled down the bed, even so. 'For what?'

'Imagine you are posing for a portrait. You need not hold yourself overly still. And do not mind Bonnie's special attention.'

'Why? What's she planning on doing?'

Bonnie perched on the stool by the dresser. Her gaze fell on Anne. It was like being subjected to an X-ray. After the initial examination, the woman dug in her shoulder bag and fished out a sketch pad which she set on her lap. She armed herself with a pencil and then exhaled through a smile. Like someone arriving at their happy place.

'As I said. She means to draw you.'

Bonnie's pencil darted about the page, taking on a life of its own. The life of some skittish insect, it seemed, tracing dark and erratic trails that swiftly coalesced into eyes, mouth, nose, hair. She kept looking at – or into –

Anne, but appeared to be seeing somewhere else entirely.

'What is all this about?' Anne demanded. Nobody answered, but the truth came unbidden.

New Mexico. It has to be New Mexico.

VIENNA.

Steam trailed after Sophia Montilla as she exited the bathroom, attacking her hair with the towel. Hit by the scent of fresh-baked brioche, she stood and breathed it in while binding the towel into a turban.

Mmm. Fruit, yogurt, a bite or three of that heavenly bread. And coffee. Definitely coffee. After that, the balcony, a cigarette and the day awaited. In that order.

Halfway to the table and the waiting breakfast tray, she stopped. She tugged the belt on her robe a little tighter and turned to face the figure seated on the end of her bed.

'I let myself in. I hope you don't mind.'

Somehow it was more startling to see a familiar – and friendly – face than some dangerous intruder.

'Anne!'

Dismissing her shock, she approached, arms spread. Anne jumped up and locked in the hug. Sophia released her eventually and backed up for a proper look.

'I thought you were in Chicago. Some sort of conference?'

Anne settled back in place on the bed. 'Some sort, yes. Scientific one.'

'Naturally.' Sophia homed in on the coffee pot. 'Can I fix you a cup?'

'No, I'm fine, thanks. Yes, I had to cut it short. Something came up.'

Sophia poured herself a strong black. She was wide awake already. But she wondered, why wasn't she happier to see Anne?

'What something? Something I can help with? An

urgent history emergency?'

'You could say that.' Anne studied her fingernails. She looked ready to chew on them for breakfast. 'How urgent depends on whether you can help or not. I'm talking about our shared history.'

Sophia drank her coffee. One dark and bitter memory surfaced above all the others. She set the cup down. 'New Mexico?'

'Exactly.'

'Why, after all this time? Has it come back to bite us?'

'It hasn't. Yet.' Anne bit her lip, perhaps as a tastier alternative to her nails. 'I need to do some digging. Do you still have the samples? Something I could run some more tests on?'

'What are you thinking? They warned us–!'

'I won't tell them if you won't.'

Sophia dropped into the dining chair. Her hand patted the table, searching for a pack that wasn't there. She spotted her bag, tipped it over and spilled a few loose items on the bedside cabinet. Smokes had moved up today's batting order.

'Anne, no. Just – no. I can't do this, and I can't allow you to endanger yourself. They should stay where they are.'

Anne smiled, leaning forward. 'You don't need to have any more to do with it. Just tell me where they are, and I'll take care of them.'

'It's not that simple.'

'I'm sure not. They weren't the sort of thing you could just leave lying around in a cupboard.'

Sophia laughed. Anything else, there was a strong chance she might have done. But not with these. Some souvenirs needed to remain securely out of sight – and out of reach.

'Look, I'm sorry, you must think I'm being ridiculous.' Sophia rose and walked to her cigarettes. 'But

I've had a gun pressed to my head on precisely two occasions. It's surprising how fresh the memory remains. One little reminder – like you showing up and talking about it – that's all it takes and I'm back in that desert and... Well, there's a reason I've left those things where they are. Undisturbed. Unlike me, now.'

'Listen to yourself. That's not Sophia talking. That's the bones. You know how they can—'

'Oh no. No, no. This is not that. This is all me.'

Sophia marched back to the table. Anne's expression softened to kindly concern.

'I understand. I do. It scares me too. It would be stupid not to be scared. And neither of us is that.'

Sophia lit up and tossed the pack onto the table. She could almost hear the skeletons rattling around in her head. The same trouble stirred behind Anne's eyes, no matter how hard she was working to soften it. All that seriousness spelled out necessity. But it also spelled bad idea.

'No, Anne,' she insisted. 'I can't—'

A knock at the door gave her a start. Anne didn't react.

'Who is it?' called Sophia.

'Señora Montilla. Room service.'

Sophia eyed the breakfast tray. Nothing missing. 'I didn't order anything else.'

'So, you've seen through my ruse,' said the muffled voice. 'It's not room service. It's a friend.'

Somewhere along the way, the voice inherited an accent. Russian. She went and opened the door to—

Grigoriy Yevgenyevich Bugayev. In the flesh. Also, in leather jacket and slacks. His arrival at her door was surprise enough. To see him looking so casual was bewildering. Although he searched the room past her with eyes that seemed very much on-duty.

'Captain?'

'Major,' he corrected her, with a slice of a smile. He dangled two plastic evidence bags. 'I wanted to get your expert opinion on these.'

It was quite the day for the past to come visiting.

The contents of the bags robbed her of breath. Sophia backed up and waved in her second visitor for the morning. 'How strange. I was just discussing those with —'

She gestured at a vacant spot on the end of the bed.

Anne was gone.

Blinding flash. Fireworks going off in her head. Smoke and confusion, airplane passenger cabin filling up with screams. Bonnie stands at the top of some stairs. There's a blur rushing up at her. She sees the pistol. Too late. A bullet punches into her brain. She falls back into —

A train carriage. A world of flames and shouts. She breaks out of the compartment. Collapses in the corridor. On fire. Heat eating up her back. Her screams turn the pain to blackness. Something snaps.

Bonnie jerked awake from a nightmare fall. She threw the pad from her lap and sat shivering and holding a broken pencil.

Down at her feet, her drawing was a dark-carved mess. Jagged flames and ranks of passengers scrawled all over her quiet scene of two women sitting facing one another in a hotel room. An enormous hole drilled through the centre and filling the circle was a demonised face. Angry lines and intense eyes. The face of the man who had entered the Vienna hotel room.

A Banquo at her table. She let the pencil fall and massaged her eyes. 'God.'

'What happened?' Seth leaned over her.

Bonnie ignored him. She bent over, head nearly between her knees, feeling like she might throw up.

'Is she all right?'

That question came from their hostage.

Bonnie spoke to the floor. 'We got interrupted. This guy showed up. A Russian. Major.'

'Major...?' Seth prompted.

'Bugayev. He had two spent bones with him.'

'Contaminated,' said Seth. Bonnie nodded. 'Can you go back in?'

Bonnie frowned. 'What good would that do? Sure, I can conjure up another Anne Bishop. But what the hell good would that do now? Neither of them – the archaeologist or her "major" friend – is gonna buy her showing up again. This trick's a bust.'

Seth straightened. 'Then we'll have to get in touch with our friends.'

VIENNA.

Vasily popped the glove compartment and retrieved his pistol. The Tokarev welcomed his grip, presenting itself like a keen soldier volunteering to be of service once more.

Outside, the day made a half-hearted attempt to throw light in under the arch of the railway bridge where they had parked. As though the effort of climbing above the derelict buildings and crawling over the wedge of wasteland with its litter of dumped refrigerators and rusted bicycle frames had been too much. Whereas Vasily felt energised at the prospect of a job to be done.

Beside and behind him, his comrades stirred. Their latest borrowed vehicle was a VW Kombi, which featured a few basic amenities but, in some respects, was more cramped than the van. Stretching and groaning as they worked stubborn kinks out of their necks and stiffness out of their limbs.

Valentina rubbed her eyes and smoothed her brows with the tips of her fingers. She looked at the gun in Vasily's hands.

'What's that for? Are you going to go out and shoot us some breakfast?'

Vasily grinned. He rather relished the idea of serving Valentina raw squirrel with its head blown off. 'Contact from the Shepherd.'

'What did he say?'

Vasily tucked the Tokarev in his belt. 'We go talk to the archaeologist. The old-fashioned way.'

CHAPTER NINE
Golden Years

1971. NEW MEXICO.

Head back, Anne Travers lapped up every breath of wind blasting in through the passenger-side window. The pick-up drove on through a stone-bake oven that had already ranged for mile after suffocating mile.

Ahead, the mesa rose from the desert like a natural fortress, ruling over a populace of mesquite and tarbush. The horizon was a long range of rain-parched and crudely decapitated mountains, but this craggy bastion bore a crown of adobe buildings that, from this distance, could be mistaken for rough-hewn battlements.

Two or three rows of tents marked out an encampment close to its base and the pick-up turned off the highway towards it, clattering along a dirt track between the straggly clumps of plant life. Anne hoped the clatter only belonged to her ride and not her equipment bouncing around in the back.

She glanced at her chauffeur. The fantastically-named Chester 'Chess' Blacksnake was impossible to age. Under a black hat banded with beads, he had a head that might have been carved by centuries of weather and sand, mounted on the shoulders of a fit young farmhand. Taciturn but courteous, he had barely said two words that she hadn't had to quarry out of him with a lot of break-the-silence small-talk that he probably thought ridiculous and unnecessary, but was too much of a gentleman to say.

The pick-up carved a lazy arc in the dirt and rocked to a halt at the edge of the camp. Through the settling dust cloud beyond the windscreen, Anne was surprised to make out only one other vehicle – another muscular pick-up – parked on the far perimeter of the small town of tents.

A waiting figure resolved in the fog of dirt.

A cowgirl, Anne thought. A *desperada,* with long raven hair tied back in a pony tail, she might have crossed the border from Mexico. Tall and slim, sandy jeans, light blue shirt, dark waistcoat, neckerchief, desert-coloured hat, the works. Sunglasses spoiled the Wild West image.

Anne hopped out. The woman trotted forward to meet her with a strong handshake.

'Doctor Travers.' She welcomed Anne with a Spanish accent that positively danced. 'At least, I hope you are.'

Anne broke the handshake to pat herself down. 'Last I checked. Señora Montilla, I presume. Such a pleasure.'

'Don't speak too soon. You haven't seen what you're here for yet.'

'True enough. Lead on and, perhaps on the way, you can prepare me for the worst. And please, call me Anne.'

'My pleasure. Call me Sophia. I'm sure in a half hour or so you will be finding other names to call me.'

Anne flashed a bemused – and amused – frown. 'I'll try not to.'

Sophia glanced past Anne. 'You brought plenty of equipment, yes?'

'Plenty,' remarked Chess from the tail end of the pick-up. He had offloaded a quartet of crates already and added a couple of sturdy cases to the stack.

'Yes, but no extra help getting it up the hill, I'm afraid.' Anne felt like some dratted colonial, leaving Chess to unload like a stevedore while she nattered away with the expedition leader. She searched the rows of tents for signs of life. 'Where is everybody? It's not a holiday, is it?'

'We are on our own. My team upped and left. You can still see their tyre tracks. That's part of why you're here. Some had started to trickle away when I called for you. Then I told the rest to leave. Chess disobeyed orders, for which I am eternally grateful.'

'I'm fifty-eight,' said Chess. 'It won't come to an eternity.'

'So you say. I think you'll outlive the hills.'

'I'll take a couple of crates, then come back. If you ladies would care to help yourselves to a case each.'

Anne let her gaze scale the cliff-face that, this close up, walled off the rest of the world in one direction.

'Don't worry, we have a baggage lift,' Sophia reassured

her.

Anne laughed. 'So, was it the climb that scared your volunteers off?'

'No. That would be the ghosts.'

Anne paused for breath on a staircase that had been hand-cut out of the rock. Walled in on both sides, there was a measure of shade from the punishing sun, but little in the way of a view to reward her for all the hard slog. The steepness had sorely tested her thighs and she was glad to have Sophia leading the way, obstructing any view of how far they still had to climb.

'You haven't considered,' she puffed, 'upgrading your baggage lift for passenger use?'

It was a simple system of pulleys and ropes and a rickety cargo pallet powered by Chess Blacksnake's arms. Anne had not hidden her relief as they had deposited their luggage. She was sure it would reach the top before them and in better condition.

The archaeologist leaned against the staircase's outer wall. 'If nothing else, these stairs will help you think twice in the event you feel a sudden impulse to run out on us.'

Anne laughed with what breath she could spare. 'Is that a risk? I've met a few things where I should've run, but I haven't run out yet.'

'Good. So, you're not afraid of much?'

'I would say I'm afraid of as much as it's sensible to be afraid of. But we fear what we don't understand. And I'd generally like to try to understand before I run off and hide.'

'A woman after my own heart.'

'Thank you. I'm sure we're going to get along fine.'

Inhaling, Anne waved, indicating she was ready to go on. Sophia nodded and resumed the climb.

'How was your trip?'

'Oh, you know. Long and bumpy.'

'How are things at home? How is the Brigadier?'

'You spoke to him. How did he sound?'

'You know Alistair, he doesn't give much away.'

That was true. 'Even less these days.' It had been nearly a year since she had left her post at the Fifth Operational Corps, but she did some occasional work for Lethbridge-Stewart, in exchange for a private lab at the Warehouse. 'More secrets than ever.'

'I know. When I first met him, it was all state secrets. But, I called for an expert, and he was able to put me in touch with you.' Sophia tossed a wink over her shoulder. 'Which makes you one secret he's willing to share.'

'Oh, I'm flattered. I'll do what I can to get to the bottom of… whatever's going on here.'

Finally, they escaped the narrow confines of the staircase. A pair of tents occupied an expanse of ground, roughly the size of the garden belonging to the house she shared with Bill back in Scotland, that formed the de facto front yard of the pueblo. The town of hard-baked adobe hovels spread all the way along the dusty plateau. Between the two tents was a campfire – currently dead – and a few cases and boxes, with an assortment of gear on top – flashlights, a camp stove, flask, large knife and a couple of walkie-talkies – and a scoped hunting rifle propped against one side.

Anne mopped her brow with the back of her forearm and did her best not to keel over and die in the merciless glare of the New Mexico sun.

'It occurs to me, I brought all kinds of electronics and completely forgot the sun tan lotion.'

'I have some in my tent. And a spare hat you're welcome to borrow.' Sophia gestured to the A-frame by the cliff-edge and the suspended pallet laden with Anne's luggage. 'Help yourself while I fetch the gear. Then I'll take you on a guided tour, if you're feeling up to it.'

'Sounds good. If you find me passed out, just give me a kick.'

She dropped and crawled into one of the tents, hunting for hat and sun block. First things first. Ghosts could wait.

Anne backed carefully down the ladder into relative gloom. Sophia reached the third rung from the bottom then dropped to the ground. She switched on her torch and let the beam have a general play around the shadows.

Torchlight wasn't immediately necessary as, courtesy of the trapdoor, the day laid down a rectangular carpet of sunshine, softened and cooled by the subterranean air. The square chamber was large enough that the walls were well outside the sunlight's favour.

Anne touched down, then activated her torch. 'Wow.'

Superficially, her torch had not found much to excite: a stone bench extended from three of the four walls, with a recessed platform in the fourth; a pair of intriguing crawl-ways were cut into its base, big enough to accommodate a rodent of porcupine proportions, but too square to be mouse-holes. While a selection of stone structures – a raised block that might have been an altar, a walled rectangular pit and the ruins of a few pillars – were arranged on the central 'arena' floor.

But there was a distillation of something in the atmosphere, or in the surrounding stone. There was age, of course, a sense of history as a quantifiable force like gravity. This rudimentary construction somehow seemed to possess the humbling power of a Westminster or St Paul's. And perhaps it carried a hint of fear, the unknown that she was here to understand and – all being well – solve.

'It's a Great Kiva,' explained Sophia. 'A chamber for religious ceremonies. And town council meetings. Ordinarily it would stop here. But there's more.'

'More? Where?'

'Below us. Come on.'

Sophia directed her torch and her feet to the walled pit and Anne only had to peer over to see the top of another ladder disappearing into greater darkness. Again, Sophia led the descent.

'How far below?' Anne asked, watching her footing on the rungs.

'Chess believes they dug down through the entire mesa.' Sophia hopped off to the next floor. 'I've mapped other shafts dropping to levels below this one. But I haven't seen engineering on such a level in any comparable site. On the surface, this is a twin for Acoma. But there are differences here that…'

Anne stepped down. 'That what?'

'That challenge our understanding.'

'Oh good. As long as it only challenges our understanding of history. It's the things that challenge our understanding of physics I tend to have the biggest problem with.'

'And what about something that challenges both?'

'Please don't tempt fate.'

The daylight had no route to this chamber. A quick pan with the torch revealed a somewhat cruder cavern, roughly circular, with several generous-sized tunnels shooting off to the four points of the compass. It also spotlighted a generator – currently inert – as well as three lighting rigs and cables, with one cable snaking into the north passage.

This was their route next. They passed another a short way along.

'How many of these rigs do you have?'

'Only enough to illuminate a couple of key areas.'

'They'll double as decent mounts for my sensors, that's all,' said Anne. 'As long as your generator can handle the load.'

'On that, I have no idea. You would have to ask someone with technical expertise. Say, an engineer. Or a physicist.'

'I'll do that.'

Anne was grateful for a reason to chuckle in a gloom that was growing vaguely oppressive. As though the dark had weight. Her torch found openings cut into the passage walls, but the light struggled to probe the shadows within. She realised she was walking past doorways and those hovels formed a sort of undertown to the pueblo on the surface.

Arriving at a crossroads, Sophia hung a brisk left and more turns and junctions followed, building a picture of quite the sprawling subterranean pueblo. Always with the cable marking their course through the labyrinthine streets. Anne started to think of the cable as Perseus' golden thread.

'Have you ever wandered in a place and sensed its history?' Sophia asked. Her pace slowed, suggesting they were nearing their destination. 'Something beyond architectural grandeur. Nothing you can see, something you breathe in. Bloody history, in particular. Say you go and stand in the fields of the Somme. Or Verdun. And you pause and reflect on what happened there.'

'But that's a kind of illusion. If you know the events, visualisation combines with empathy. And you can't help but be moved, can you?'

It worried Anne slightly that the archaeologist had chosen to raise this topic. It seemed to imply she had detected the same undercurrents that had struck Anne as soon as she had stepped off that first ladder.

'True. Nothing more supernatural than the imagination at work,' Sophia said. 'Because we know the history. But… I don't know the history here. Not yet. Of course, I can surmise based on the story of similar sites. Like Acoma. Maybe it's guilt.'

'Guilt?'

'Spaniards have a lot to answer for in this region.'

'Fair point. What does Chess say about that?'

The passage – or street – opened into another wide chamber. Roaming torch beams described a roughly square hall with a ten-foot ceiling.

'He forgives me. Actually, he assures me there's nothing to forgive. Says it's not my fault my ancestors were *bastardos*.' Sophia finally halted and turned ninety-degrees to her left. She beckoned Anne to stand beside her. 'Here we are.'

She aimed her torch ahead and invited Anne to do likewise.

Together they illuminated a buttress, flanked by two archways, dominating one end of the chamber. The projecting face of the buttress teemed with ancient graffiti. An astounding gallery of subjects – animal, vegetable, mineral – populating this one surface. Serpents and birds, bowmen on horseback, corn and cacti, hands and headdresses, a long string of strange stick-men climbing crooked stairs. The shapes appeared lightly silvered in Anne's sweeping torch beam, and seemed to dance.

Sophia supplied commentary. '*Hopituh Shi-nu-mu*, the Peaceful People. Hopi is a way of life. There is a life force contained in everything. Respect and care for all things is the path to benefit all humankind.'

Anne steadied her torch on a group of what resembled upright turtles. Then she remembered Sophia's mention of Spaniards and reasoned that they might look just like that in their armour. She didn't need a history degree to imagine what might have arisen from a meeting of the two cultures.

Sophia aimed her torch higher where just two figures stood above the throng. Not only did they appear to stand in the 'sky', they were giants.

Sophia spotlighted the one on the right.

As best as Anne could tell from the crude line-drawing, this Titan wore some sort of helmet or hood crowned with an enormous headdress fanned like a peacock tail. Blank owl-eyes and a gaping mouth gave it a rudimentary – and faintly unnerving – face, and the remainder of the figure was bulked out with angular sections of armour or cladding.

'This *hombre* here is a kachina – one of the beneficent

beings that accompanied the Hopi from the Underworld. Unfortunately, it's not so easy to identify which; there are thousands and they can represent anything. Any of the subjects in the petroglyphs for example – and more besides.' Sophia slid her beam over to the giant on the left. 'This one,' she said, 'is the bigger mystery.'

That one induced shudders. It was a skeleton, with wings spread wide, but the lines marking out the wings were too minimal to suggest feathers. It could have represented some fantastical bird of prey or a dragon, but it had arms of bone incorporated into the wings, and the skull was a strangely warped and horned thing that suggested a beast outside ordinary zoological classifications.

'All the kachinas were slain, their spirits returned to the Underworld. Leaving the people to impersonate them wearing masks and costumes in ceremonies – and crafting dolls for the children. All I can think is that this figure is intended to depict one of the slain kachinas. Returned. That, or it's an unusual interpretation of Masau'u – otherwise known as Skeleton Kachina. But with those wings… It could be an angel. It could be a demon.'

Sophia shone her torch up at her own face and arched an eyebrow. Then returned the light to the petroglyphs.

'What worries me,' she continued, 'I can't blame the volunteers who ran. Volunteers, so they're not sticking around to get paid, that's one thing. But the fear. I feel it too. Especially here. As though we have unearthed emotions locked up in the ruins. An undercurrent of… dread.'

Okay, thought Anne. *So we both felt it.* Two rational women susceptible to the heebie-jeebies. 'Wonderful. Perhaps we can sit around the campfire tonight and spook each other with ghost stories.'

'All right.' Anne rose from her handiwork and kneaded the small of her back. She tossed her screwdriver into the toolbox. 'We are all set.'

It had taken a long afternoon underground, affixing sensors to the lighting rigs and carrying the rest of the gear into position. But the temperature below was more bearable and with the generator grumbling away she'd had plenty of light to work by. The engine noise really travelled in the tunnels, but she soon demoted it to the background and the assembly and myriad connections didn't require masses of concentration.

'You know,' said Sophia, 'I pride myself on being able to decipher the nature and purpose of any artefact or relic I find. Eventually. But I have no idea what any of this is or does.'

Anne smiled at her initial expression of bafflement. To the archaeologist, the collection of instrument boxes must have looked something like an elaborate stereo system. The stack was fronted with a host of dials and switches, miniature gauges, oscilloscope screens and a single monitor no larger than an average lunchbox. The back was a jungle of jacks and sockets and wires. Anne had a CCD video camera wired to that monitor, mounted on a tripod and rigged for constant 180-degree sweeps of the chamber.

'Would you like the full technical rundown or the Ladybird version?'

'Ladybird?'

'Sorry. Childish joke.' Outlining technical specs in layman's terms wasn't half as tricky as remembering which parts were subject to the Official Secrets Act and the like. 'In the past, I've had occasion to develop what, for simplicity's sake, we'll call a psychic barrier.'

'You mean for my sake.'

'I never said that. Anyway, suffice to say I've adapted some of the tech involved. I should add it is in no way psychic, but the sensors direct active pulses on a cycle of electromagnetic wavelengths commonly associated with psychic phenomena hotspots. In short, we have what – again for simplicity's sake – we can call a psychic radar.'

'And – what? – signals bounce back if it detects anything?'

'Not quite. What this box of tricks will be doing is seeking to match the frequency of localised activity – if any – and, well, provoke a response.'

'Ah, so we're poking the ghosts with a stick?'

Anne laughed. 'An electromagnetic stick, but yes. Our camera will record anything in the visible range, the rest will record everything else and this unit right here' – she pointed at a console that protruded from the main tower – 'is detachable. So we can be safely tucked up in camp and the main system will relay alerts and wake us if we get any hits. Actually, I may notch up the volume. I don't know about you, but after today, I fancy I'll be sleeping like a heavily sedated log.'

She spun a dial to MAX. Then flicked switches and punched buttons and fine-tuned dials in her well-rehearsed activation sequence. Screens warmed to a soft glow, needles danced and the machinery hummed.

'There,' she declared, 'that should—'

The machine *screamed.*

Sophia knocked her hat off in the rush to slap a hand over each ear. Anne covered one ear and rapidly attacked the console with her free hand, grimacing against the painful siren wail. Through her squint, she watched oscilloscope waves thrash about like eels. The shrill sound continued to pierce her eardrums.

The monitor showed nothing. No, wait – it showed nothing *where a wall should have been.* The camera panned across an opening where all the petroglyphs were supposed to be.

She looked. Her eyes told a different story: the wall was there, complete with all its graffiti.

But a phantom image flickered in and out – like the drawings, but etched in the air. Scratches of radiant light described a skeletal, winged creature.

Anne killed the output.

Sophia blinked and opened her mouth like a woman trying to combat a change in air pressure. The scream remained trapped in Anne's ears. And the image burned for a while in her retinas.

Just like Sophia had said: it could've been an angel. But its skull said demon.

CHAPTER TEN
Neighborhood Threat

JULY 1981. VIENNA.

Something about the VW camper turned the back of Alistair's neck prickly. Its orange and white colour scheme wasn't terrific camouflage, even in the highly decorative touristy part of town. The hand-painted flowers and the slogan FRIEDEN! on its rear were further advertisement.

He tucked the rental car alongside the curb on the opposite side of the street, observing with a wary eye.

The Hotel Ruby-Gisele boasted a grand façade that might have belonged to an opera house, and ought not to take kindly to shabby hippie-vehicles parking right outside their front door.

The camper's side door was open, an eclectic half-dozen people gathered round. They collected an assortment of suitcases and bags from the vehicle and started to look a little more like hotel guests. Still, their mode of transportation didn't fit the picture.

Alistair scratched at the base of his neck. Definitely itchy. He checked his watch and wondered if Bugayev was there already. His call had been scant on details, but strongly suggested some overlap in their investigations.

Even if it proved to be a wild goose chase, it was preferable to being messed around by Whitehall foxes.

*

Vasily hauled out the large blue sports hold-all. He presented it to Valentina. 'Guard it with your life and make sure it gets where it needs to go.' She slung it over her shoulder. It was a poor match for the pink suitcase on wheels that made up the rest of her luggage. She cocked her head, like he'd just lectured her on how to ride a bike.

Vasily ignored her. 'All right, everybody stick to your assigned routes. Leave a souvenir or two in each city. Select your sites well.' He closed up the camper. 'Good luck everyone. We will see you in America.'

Ekel, Valentina and Abdulin headed their separate ways. Tsarsko idled against the van.

'Shouldn't we all do this? Together?' asked Irena. The girl pouted and watched the others depart, like a kitten stressing at the prospect of abandonment. After all these years, Vasily still thought of her as a girl. Fear could make a man appear older. In her, it cast the illusion of youth.

'No, *Krolika*. We were due to separate here in any case.' He pointed to the hotel's upper floors. 'There is nothing up there we cannot handle. Once we have the location we can dispose of the archaeologist and reunite on the other side of the world.' He planted a paternal hand on her back and propelled her towards the front of the vehicle. 'Now, go play your part.'

Tsarsko sighed and shook his head.

Vasily glared. 'And what is your problem?'

The driver's door slammed. The engine turned over.

'We're trusting a mouse to be our getaway driver?'

Vasily hooked Tsarsko's arm and yanked him to the pavement. The camper drove off. It quickly turned and dropped out of sight down the ramp. 'She is no mouse. Irena is our little rabbit foot. You... Just you do your part. Keep them in their room. Take the elevator. I'll take the service stairs.'

Tsarsko shook off the hold and sulked. For all his

103

education and unkempt beard, he acted more like a child than Irena.

'Is this a private argument or can anyone join in?'

Vasily's hand shot to the gun in his belt and spun to face the voice. Some pale traveller with a red mane. In her British Army longcoat and scuffed boots she looked like a lipstick-painted tramp.

'Who the hell are you?' he demanded.

The itch turned to a cold rash.

Alistair grasped the door handle. He watched her. Half-expecting her to shimmer and vanish or transform into someone else.

But no. It was her. No backpack; travelling light. Talking to the pair of shady characters who had stayed behind after the party split up and the camper had run down the burrow into the hotel's underground car park.

Experience had long ago taught him that there was no such thing as coincidence.

The trio – his suspect and her two new associates – turned and headed for the hotel entrance.

Alistair leaped from the car. Instinctively he reached for his mobile phone but, it wasn't there, so he raced to the phone box at the corner.

Vasily marched at the hotel entrance. The woman refused to stay at his heel. Tsarsko shambled along at the rear.

'When I say you need me,' she insisted, 'I mean all of you. Your little *cell*. And your American allies.'

'No. What we need is calm. Order and co-operation. You are the polar opposite. You are a disruption. We have no vacancies.'

Vasily stopped under the hotel's portico. The doorman glanced at their impromptu huddle. Secrecy would not be a problem if necessary, but the attention still agitated.

'Maybe you'd appreciate a demonstration.'

'Is that a threat? Take care, little girl.' His hand hovered near his belt. 'If you wish to make threats, make sure and be one.'

'Say "little girl" again.' She searched his eyes. 'No? Don't fancy your chances? You reckon age gives you seniority. As if age is even measured in years. Screw beauty. *Life* is skin deep. If you have the eyes to see it. Yours is all there in your face. As well as that old service pistol you're struggling to keep your hands off right now. How far can you see? I'm right in front of you. Do you see me?'

He saw… energy. Wild, untamed, unschooled. Volatile. Like lightning, bottled up in black clouds and hunting for a target.

'Maybe we should give her a chance,' suggested Tsarsko. He drew his jacket lapels up and threw over-the-shoulder glances everywhere. He had the surly, shifty look of a criminal in a police line-up.

'No,' Vasily said. And he pushed on into the lobby.

It was a palatial space of marbled floor-tiles, brass ceiling fans and tall plants in every niche and corner. Handfuls of guests stood or sat around, while a couple sought service at reception. Romola grabbed Vasily's arm, arresting him a few feet inside the entrance. He spun and jerked his arm free.

'Maybe you haven't caught up on UK news?'

'Forgive us, we have been travelling.'

'You've missed a lot,' she said. 'It was all me. And I didn't need *enhancements*.'

'What enhancements?'

'Give it up, Vasily,' said Tsarsko. 'She knows. Everything, I expect.'

'Your friend gets it. Yes, I *know*. And all I've done up to now, that's just raw me. But have a little think when you can spare the brainpower, think what I can do with a boost. I do everything you do. Only better.'

'Better?' Vasily scoffed.

But she saw through him. Vasily's face began to burn like that of a schoolboy caught in a lie.

The couple from the reception desk passed by. Polite smiles failed to mask their distaste for this unsavoury conference near the doorway.

Romola cupped her palm. 'Give me one.'

'You're insane.'

'One. That's all. I'll give you a *big* demonstration.'

Tsarsko fidgeted from foot to foot. His shrug was nine-parts impatience to one-part indifference. 'Let her have one. At worst, she would become a diversion, a decoy for the police.'

And at best? Vasily dreaded to think. If she was everything she claimed, then her best might be something all men should fear.

'No,' he hissed. 'We have our plan. It does not involve you. Go. Leave. Do whatever you think you can do. But do it alone.'

A calm descended over her, like a falling veil. She turned and walked to the exit. Tsarsko gave her plenty of room. Probably a smart move.

That woman made Vasily feel something he hadn't felt since he was a little boy in Berestechko. She scared him.

That was reason enough to hate her.

The phone interrupted Sophia's story. She smiled an apology as she waited out the ringing. Bugayev went to the desk and picked up. 'Hello?'

He listened. Nodded. Listened. Nodded. Much like he'd been doing as he heard out her tale. For a few seconds, in the wake of Anne's vanishing act, she had wondered whether he was really there. It might have been so good to see him, if only he hadn't brought those

106

accursed bones.

He discarded the phone, and made straight for the door.

'That was Alistair. We need to go.'

'The Brigadier?' Okay, now the past was just playing games with her.

'Lethbridge-Stewart. He accepted my invitation.' Bugayev opened the door to scout the corridor. His usual intensity kicked into overdrive.

'That's – nice,' Sophia said.

'We'll all catch up later. Throw some clothes on. We need to go.'

'What? Why?' Sophia planted her hands on her hips. 'Has it really been that long that you forgot I don't take orders?'

'Pretty please.' He beckoned her to the door. 'There are people on their way. Plainly, they don't want us to leave.'

Sophia eye-rolled and marched to the door. She peered out, left and right. The corridor was choked, wall to wall with barbed-wire. Tangled bundles of it reaching to roughly waist-height all along the passage in both directions. She was accustomed to being *called* crazy. This was new.

'They're here.' Bugayev tapped his temple. 'They're in our heads.'

He hurried to the bed. Sophia closed the door, feeling like the world was rushing about her while she was trapped in slow-motion.

'If it's not real, we can walk through it, right?'

'How real did you think your friend was?'

Anne. Again, Sophia suffered fleeting doubts whether Bugayev was really there or if she was she losing her marbles.

'Well, I spoke with her. We hugged.'

Bugayev attacked the bed, tossed the duvet aside.

'You can try hugging the barbed-wire. But I wouldn't take that chance.'

'So we're stuck here?'

'Not if I can help it.' He tugged the sheets flat, then whipped out a knife and stabbed, shredding a patch of linen to thin ribbons. He glanced up briefly. 'You feel like getting dressed now?'

Sophia grabbed some things and dashed to the bathroom.

Alistair trotted back towards his car. Throughout the phone call he'd exhausted all the elasticity in his neck craning for a view of the hotel entrance, but the morning traffic had begun to pick up and he had quickly lost sight of his suspects behind passing cars and buses and the occasional rattling tram.

He jogged across the road, dodging bumpers. A car braked with a sharp screech and the driver shook a fist through his open window. Alistair waved his apologies and ran on.

The enemy were almost certainly on their way up to an encounter with Bugayev by now. He trusted the Russian would give them a warm reception. Meanwhile, there was another suspect, stowed out of sight and offering the enemy a likely means of ex-filtration.

Alistair strode down the ramp into the underground car park.

Sophia emerged from the bathroom, thinking, *Shoes!* Slipping into her pumps, she froze. And wondered if the attackers had already been.

In the time it had taken her to throw on white slacks and black blouse, Bugayev had finished murdering the bed. The door was open to the corridor. And her duvet and pillows were missing. The minibar was wide open and he was busy using the dresser as a workbench.

'Drink and a smoke.' She wandered over. 'Well, that's the best idea you've had since you got here.'

He had bundled two batches of miniatures, seven or eight apiece, bound tightly with rags. He quickly wadded a last strip of linen into each of the centre bottles. Done, he handed her one of the improvised incendiary devices. Then scooped up her lighter from the dresser.

'Useless little bottles.' He weighed his bundled miniature Molotovs in one hand. 'Together they'll have some heft though.'

'Wait, we can't go torching the place. What about the other guests?'

'This won't trouble them. Trust me.'

Bugayev beckoned her to follow and rushed out to the passage. She saw little change in the scene immediately outside. Except for her bedding draped messily over a span of barbed-wire left of her door.

'Uh, are we sure it's not real.'

'Looks like the illusion adapts to what we do. The bedding is actually on the floor. Has to be.'

He held the lighter to the fuse on his small but expensive bomb. One flick and a flame leaped eagerly onto the cloth. He chucked the Molotov cluster at the wall above the heaped duvet and sheets. Fire splashed over the waiting bonfire and a burning puddle started eating up the wallpaper.

Bugayev reached back, palm open.

Sophia blinked. 'It's my lighter,' she reminded him.

'Really?' he said. But shook his head and returned her property.

Smiling, she lit her Molotov and threw it at the wall opposite the gathering blaze. More splatter caught nicely on the piled bedding.

'You do realise the main stairs and the lifts are that way?'

'Which is why we'll be taking the service stairs.

'Bugayev turned from the steadily growing bonfire. The corridor to the right was still choked with wire. 'Any minute now...'

Sophia glanced back at the flames, watching them creep this way. Whatever Bugayev was hoping would happen next, she willed it to hurry up.

Vasily climbed a stairwell of cold grey brick. Taking his time. Less from patience, more in the interests of conservation of energy.

This 'major' was an unknown quantity, but he was familiar with the type. Enough to breed lifetimes of contempt. Even confined in the room he would be no slouch.

Put him down, thought Vasily. Fast. A swift execution should be enough to persuade the woman to talk. No illusions required.

The sign on the wall informed him he had reached the third floor.

The fire alarm rang out, deafening in the stairwell. That confirmed his reasoning about his foe. Definitely no slouch.

Vasily drew his pistol and launched into a run.

Tsarsko closed his eyes and basked in the elevator's contained stillness. He didn't need an isolated environment for his work. He was just glad to have Vasily out of his hair for a while.

He held the corridor scene in his mind: meshed barbed-wire like steel bracken. Vasily ought to be impressed. But no, praise from Vasily was a pipedream. And Tsarsko didn't want the man's approval anyway.

A bell rang. And rang and rang and kept on ringing. Rattling metal hammered at his thoughts and chiselled at his teeth.

Damn and hell!

His vision shattered like a painting on glass.

The barbed-wire vanished. One second there, one second gone. Like a jump-cut in a film. The bedding – just as Bugayev had said – lay on the floor. Burning. The flames asserted their reality.

'Come on.' He led Sophia in a run, leaving the blaze behind.

They hit a corner and he backed against the wall, peeked around, then led her onward. To a fire door. He eased it open, scouted, then beckoned her through. A grey-brick stairwell offered a choice: up or down.

Sophia registered the wall-mounted extinguisher and the glass-fronted case in the corner.

'In case of emergency...' Bugayev elbowed the glass. Grabbed the axe.

He started down the steps. Sophia moved to follow. A shot cracked out. Bugayev ducked back. The ceiling shed plaster chippings.

He reversed, waving her back through the fire door.

Sophia retreated into the corridor, expecting to hear another ear-splitting shot any second.

Vasily tucked into the corner of the landing, his pistol trained up the last flight of stairs. The fire door swung closed, targets gone.

He cursed himself. He had fired *too* fast. Now he was going to have to pay with a little patience.

He crept up. Breathing fast, moving slow. His automatic waiting – just waiting – for the slightest twitch from that door.

He couldn't hear anything apart from the bell. He tried to see the corridor, but the bell curdled his concentration. Never mind. Running from him would only send them to Tsarsko.

*

Tsarsko stormed out of the elevator in an ugly mood. The damn bell was deep in his head. He drew his hunting knife and homed in on the smell of smoke and a small choir of screams.

He rounded the corner into the burning corridor. Before the flames though, his way was barred by a clot of guests squealing like lemmings. They bombarded him with pleas and questions. He shoved his way through.

'Do I *look* like the help?' he growled.

Most fled in the direction of the elevators. On his left, a couple peered out from a doorway, trapped by fear and indecision. Tsarsko thrust his knife at them, helping them make up their minds. They retreated inside and shut the door. They preferred to take their chances with the fire than him.

He marched on towards the blaze.

The fire formed a portal framing the corridor. He sized up the gap. Flames occasionally licked at each other from either side.

He turned his march into a run-up.

He jumped. Heat snatched at him. He sailed through, hit carpet on the other side and stumbled. He recovered, managed to not look a complete clown. He glanced over his shoulder. Past the blaze, the corridor was clear of spectators.

Then it started to rain.

Sprinklers set the flames hissing. Tsarsko hissed back.

Vasily tensed, then pulled open the fire door. The sprinkler system was dowsing the corridor. Alarms and now water to contend with... Oh yes, he had to be rid of this major.

He advanced, gun-arm fully extended and trigger-finger ready to squeeze at the first movement. He spun left into the downpour.

A figure rushed him, swinging something. He

hopped back to buy space. Fired. The something smacked his wrist. Steel on bone.

He yelled. His pistol flew free.

Stinging vision made out the axe arcing up. Vasily lunged right, evading. He grabbed. Wrestled for possession.

'Go! Go now!' the major barked.

A second figure darted past through the shower. Vasily heard the fire door batted open, as he spun in a violent waltz. He shoved this opponent against the wall. His wrist lodged livid protests as he fought to press the axe-shaft into the major's windpipe.

A kick hooked his leg out from under him and slammed him to the floor. The axe twisted out of his grasp.

Through the spattering water in his eyes he spied another shadow in the rain. Moving up on the major.

Vasily grinned. *Tsarsko.*

Alistair roamed the aisles, doing his utmost to appear casual. He assumed more the role of an absent-minded driver seeking out his own car.

The car park was a generous size and occupied to near-capacity, split on two levels and with pillars that seemed deliberately spaced to obstruct a clear sweep. He wandered down a second row, his show of frustration growing more authentic. His footsteps were the only punctuation of the silence. Might as well be exploring a graveyard of cars.

But no orange Volkswagen camper vans.

He stopped in front of a silver Audi Quattro. Had there been an odd flicker reflected in the radiator?

He looked to the ceiling lights. Steady illumination.

A shot cracked, several floors away. He looked to the far end of the car park. An engine snarled – and the camper leaped from the Audi's space. Alistair threw himself aside – a whisker too late.

He caught the image of a frightened young woman behind the windscreen. And a corner of the camper in his ribcage.

The VW swerved and bolted down the aisle, leaving him rolling on tarmac.

Bugayev hopped clear of a defensive kick from Vasily and chopped with the axe. Vasily rolled aside.

The man's grin was a poker tell: Bugayev knew there was a joker coming.

He sent the axe down again, spike first. Vasily rolled the other way, but the point bit into his thigh. Vasily screamed. Bugayev yanked the spike out and spun to face the newcomer.

He was right there, looking like a drowned rat, coming at him with a hunting knife. He slashed at Bugayev's throat.

CHAPTER ELEVEN
The Terror of Knowing

JULY 1981.

Sophia ran to the head of the stairs. The fire door swung closed, muffling the sounds of the fight behind her. She hesitated. Torn.

She forced herself down two steps. Four. A hellish yell – a howl of rage and pain – stopped her on the fifth.

She turned and dashed back up to the landing. Straight to the corner.

Tiny black stars swam in Vasily's vision. His world reeled. He dragged himself across water-logged carpet. The sprinklers failed to put out the fire in his leg.

He flapped an arm about, feeling for the lost pistol.

Tsarsko's knife-arm met the axe-shaft. Tsarsko kicked at his opponent's knee, but the man blocked with a kick of his own. He turned the axe fast and swung at Tsarsko's middle. Tsarsko skipped backwards. The axe fetched him a brushing blow across the chest and dented the wall. Tsarsko ducked left and charged in for a stab.

Vasily's fingers closed around the friendly pistol-grip. Finally, the pain didn't feel so bad. He flipped himself over and sat up. Aimed at the two shapes thrashing about in the corridor, trading brutal blows in the downpour. Mere yards from him, the profiles merged, broke apart, merged. Axe and knife sliced and swiped. Legs and arms lashed out.

Vasily willed them to separate. Any second now…

The fire door bashed open.

Vasily swung his pistol to bear. He saw the archaeologist. He saw a cylinder. He saw red.

The extinguisher banged the side of the terrorist's head. The weighty cylinder made for an unwieldy club and Sophia lost hold with the impact. It hit the floor with a dull thunk and splash. It rolled a short distance.

By then the gunman had crashed over, sprawled in the wet. And the pistol had landed near the extinguisher. Result.

She hopped over her victim and stooped for the gun. A hand clutched her ankle.

Bugayev twirled the axe like a baton and jabbed the handle in an uppercut to Tsarsko's chin. The head jerked back and he staggered.

Which bought time to check out the noise behind him: Sophia was down and fighting to beat off Vasily with kicks. Bugayev hopped over the fire extinguisher, came around Sophia and stamped a boot on Vasily's arm. Sophia scooted clear. Vasily snatched at her.

Bugayev brought the flat of the axe-blade down on Vasily's back.

Past Sophia, Tsarsko recovered from his stagger. He rushed forward with the knife.

Bugayev dropped, scooped up the Tokarev and put three in Tsarsko's chest.

Vasily twitched, then lay still.

Ekel wandered the market square, feeling like a sticky-chinned boy set loose in a sweet shop. Pretty cake-box buildings, pastel façades and white trim, market stalls adorned with pastries and confections, and a wealth of other foods. There was a deliciousness to the people too, bustling about their sugar-plum streets, oblivious to his smiles or frowns.

He tested some of them: he beamed placidly at a woman burdened with a stuffed grocery bag; he scowled like Mary Shelley's Creature at the child she towed along behind her. Nothing from either. He could taste their youth. The syrupy scent in his nostrils.

Everyone was young to him. Infantile. Beneath him. Playing at life while starved of understanding. It was as well they did not see him. He must not dally with these people.

'Leave your old appetites in the past, Ekel,' Vasily had lectured him time and again. As though Vasily feared he needed constant teaching to keep him on the right path. Perhaps he did.

He was tired.

A fountain formed a picturesque centrepiece to the square. Ekel walked to the bench that surrounded it and sat, listening to the splash. He set his small suitcase on the ground between his feet. He watched the people. East, he thought, was savoury. The West was sweet.

'Ekel.'

A woman sat beside him. She had hair red as autumn, fiery as summer. She made him feel younger. Small. Nervous.

'The Creeper.' English. She was an English rose. Her lips were so red. There were thorns in her voice.

'That was my name in the newspapers. That is not me anymore.'

'It's not me you have to convince. Vasily sent me to relieve you of your baggage. He wants to see what I can do with those magic charms.'

Ekel stood. 'No. I do not believe he did.'

'Not in so many words. But people say so much with their body language, don't they?'

Ekel closed his legs, trapping the case. The woman jumped up and there was a knife in her hand. Silver flashed – then slipped from view. It turned to a blade of pain sliding between his ribs, drilling into his heart. It couldn't be real. But it was killing him anyway.

Nobody in the square could see him. For the first time in decades, he wished somebody – anybody – could see him.

Alistair hunted for the source of the gunshots.

Nursing the ribs that the VW had clipped, he quickly located the service stairs to the hotel. He was spared the trouble of dashing up too many stairs by the presence of Señora Montilla, dripping wet, hurrying down. Bugayev, equally soaked, was a few stairs behind her, slowed a little by his burden: a body.

In spite of his battered state, Alistair recognised the chap: one of the suspicious characters from the VW camper. One arm hooked over Bugayev's shoulder, head hanging uselessly and feet dragging on every step, he appeared lifeless, but Bugayev would not go to all that trouble for a corpse.

'Alistair. Good to see you. Just in time.'

Remarkable to see Grigoriy so much younger. Whether his relative youth was reason to excuse his informality or not was another matter. The sight of the Señora alive and well was a jolt that put the matter into perspective. A sharp reminder of another funeral yet to happen.

'In time for what?' Alistair glanced at the Señora. She greeted him with a smile, but it wavered and she aimed her gaze elsewhere. Alistair nodded up the stairwell. 'Any more up there?'

'None we need worry about,' said Bugayev. 'Give me a hand with this one.'

Between them, they carried the man down the last

flight and pushed through the door into the car park. They conveyed him to the nearest rank of cars and sat him on the ground, propped against a bumper.

Sophia loitered in the background.

'Are you all right?' Alistair asked.

'I'm sure I will be.'

Bugayev crouched near the suspect and performed a brisk pat-down. He turned up a pistol clip and transferred that to his own jacket pocket. Otherwise, nothing. He slapped the man's rather gaunt cheeks, coaxing him towards consciousness. The eyelids flickered, but if there was anybody home they were slow to answer the door.

'I'm afraid their getaway vehicle got away,' Alistair informed Bugayev. 'The others split up. And *my* suspect showed up. Had some words with this one.'

'Your IRA woman?'

'Romola – if that's her real name. As to her affiliations...'

'If she was capable of what you described, I would wager she is a remote-viewer like my fugitives.' Bugayev appeared to catch a spark or something in the suspect's eyes. 'Oh, hello. *Dobroye utro,* Vasily.'

He flicked the bridge of the man's nose. Vasily flinched, suddenly more awake. Conscious enough to be mad, at any rate.

'Remote-viewers?' Sophia asked quietly.

'Psychic spies,' Alistair supplied.

'As good a label as any.' Bugayev watched Vasily like a cat waiting for a mouse to make its move. 'But let's not deceive ourselves. These are not telepathic James Bonds. They are misfits and criminals with dangerous delusions of grandeur. Detained for a while, recruited and trained by the KGB. Finally free after years of servitude and full of resentment.'

Romola. Does that explain her? Alistair wondered.

119

Product of a similar programme? The UK was always under an obligation to keep up with the Soviets in every potential arena. 'So that's what we're up against: a sort of slave rebellion.'

'In essence. And this is their Spartacus. Vasily Kirillovich Savvin.'

Vasily listened to all this with a developing sneer. 'My part is over. Evidently.' Alistair wasn't sure whether he had ever seen a man so beaten and bruised look so victorious. 'You have won nothing. My comrades have flown, and Europe is rich with destinations. Perhaps you should concern yourselves with my American friends and the scientist.'

Alistair advanced on the prisoner. 'What's that supposed to mean?'

'Anne!' Sophia blurted. 'Ask him about Anne!'

At the mention of Anne, Alistair moved to stand right over their man. A warning, if he was intelligent enough to interpret it. 'You're in the West now. Time to start exercising your right of free speech.'

Vasily's sneer returned, but with an extra slice of sour humour. 'You gentlemen would like a story? I prefer show to tell.'

A blade twirled in Bugayev's fingers. Alistair was still wondering where the knife had come from when the major pressed the blade down on the prisoner's thigh wound.

Anne felt she was trapped in a bad play in a cramped theatre. The drama was more of a tableau and the suspense wasn't exactly killing her, but the ending could. Despite the best efforts of the air-con, the atmosphere was getting close and claustrophobic. But that was nothing to her crowded headspace.

'Look, if it's not too much trouble, I need the toilet.'

Seth assessed her like she was a badly written

equation chalked on a blackboard. 'Do you, my dear? Or is that one of those clichéd ploys of hostages who need a little private time and space to plot their escape? Your *toilet* has no outside window. Even if it had, I cannot see you testing your abseiling skills with a shower curtain and a few towels. No. All that leaves you with is a scrawled plea for help in a condensation-covered mirror, or climbing into the bathtub and ending it all. Did you pack a razor?'

The man curdled Anne's stomach. She realised there wasn't much in there. She didn't suppose Seth would permit her to phone for room service.

'I can do it,' volunteered Rufus from his shadowy corner, where he had propped himself against the wall. 'If we mean to get rid of her.'

'Oh, thank you, Rufus, that's most generous.' Seth sounded like a teacher thanking a pupil for bringing him an apple. 'But I believe we will… *take* her with us. Yes,' he decided.

'She may be a useful unit of exchange if the archaeologist proves uncooperative. Some sterling British currency.'

Good news, bad news, thought Anne. And both were grim.

Sophia would not submit quietly. To anything. That was guaranteed. What that meant for her… Well, Anne was looking at a stay of execution and an extended prison sentence. Caged up with these lunatics.

She mulled over the menu choices she might have ordered from room service. They all made her sick.

Oddly, Bonnie wore a similar queasy expression, fixed to her chair and gazing down at her pad. She'd said nothing in an age.

'Rufus,' Seth said, 'let's leave a little present for the hotel. Ready for when it's time to get the hell out of Dodge.'

Rufus dug in the small holdall which had lain neglected since Bonnie had set it down. Whatever he brought out, he walked to the head of the bed and carefully placed it on a pillow like a complimentary chocolate.

Light from the bedside lamp played in its pearlescent contours.

Seth tutted. 'No, no, no. At least conceal it, there's a good boy.'

Rufus grumbled, retrieved the bone and traipsed about the room searching for a hiding spot. He looked like a beginner Easter Bunny, new to his trade. Eventually he settled on a drawer in one of the bedside cabinets.

Seth smiled. 'There now. We can't have some maid coming in to turn up the sheets and undo our arrangements.' He examined his watch, at some length, like a man unhappy with the spacing of each tick. 'We will wait until first light for word from our friends. And then we shall depart. Is that clear? Bonnie?'

'Uh huh, sure, whatever.'

'And then a little road trip, Mrs Bishop. Won't that be pleasant?'

Anne shook her head. 'You people are insane.'

Seth made a child-like frown-face. 'Rufus, if you would, please.'

Rufus lunged. He smacked her mouth with the back of his hand. She reeled. When she looked up, Seth had taken Rufus' place. He leaned and dropped to her eye-level, all gentle, nauseating smiles.

'Every time Pinocchio told a lie, his nose grew,' he said, as though reciting a fairy tale to a toddler. 'Every time you give me any of your lip, it will grow. Do I make myself clear?'

Anne tested her lip with tentative dabs of her fingers. Definitely bigger. 'Yes, Geppetto,' she said, loading the words with quiet spite.

She braced herself, but nothing came. Seth appeared content that her defiance had emerged as a whisper.

'Really, Major! The man is our prisoner. I will not be a party to torture.'

On top of everything else, the move had inflamed every fibre of military discipline. Alistair was ready to tear into Bugayev like he was reprimanding a subordinate. Futile, when they were on the same side, but not.

Bugayev eased up on the blade pressure. The prisoner seethed, riding down the pain.

'No, Brigadier.' Vasily's grimace faltered on the edge of a grin. 'This isn't torture. As much as it hurts.' He laughed, loud and fierce. 'This is security. Prevention. This Grigoriy Yevgenyevich Bugayev is a smart foe.' He managed a weak, mock salute. 'I really should have killed him.'

'I'm not entirely sure I follow.'

'I think I do,' said Sophia. She looked a little queasy. 'Which is not to say I enjoy seeing it.'

'For which, my apologies.' Bugayev wiped the blade on Vasily's leg, near the leaking wound. 'But pain is a great concentration breaker. If I get a hint that Vasily here is thinking too hard, there will be more. For which, I encourage you to look away, Señora.'

She huffed and turned away, but not to spare herself the sight of blood.

'Yes, well, I can't say I altogether approve either, Señora,' Alistair said.

'You're British. You're obliged to act differently with ladies present.' Bugayev stood and tucked the knife in his belt. 'Now, what about you, Vasily? Are you ready to tell not show?'

Vasily maintained a tight lip.

'Okay,' said Bugayev. 'You know what happens now?

If there's no more useful intel you care to give us?'

'What? You hand me over to the Austrian police? Who knows? I might talk more freely to the Austrians.'

'Might you? Well, you make a convincing case for killing you.' Bugayev drew a pistol, a somewhat antiquated automatic.

'No, Major!' Alistair snapped. 'Breaking his concentration was one thing; he's no threat now.'

'Um, are we sure about that?' Sophia asked. She made an unhappy face and threw her arms out for balance.

Then Alistair felt it too.

A murmuring thunder beneath his feet, like the approach of an underground train. The noise rose, climbing into the pillars, into the ceiling. Vehicles rocked on their suspensions. A number of car alarms chorused their protests. Alistair's knees wobbled. Sophia laid a steadying hand on a trembling car.

Bugayev crouched in front of their prisoner and cracked the man's nose with the butt of the pistol. Vasily yelped. He reached for the wound, but flinched when he touched bone.

'It's not me!' he yelled.

'I warned you!'

The parked cars were going wild, horns blaring amid the mounting rumble. The quake had a hold of the building now, as though trains were converging above and below. Suddenly, Alistair was down, backside hitting the ground. Señora Montilla pitched against the car and slid down its flank. Bugayev stumbled about on his haunches until he too keeled sideways. Vasily laughed even as blood poured down to colour his teeth.

With eyes that wouldn't stop rattling around in their sockets, Alistair sighted a figure standing – steady as a statue – at the end of the aisle. A shaking silhouette of long coat and long hair. She tossed something to the ground. It landed and rolled, coming to a rest not far from

Alistair's right hand. He expected a grenade. But it was a bone. A shiny finger bone.

'Major!' Alistair pointed to the figure.

Bugayev spread himself flat and aimed. But his arms were all over the place and the shot sailed wide. A car windscreen blew inwards. But not from a bullet impact. Giant cracks ripped across the ceiling and ate through the pillars. Masonry rained hard on the vehicles.

The woman walked through the chaos.

The ground split under Bugayev. He let go of the gun and grabbed for a hold as an abyss opened. 'It's not real!' he shouted. 'Just lie flat!'

Alistair dived for the bone, not sure what he could do or if it would help. The ceiling crumbled apart. What felt like meteorites thudded into his back and punished his legs. He crawled through a storm of dust. Making no headway. He looked back. His legs were crushed under multiple slabs of concrete. Sophia was gone, a burial mound over her and most of one car. He searched and saw Bugayev's hand reaching from a grave of rubble.

Romola strode through the veil of dust. She stooped to pick up the abandoned pistol. Turned it over. She pointed it at Alistair's head.

Alistair coughed and fought to wriggle free.

She shoved the gun in her coat pocket and collected Vasily.

The woman dragged Vasily into a war zone. Not a Stalingrad hell – nothing could equal that. But perhaps Vienna that morning could pass for a blitz-battered London or a German city punished in an Allied air raid: buildings with pulverised faces, the entire front of the Hotel Ruby-Gisele caved in, the road a broken field of rubble and exposed gas pipes, crippled streetlamps and littered vehicles. Several cars were crunched into one another, one into a newspaper kiosk further up the street.

None of it real.

She hauled him to one of the cars, left him to stand lamely. She wrenched the driver-side door open. The driver – a young Austrian with a bushy blond moustache – was in there, lightly blooded head rested on the wheel. She pulled him out and dumped him on the road. The man didn't stir as his skull cracked against tarmac.

'Get in,' the woman ordered. She turned the key.

Resentment crawled in his gut. But he hobbled around to the other side. He collapsed into the passenger seat. She backed them up and manoeuvred around a minor pile-up. The rubble melted away, the cracks and craters and ruined buildings repaired themselves. Some of the vehicle wrecks remained.

Vasily watched his driver from the corner of his eye. She scared him more than before. He despised her for that.

But the Americans had taught the world one major lesson in the Pacific War: you could fear a weapon, dread it even, but still use it without compunction.

The gag pulled at the corners of Anne's mouth as Rufus shoved her out of the lift and strong-armed her across the foyer and out through the revolving door. Bonnie and Seth followed.

Her muffled shouts achieved nothing. Whatever show these conjurers were giving the guests and staff, Anne was part of their silent movie. Nobody batted an eyelid at the sight of her checking out against her will.

Early sunshine played on the glassy buildings. Her head was thumping. She was starved and dehydrated. (They had let her visit the toilet, but that was small consolation and a distant memory.) The morning traffic was more noise and motion than she could handle. And the few occasions she was stupid enough to look up, the tops of the high-rises wheeled against a canvas of blue.

Rufus propelled her across the avenue and marched her down a narrow backstreet. Ahead there was a large Winnebago parked snugly behind a dumpster. Anne figured she was headed for one or the other.

The Winnebago, as it turned out.

The side door opened and a figure ducked back out of the way before Rufus bundled her inside. That was all she got to see of the other passenger because Rufus shoved her towards the bunk at the rear.

'Get us under way, would you, Earl?' said Seth.

'Sure thing, Shepherd,' said Earl.

Rufus headed to the front. Bonnie sat next to Anne. The artist cradled her bag.

'We need to swing by Blick's,' she said.

'What?' Seth showed his distaste for surprises.

'I need a new pad. And pencils. Mostly the pad.'

'What, pray, is wrong with the one you have?'

'I can't look at that face. He's pressed into every damn page. That's the face of the man that's gonna kill me.'

Seth forced his facial muscles into an imitation of patience. 'Bonnie, my child, what did you see? Exactly?'

The engine grumbled. The vehicle creaked and clunked, pulling out around the dumpster with three or four reluctant manoeuvres.

Bonnie had to speak up: 'I ain't your child, Shepherd.'

'Still, I am your Shepherd. Tell me.'

'The plane hijack. Bugayev. He comes rushing up at me. Pistol aimed right here.' She touched the centre of her forehead. 'I can feel the bullet.'

The Winnebago lumbered down the backstreet and swung out into the main stream of traffic.

'Bonnie, that is not your future. That is the past. A false past at that. Residual patterns. Traces imprinted in the materials, not unlike impressions on your precious pages.' Seth patted the back of her hand.

Bonnie snatched it clear and pulled her pad from her

bag. She tore out the last sketch and crushed it into a ball. 'That's as may be,' she said. 'But I ain't having him in my drawings.'

'Very well. Blick's it is. On our way out of town.'

Seth sighed and settled opposite Anne. He glanced out the window. Smiled. Then he was on his feet and reaching over her. He tugged the curtains back as far as they would go, then sat back down.

'Here. We wouldn't want you to miss this.'

Against her better judgement, Anne turned to look at the receding view of downtown Chicago. Loose strings of vehicles trailed in their wake. The front of her hotel erupted, blowing smoke and fire and concrete and glittering shards out over the road. Cars swerved or screeched to a halt before the crashing storm. Others careered headlong into its belly. Debris rained mercilessly on the traffic that had strayed too close, and the slow-swelling cloud blotted out Anne's farewell shot of the city. Within minutes, wailing sirens tore up the Chicago morning.

The Winnebago left it all behind.

CHAPTER TWELVE
Run for the Shadows

1971. NEW MEXICO.

Sophia poked the campfire with a stick. The flames rewarded her with a comforting crackle.

She was not one to be troubled by a little solitude, much less the dark. But something about this site made the absence of company an emptier space than usual. Even now that she had seen the 'ghost', she refused to believe it. What bothered her most was not what she had witnessed, but the invisible intangibles that crept in to prey on her in the quiet.

Anne was busy working on some means of rendering them more visible... But hopefully not too tangible.

She checked her watch. Anne had been underground for the past two hours. It had been an hour since Chess had swung by, collected his rifle and headed down to the solace of his own tent for the night. She bid him, '*Buenos nochos,*' and he had assured her, 'If you need me for anything, I'll be asleep.'

Yes, even if Anne's efforts revealed actual ghosts, Sophia was persuaded that Chess would remain her true prize find on this expedition.

She rose for a leg-stretch and picked up her walkie-talkie. She thumbed the button. 'Anne. How're you getting along down there? You know you're not on a deadline, right?'

Anne's voice came back pretty quick. 'Modifications are about done.' She yawned. 'I am also in need of about ninety winks – which I might round up to the full hundred – so I'll be up shortly to take those.'

Sophia was about to hit send, but put her reply on hold. She strained to listen. There was a low rushing sound building in the background, but no wind on her cheeks. Homing in on the noise, she wandered towards the edge of the mesa.

From high on her mountain island, the desert was a black sea. A solid unmoving expanse that had no power or inclination to reflect the night's stars. And yet, there were lights traversing that space below. Multiple bright pairs of eyes, as if a family of armadillos or skunks were foraging along the road in single file. Except, of course, their shadowy outlines were a shade too large to be desert wildlife. These were the headlights of a convoy; two lead cars, an eighteen-wheeler, plus a follow-up car.

Skunks, Sophia decided. Even at this distance, there was a stink about them.

She thumbed the walkie-talkie. 'Chess. Come in. Chess. Wake up. Now.'

The line of vehicles snaked off the highway, ploughing up small dust storms in their headlight beams.

'Chess!'

'What's going on?' Anne broke in.

Sophia hurried back to the camp. 'Stay put, Anne. I was up here feeling lonely and now we have company.' *Careful what you wish for.* 'I'll be down with you shortly. I just need to get a hold of Chess.'

Sophia kicked the campfire to death. Far too late. Someone in those vehicles would have spotted the beacon by now.

'Who are they?' Anne came back.

'No idea. But how's your Tolkien?'

'My what?'

'We're on Weathertop and the ringwraiths are coming.'

Sophia ran back to the edge. 'Chess! Where are you? Come on, come on, wake yourself up right now!'

Headlight beams illuminated a destructive rampage taking place below. The party-crashers were demolishing the campsite. One gunman played traffic-warden, guiding the big eighteen-wheeler into reverse over a row of tents. Others paired up to turf over the rest of the camp, ransacking tent interiors before exiting and tearing the shelters down.

Frantic, Sophia struggled to identify which tent Chess had commandeered. If he wasn't awake yet, he might never be again.

'Chester Blacksnake, I swear if you do not answer–!'

'Here. I'm safe. For now.' His voice was a whisper, no louder than static. 'I'll try to make my way up to you.'

'Negative,' said Sophia, crediting herself for sounding so

130

military. 'You get yourself clear. Go. Anne and I will take care of ourselves.'

She watched the mayhem below begin to settle down. Three pairs of men merged and scurried across the open ground towards the base of the mesa.

'And don't you dare be stubborn this time. Do you hear me?' she added. The radio hissed. 'Do you hear me?'

'Loud and clear, Señora. Stay safe.'

The six passed in front of one car's beams, inadvertently advertising their weapons – shotguns, submachineguns, pistols- and bulletproof vests. They hustled towards the long, steep stairs. The first teams were commencing the climb.

Sophia dropped to the kiva floor and kicked the ladder over. She climbed down the next shaft and gave the second ladder the same treatment. There was no sense making life easy for her pursuers.

A booming warning broke overhead, like a thunderstorm with the power of speech: 'This site is the property of Central Intelligence Agency. Surrender yourselves immediately. You are in no danger.'

The megaphone robbed that last part of all sincerity.

She raced through the labyrinth. In an ideal world, she would have killed the generator, chugging away, but Anne was going to need that. She hoped these claim-jumpers – CIA or not – didn't think to cut their power before they were done with it. She followed the cable, knowing the hunting parties would likely do the same, and she burst into the chamber where Anne waited.

The scientist was armed with her box of tricks – the detachable console – and a moderately anxious raised eyebrow or two.

'Okay, we are definitely on a deadline now,' said Sophia. If the cable didn't lead them there, the lighting rigs would. She wondered about knocking those out, but they were also perches for Anne's sensors, and were probably crucial to whatever she had in mind. 'So, any time you're ready.'

'Are we sure we still want to do this?'

Sophia nodded. 'Damn straight. I can't leave without answers.'

'You're the boss.' Anne smiled. She fiddled with a dial on the box of tricks.

Sophia readied her hands as ear-muffs. She looked to the

wall decorated with petroglyphs–

To see it vanish. Like before. Only this time, without the accompanying apparition. Or the screams. Hers, Anne's or the machine's.

'The wall was never there,' Anne explained. 'It's a psychic barrier, if you like. I'm currently directing an interference signal from all the sensors in this chamber. It appears to also inhibit the other effects we observed.'

As she heard out Anne's commentary, Sophia advanced towards the recessed vault that had opened behind 'the wall that was never there'. A solid stone altar occupied the centre, but what dominated were the figures embedded in the back wall. They looked like bas-relief representations of the skeleton-creature from the petroglyph. But slow scans with the torch-beam revealed they were comprised of actual pearlescent bones, nestled in accommodating hollows in the stone. Between them, the same wall was marked with a crudely carved face, with a gaping arch at the base providing the mouth; which appeared to serve as some sort of crawl-way or ventilation duct leading to another space beyond.

Both side walls were home to bas-relief kachina-figures, which similarly revealed themselves as sections of suits or costumes. The skeletons stood perhaps eight feet tall. The 'suits' might have added another foot. An uninspiring slate grey and devoid of the colours Sophia normally associated with traditional Hopi designs. She would have to examine the materials more closely – along with the pearlescent bones.

She stepped inside. Anne followed, staying close.

'Could this be what the Nine are after?'

'Six for now. Possibly more on the way.'

Voices travelled the approach tunnel to the main chamber. Flashlight beams bounced around the walls, far along the passage. Their deadline was about to be brought forward.

'Speak of the devil…' Sophia said.

'Hang on,' said Anne.

She tweaked some controls on her console again. The wall that was never there returned. The perfect concealment. The downside: it sealed them in total darkness. Sophia pulled out her flashlight. She shone it at the wall. No petroglyphs on the interior face.

The voices – and footsteps – were heavily muffled, even though they had to be getting closer. Sophia touched the wall that didn't exist: solid as any wall. She wondered at its capacity to block sound. Behind her, something scraped stone.

Sophia spun and aimed her torch.

One pearl skull projected from its mould. She panned over to the other skeleton. The neck flexed and thrust the head outward. An arm jerked, tugging the wing from its upright bed. The skeleton extended a leg, stamping a taloned foot onto stone.

Sophia grabbed Anne's arm and together they dropped, sitting with their backs to the altar.

A symphony of scrapes and stomps played in the darkness, an ominous soundtrack to the creatures' emergence. It was difficult to shake off the notion that they had awoken a pair of demons. Two – three – four leaden steps and then they fell silent. Which was strangely worse.

Sophia popped her head up for a peek, risking a flash of the torch. She stared and quickly shut her mouth to prevent a gasp. And dropped right back down and shut off the light. The image of the figures stayed with her.

They were stationary. Fixed sculptures of dragon skeletons, standing tall on digitigrade legs, fashioned in pearl. Arms extended at two points along each wing of bones, and the skull was like an enormous warped gemstone, with crests and ingrown horns. Moreover, sections of armour were floating from their niches in the side walls, drawn to the skeletons as if by some magnetism, and assembling around the frames as cladding. The pieces knitted together somehow, arranging themselves into formidable suits. Building, in effect, a pair of monstrous knights around the dragons.

'What?'

Sophia shushed Anne. She leaned close to find Anne's ear. 'I think they're getting dressed for battle.'

'What!' Anne's hiss almost escaped as a squeak.

'I think we have to get out of here.'

'Listen,' Anne said. Mumbled conversation and human-sized footsteps reached them through the wall. The CIA claim-jumpers were close by. 'We should go further *in.*'

In, thought Sophia. *Of course. The mouth. Past this altar. But also past the two monsters.* 'And how do we–?'

It was Anne's turn to shush her. 'Shine a light.'

She guided Sophia's hand, directing the torch over her console. Sophia switched on and cupped a hand around the

133

beam to limit its cast. Anne fiddled away in the mini-spotlight. Light flooded the vault. The 'psychic' wall was gone. Sophia and Anne were lit up like performers on a stage. A potential audience of three gun-wielding agents were out in the stands, waiting for the show to start.

They turned their heads, as though realising the curtain had gone up.

'What the hell!'

'Back up! Back up!'

They withdrew towards the exit, clustering together and covering their retreat with weapons raised.

Sophia knew she wasn't *that* scary.

A heavy thud got the men extra nervous. Sophia too, to be fair. Then came another and another. Like beats on a stone drum. And she and Anne were *in* the drum. A great armour-clad foot stamped the ground close by. Sophia held her breath. The creature advanced, past the altar, looming large on her right. Its partner stepped forwards on Anne's left.

'You ladies best come on out!' One of the agents beckoned them. 'Move! We'll cover you.'

The creatures lurched into the chamber, advancing on the knot of agents. Sophia watched two full-fledged kachinas. Moving. Living? Not breathing, without lungs. Their armour brought them more alive. The sections inherited a strange translucence, infused with glimpses of the fluid rainbow colours of the pearl skeleton within. Spectral rays emanated from around the helmets, fanned like feather headdresses. Demons with a hint of angel.

Anne tugged her sleeve. Sophia gave a nod. They parted company, crawling around their respective ends of the altar. They met again at the mouth in the back wall. Sophia hung back, letting Anne scuttle through first. Sophia wasted no time following.

Gunfire erupted, made worse by ear-splitting echoes. The thud of kachina footsteps continued undeterred.

'Fire in the hole!' one agent yelled. Heralding nothing good.

From ear-splitting to earth-shattering, the explosion rumbled on as though the sound was burrowing through the rock like some gigantic worm.

Sophia rose in a second vault and immediately waved her torch around for a brisk survey. Petroglyphs colonised every wall, an array of pictograms that would take a lifetime to study. More kachinas, more animals, plants, more history mingling with myth. In place of an altar, the vault housed a central sarcophagus. A simple open coffin of stone.

Sophia dipped her flashlight to illuminate the inside.

Anne gasped.

Bathed in the light, lay another skeleton. Wings of bone and – relatively – tiny arms folded across its ribcage in repose, digitigrade legs, and that curious malformed skull with its selected Möbius contours. But approximately twice the size of a human infant.

Shots and drumbeat footsteps continued to hammer away outside, but the din seemed to be receding. The shouts of the agents sounded no less desperate, but definitely more distant.

'Is it…?'

A child. Sophia could practically hear the words choked in Anne's throat. 'Must be.'

Accounts of the Spanish slaughter and enslavement of Hopi were readily transposed onto the site. In the Sky City the conquerors had built a chapel among the humble pueblo dwellings, as though to proclaim their actions as 'God's work'. The idea of similar tragedy befalling these kachinas, as well as the pueblo inhabitants, was harder to bear. Faced with the remains of one of their young, it was easy to revise first impressions of these creatures from monsters to something nobler. Perhaps something more akin to the *kachina* spirits as viewed by the Hopi. There was no chapel atop this mesa. Perhaps the Spaniards had feared something unholy here. Perhaps their consciences secretly ruled their own actions unholy.

Sophia cursed her ancestors. Not including her grandparents on her mama's side, who had been lovely.

'What can we do?' Anne asked.

Sophia saw these bones, the skull, being drilled, sliced, probed, vivisected in some government lab. Possibly underground. The details were vague, but the idea provoked more than enough motivation.

'Save what we can.'

Battle-noise, mostly gunfire, now mixed with sporadic screams and shouts, had drifted further away. If the *kachinas* were still advancing, then their steps were lost in the passages.

She shone the light on Anne and held up a finger. 'Wait

right here.'

'What? You're going back out–?'

Sophia dropped on all fours and crawled back through the mouth. She scuttled immediately to the altar for a spot of cover and peeped around. All clear. For now. Some of the lights were out – presumably victims of the blast – but the sensors were keeping the psychic wall 'down'. Good job, because knowing the barrier was an illusion would probably not help her to pass through. She supposed she would have to be a ghost for that.

Glad to be corporeal and staying low, she scurried towards Anne's equipment stack. On her way over, she spotted the very shallow crater where the blast had struck. There were artefacts scattered in the dust. Curiosity was a terrible temptress.

Sophia detoured to investigate.

She brushed one clean of dust, revealing a section of kachina armour. Broken loose by the explosion, she deduced. It resembled the banded carapace of a woodlouse. Complete with a multitude of tiny 'legs' lining its underside. In fact, it looked so much like a mutated and overgrown bug she was initially reticent to handle it. But she held up two; and the tiny legs wriggled, the limbs of each reaching for the other. Part of the interlocking mechanism for the armour?

Fascinating, in any case.

She scooped up five pieces and carried on to the equipment. The toolbox, she decided, would do nicely. She picked it up and tipped it upside down, dumping the contents. A touch more noisily than she'd intended.

The guns and yells had fallen worryingly silent.

She hastened back to the vault and Anne. And presented her with her toolbox. Anne gave a brief sigh of mourning for her tools, but then assisted Sophia with the careful collection of a few bone specimens from the 'crib'. Sophia gently lifted and transferred the skull. Anne shut the toolbox.

'Let's find out if Chess was right about those lower passages.'

Squeezing through a crevice, Sophia emerged onto a ledge that was five or six feet above the desert. Anne passed the toolbox through and squeezed out beside her. Sophia sat and slid over the edge, landing a little awkwardly on loose stone.

Probably the remains of a small staircase that had crumbled away.

She reached up and caught the box from Anne. Then Anne dropped.

They were a fair distance around the mesa from the camp and the CIA vehicles. Clear desert stretched away for miles, and if they could make it over the nearest ridgeline they might make good their escape.

Sophia knelt and plucked her trowel from her belt. She cleared some of the larger stones aside and began to dig.

'What now?' Anne asked. Something about her expression suggested she didn't fancy a night-time jaunt across the desert.

'We bury our treasure. Then we surrender.'

'We do?'

'At least one of us does,' said Sophia. She gauged the size of the toolbox against the hollow she had dug out so far. 'By which I mean, me. If we give them someone, maybe they won't search so far or wide. For this or for you.'

'I can't let you do that alone.'

Satisfied with her shallow grave, Sophia lowered the toolbox into it. She scraped plenty of dirt in over it, then started relocating the chunks of stone. 'You don't owe me anything. You can disappear when they're gone.'

Anne shook her head, stubborn as Chess. 'Nonsense. Anyway, with a bit of luck they'll give us a lift out of here.'

CHAPTER THIRTEEN
Afraid of Americans

JULY 1981. MEDITERRANEAN.

My God, Barney Hackett thought. The Americans knew how to stamp their authority on the world's oceans. From the frigate's helipad, he had a grandstand view of a sizeable contingent of the US Sixth Fleet carving through the light swell. USS *Forrestal*, a veteran and a veritable Leviathan, owned the Med for a conservative hundred nautical miles in all directions. A Leahy-class missile cruiser and five destroyers arrayed around their carrier added up to an intimidating presence that enemies would undoubtedly feel but, in all likelihood, would never see.

By all accounts, *Forrestal* was also known as Firestal or the Zippo, owing to a number of unfortunate blazes that had broken out on board, but those mocking nicknames did nothing to dent her formidable demeanour. Few cities were without the odd incident. And that was what she was: a floating city. A fortress.

Power projection. The *raison d'etre* of a Carrier Group, and something of a defining characteristic of Americans.

Barney was glad to be on their good side. Out in front, HMS *Broadsword* was running defence alongside a Spanish frigate as part of the Group's ASW screen. Thus far, the exercise had been just that, but they had yet to make contact with the poor blighters who'd drawn the short straw to play the Ruskies.

Operation NATO Mediterranean Venture 81 was about to get exciting. Especially for him.

The captain had Barney jerking to attention with a simple throat-clearing. McNicholls had a good ten years on him, but only the one extra stripe to his cuffs. Barney hoped to command the same level of respect as the man's relaxed manner one day.

'Everything packed, Barney? Ready to be thrown overboard?'

'Taking a good look at my new home for the week, sir. Must say, I'm thrilled at the prospect.' The Americans were sending *Broadsword* one of theirs; Barney had left his cabin in perfect order for the fellow. 'As long as it doesn't involve an actual dunking.'

'Do us proud. Best foot forward and all that. And don't just take notes. Teach them a thing or two whenever you get the chance.'

'Will do, sir.'

Broadsword's wake developed a curve, turning fifteen-degrees across the Carrier Group's path. A healthy blast of breeze blew across the helipad from starboard. A Lynx helicopter veered into view, roughly the size of a bluebottle at its current range. It dropped smartly into an approach vector.

Barney's taxi was on the way to pick him up.

GENEVA.

The capital of peace was busy. Lac Léman was a playground for a menagerie of windsurfers, swimmers and boats. From the café's waterside veranda, Bugayev watched the *jet d'eau*, a giant water cannon firing 140 metres into the air. There were no riots to break up there.

A sort of paradise. And the sort of place that would probably kill him within six months. The city was a bubble, isolated from the realities of the world. Terror only reached here as a story. Like the headline on the *USA Today* that Sophia had walled herself behind within minutes of their 'good morning' exchange.

She had surfaced briefly to thank the waitress for their coffees, only to return to her appetite for news like a pregnant woman craving the worst foods. The dramatic scene and words of the front-page suffered sporadic tremors as she flicked through the paper, hunting for scraps that would tell her nothing and only harm her digestion.

He tugged the upper edge of the paper. Sophia slowly lowered the tabloid. Bugayev laid a hand over hers.

'You will not find any information in there to set your mind at ease. Alistair will have some harder intelligence.'

'I'm digging for clues. It's what I do.' She freed her hand and returned to devouring column-inches, but with the paper spread open on the table.

Bugayev took a swig of coffee. It had gone cold. He snapped his fingers to attract a waitress and pointed at his cup. She collected the nearly-empty and disappeared indoors. Sophia tutted. He had an inkling it was more about him than the news.

The woman had natural edges. Which only sharpened when she too was on edge. For a full day, the news that had erupted out of Chicago had preyed upon her. Alistair too, he was sure. He didn't know Anne Bishop personally, but a 'friend of a friend' couldn't be ignored. Mostly, it confirmed an active American faction, probably in league with Vasily's lot.

Attacks on United States soil were none of his business. Sivakov and Yubkin might frown upon a one-man invasion in pursuit of his targets, to say nothing of the American view on operational jurisdiction. And then there were deeper issues: he wanted to eliminate Vasily's American counterparts as well and he had yet to determine whether that arose from professional completionism or something more personal.

The waitress returned with a fresh cup. '*Merci*,' he said.

Sophia appraised him like a pottery shard that had shown up in the wrong era. 'So, Captain, you appear to have rediscovered your manners.'

'Major.' He suffered his demotion with wry good-humour. 'And as a gentleman, I invite you to tell me what it is you are truly angry about.'

Sophia closed her paper. 'Would you have shot that man? Vasily?'

'The terrorist? Yes.'

'The prisoner.'

'Men like that don't stop being terrorists just because you have them in custody. Least of all when the custody proves so temporary. Do you imagine he is going to go lick his wounds and then mend his ways, retire perhaps to somewhere like this?'

He gestured at the scenery. Not the stereotypical tropical paradise, but warm today and very much an island, cradled by the Alps and Juras. Peace was a small country.

'Still, he was at your mercy.'

'Am I the problem?'

She sighed. 'You. Or me. I'm having trouble deciding if you are the man I remember.'

'What do you remember?' He knew the exact moment she was replaying behind those eyes. A close-quarters pistol-shot was a rude introduction at best. 'A killer, or the man who saved you?'

She snatched up her cigarette pack, but only used it to rap the table a few times. A kind of gavel, he reasoned, to call her thoughts to order.

'Whatever side of you I saw at the villa, I'm in the uncomfortable position of having to be grateful for that. What I saw in the garage – I'm not sure how that is something I'm supposed to be grateful for. Terrorists, psychic spies – psychic terrorists, even – whatever those people are, it doesn't absolve us of who we are. Of the people we should be.

'When the world can be rid of their sort, it can retire my sort.'

'And in a moment like that, how do we tell one type from another?'

'At a glance – perhaps you can't. But the difference lies in our reasons.' Bugayev recalled a single shot glass and his conversation with Grushkin. 'Drinking doesn't make you a drunk. The reason you drink, that's what decides it. Same for killing.'

'And the terrorists – they have their reasons too. Which I am sure strike them as *reasonable*.'

'They have motives, but they lack reason. Think, what is your first reaction when you read this?'

He tapped the USA Today. On the surface, a poor example. No bloody victims and no visible destruction. There had been injuries and a single fatality from vehicular accidents, direct physical consequences of what drivers had witnessed. But the story's accompanying picture painted a harrowing and chaotic scene even without any of that. Civilians, distraught, doubled over, assisted across the street by officers and paramedics. Patrol cars, fire trucks, ambulances ringed the area like a lot of frantically circled wagons on a cityscape that had become a war zone. And embedded in that image would be all of Sophia's anxieties about her friend.

'Anger,' she admitted. 'Worse. Rage. Fury. And – yes, I want these people dead. But that's my evil side. That's what the terrorists want to bring out in us. We feel it – it's natural – but we don't give in to it. Whatever stirs in the heart, you allow it for a while, then you put your head in charge when it comes to how to act.'

Bugayev nodded. 'Exactly. I'm human too. I am not

142

immune to the impulse of revenge, but I cannot allow it to give the orders.'

'So, you are clear then? Why you're hunting these people? Are you sure of your own reasons?'

'The truth? No.' It surprised him, how ready he was to admit that to her. 'I'm trying to make it about my job. Keep it professional. All the lines are blurred in any case. Is it warfare or policing? Am I bringing criminals to justice or am I fighting enemy soldiers? The battlefields are parks, playgrounds, hotels, airliners. Only one side comes armed – with guns and bombs. The other side carries shopping bags and holiday luggage. I can't accord these cowards the respect owed to enemy combatants, but I am not sure they deserve the justice afforded common thieves and murderers.'

'You are a complete mess, Major. Clearly.'

He laughed. Wit and intelligence were Sophia's primary weapons. It was as well she used her powers for good. 'It's a temporary condition. When I track them down, I will act with clarity and without hesitation.'

Sophia drew a cigarette from her pack. 'You've made up your mind then? To go with the Brigadier?'

'I think I already had.' He had acquired everything he needed from the KGB safehouse. Their turnaround on documentation was more efficient than a high-street copy shop. He'd told himself it was a matter of readiness, but now it felt more like facilitating a course pre-decided. Professionalism was all about going the extra mile. What was another eight thousand? 'And Alistair is on the point of retiring. He'll be sure to need a younger man's help.'

'Oh, he'll be sure to thank you for that.' Sophia finally treated herself to that smoke she'd plainly been hungering for these past minutes.

'Speak of the devil.' Bugayev nodded towards the lakeside promenade. Alistair was heading their way, gaze casually taking in the view he must have seen a thousand times.

Answers were incoming. Some of Bugayev's had already arrived.

The Royal Navy Lynx carried Barney in over an angled flight deck the size of three footie pitches. Nobody was playing ball down there, but the linesmen waved paddles in place of flags and the activity was as thrilling to watch as beautifully orchestrated team play.

F4 Phantoms, A7 Corsairs were parked in neat rows. An E2C Hawkeye, saddled with its distinctive radar-saucer, taxied into position. He was just another arrival at a busy seaborne airport. The Lynx descended, fanning wreathes of steam from the catapult tracks. A freshly launched Phantom thundered into the wind as Barnaby touched down.

He hopped out, gratefully took his kit-bag from the crewman. Down-draft from the rotors beat at his back as he trotted to meet his reception committee. A USN commander and a pair of marines. Salutes were traded. One of the marines took Barney's bag off his hands.

'Lieutenant Commander Hackett, welcome aboard!' To Barnaby's admiration, the American nailed the pronunciation in Queen's English. *Lef-tenant.* Along with some hearty volume to compete with the flight-deck noise. 'I'm Commander Perry. The captain's eager for a meet and greet, but come with me and we'll get you quartered.'

Barney threw his voice like he was shouting from the terraces. 'How are the accommodations?'

'Nothing but the best for Her Majesty's finest.'

Barney followed Perry at a brisk walk. The marines fell in aft. Behind them the Lynx was already aloft and wheeling away for the return flight. In the wake of the chopper's departure, Barney still had to contend with the taxiing jet.

'Well, I trust you haven't gone to too much expense on my account. Not on Uncle Sam's dime.'

'Uncle Sam's dime' was for Commander Perry. *Fair repayment*, Barney thought, *for the chap's gesture of pronunciation.*

'*Un cafe, s'ilvous plait,*' Alistair told the waitress as he took his seat.

Bugayev raised his coffee cup in an informal toast. The Señora leaned back in her chair, puffing on a cigarette. She toyed idly with her fancy gold lighter, making it spin on the table. A copy of *USA Today* lay in front of her, gloomy side up. Perhaps the trace of atmosphere he detected originated in the headline.

CHEMICAL TERROR ROCKS CHICAGO.

He spun the paper towards him and glanced over it for a précis of what the US government had deemed fit for public consumption. He read aloud: 'FBI forensics teams have confirmed use of a prohibited neurochemical agent that has left its victims reeling and profoundly scarred from widespread hallucinatory effects.' He shook his head. 'Hmph. I bet old Duffer wishes he'd thought of that.'

'Your coffee, sir.'

'Hmm?' The waitress set down his cup and withdrew to patrol other tables on the veranda. '*Merci.* Much obliged.'

He reached for his coffee. Sophia stopped her lighter's pirouette. Alistair realised he was the subject of much scrutiny from his companions.

'Duffer? Oh, it's nothing,' he explained – or didn't. 'Well, it's something. Quite possibly connected to your Russian mob and this American faction. Those "bombings" in the UK are all of a similar nature. Freddie Hackett; he's an old friend, but he's shut me out.'

'So, what is he holding out on?'

Alistair awarded Bugayev a protracted sidelong look. 'If I knew that...'

'No, listen.' Bugayev waved him quiet. Alistair arched his brow, unsure if it would ever come down. 'Could it be one of these bones? If this Romola of yours is connected, did she leave one at the scene?'

Bones, Alistair thought. Bugayev had shown him the two in his possession and now they had another, courtesy of the near-burial in the Vienna car park. The damned things screamed of extra-terrestrial origin and, frankly, Alistair could have done without alien artefacts complicating matters.

'No, nothing like that —' This time Alistair interrupted himself. 'Remind us of that theory of yours.'

Bugayev had outlined what he had been willing to divulge of the incidents on the Moscow plane and the train near the Ukrainian border. But that already seemed an age ago.

'Okay. I think they're target designators. Left at each scene as a focus. With perhaps some capacity for amplification. My feeling is, they'll want to leave a souvenir in as many cities as possible.'

Alistair nodded. *Focus*. An object left at the scene. His gaze latched onto Sophia's elegant lighter. 'Yevgenyevich,' he muttered.

Bugayev tilted his head. 'Excuse me?'

'Is he having a stroke?' the Señora wondered.

'Patronymics,' Alistair explained. 'I have to go and make another round of phone calls.'

Sophia sat forward. 'Not yet you don't. What about Anne?'

'Ah yes. Anne,' said Alistair. He reined in his thoughts before they raced off in too many directions at once. 'According to channels, there's no evidence that Anne was there. That is to say, she was not among the victims escorted from the site and accounted for by the

146

police. However, belongings positively identified as hers were left in her hotel room.'

'So... We know she was not in the blast.' Bugayev patted the table. 'That's good news.'

'Yes, she left. At some point. Clearly,' said Sophia. 'With the terrorists, I imagine.'

'We don't know that.'

'Then we need to find out.' She crushed her cigarette in the ashtray.

'Anne is important, of course. But let's not lose sight of the wider picture. This is a global landscape, not a portrait of one individual.'

Sophia applauded. 'Oh bravo, Major! Your powers of metaphor should have this solved in no time. What were we talking about just minutes ago? Reasons. Well, Anne is my reason. I'm the reason she's involved at all.'

'Well now,' said Alistair, 'Señora, you mentioned that you had some means for us to secure these artefacts that this "phantom" Anne was fishing for. Those are the key. We acquire those, our enemies will come to us.'

'Yes, of course.' Sophia bent to ferret in her bag. She came back up with two folded slips of paper in hand. They were both folded multiple times to form small envelopes. 'It's not particularly high-tech and it's not a hundred percent secure, but it seems the best way to go about this when these remote-viewers might be eavesdropping.' She tucked the envelopes under Alistair's saucer. He collected both, and she quickly raised a hand. 'No peeking. There is no shame in behaving like a paranoid conspiracy theorist when the conspiracy is no theory, right?'

'Couldn't agree more.' Alistair commended her precaution. One envelope was marked with a 1, circled, the other a 2, likewise ringed.

'Anyway,' Sophia pressed on. 'When you are ready to leave, I will tell you where to fly. When you arrive, you

147

open Note Number One. When you arrive where that directs you, you hand Note Number Two to the person you meet there. Nothing could be simpler; as long as you can decipher the handwriting of a crazy lady working in the dark.'

'You wrote them in the dark?' asked Bugayev.

Sophia plucked a fresh smoke from her pack. 'Naturally. Paranoid conspiracy theorist, I said. But...' She allowed a smile to grow at the pace of most house plants. 'It's only a temporary condition. Until this is all over. You understand?'

'You've thought of everything,' said Bugayev. '*Gracias*, Señora. And trust me, rescuing your friend is very much among my mission objectives.'

'I do. Trust you.' She lit her cigarette, it seemed to Alistair, as a means of cutting a longer speech short.

Alistair pocketed the notes. First stop, his office and those phone calls. Then America.

NR SPRINGFIELD, MO.

The highway rolled endlessly by. Anne watched for landmarks and road signs to indicate where they were headed, although she had a nasty feeling she knew. Also, she hoped the repetitive view might erase that departing shot of Chicago from her mind. Eventually.

Bonnie plodded over from the kitchenette. She proffered a plate bearing a sandwich. 'Egg mayo.'

'Thank you, but I'm—'

'Don't tell me you ain't hungry.'

Anne eyed the bread and the creamy mush of egg spilling from between. She hadn't the energy to argue. She took the plate and set it on her lap. She searched Bonnie's gaze. 'Why?' she said.

Bonnie swayed in place with the rocking of the vehicle. 'Seth, he figures the whole world is coded and we all fit somewhere.'

'And this is where you fit? Surely there must be better things you can do with your talents.'

'You do what you do 'cos that's who you are. My man, Alvin, reckoned I was never good enough at any of the things he wanted me to be. "Quit yo daydreaming, girl," he'd say if he caught me with my paper and pencils. Then these other folks, they had me do something I didn't want to do. Turned out I was good at it. Real good. So, I finally figured, maybe that's who I am. Just like you must've figured you was a scientist, huh?'

'But I try to use my skills for good.' Anne fished gently, keen to connect with at least one of her abductors. 'Whatever happened to make you this—'

'Oh, I ain't trying to justify nothing. All the horror show lives any of us have had, it can't justify the stuff we do. Good or bad don't really come into it, you know? World goes round, and we just do our part.' Bonnie drifted into a kind of bittersweet trance. 'It's like, I used to take my boy to Santa Monica Pier. And he'd get up on that carousel and ride them painted horses goin' up and down. And he'd kick'em. Giddy-up, giddy-up. Ride's gonna turn just the same, but he was bein' hisself.'

Seth butted in behind Bonnie. She squeezed herself tight against the counter, evading contact. Seth appeared to appreciate the consideration.

'Ladies. Everyone all right back here? How are we getting along?'

'Just shootin the breeze,' explained Bonnie. 'Killin' time.'

Nice word choice, Anne thought. She glared at Seth. 'What *are* we doing?'

'We are en route to collect Florence. Last of our party. Chicago was her craftsmanship. Bonnie is not our only artist.'

Anne masked her disgust at the notion of terror as an artform. 'You know what I mean. What's your ultimate goal?'

'Ah, the scientist in you. You want reasons, explanations. Cause and effect. I can understand the urge. But believe me, when you see the patterns as I do, they cannot be summed up in words.' Seth took the seat opposite, putting her off her sandwich.

'Numbers then? You're going to justify your actions with an equation and leave me to solve it?'

'No, Mrs Bishop. I shall dumb it down for you.' He rested an elbow on the small side-table, annoyingly relaxed. 'This world is rooted in terror. East scared of west, west scared of east. Such opposite poles repel. Our opposites are predators who threaten our society, our lifestyle. Fear is the trigger for our natural defensive instincts, to protect ourselves. It is our overriding impulse to feel safe. So why do we excel at creating demons? The Soviets. The Chinese. The Red and Yellow Menaces. And from the other side of the fence, they demonise us: bourgeois capitalist pigs.'

They were right on one of those in your case, Anne thought.

'The point is… Enemies. Monsters. Terror. The world thrives on fear. We may chase the things we want, but we must protect them from others. That is the pattern. We are not out to change the world. We are merely components of that pattern. Seeking to fuel it to its true potential.'

Bonnie's carousel. Anne wanted to tell the man he was insane. Again. But she reconsidered, thinking to spare her lip further pain. There was a chance she might want the sandwich after all. Once Seth was no longer around to turn her stomach.

On the far end of the line, Freddie was immediately on the defensive. 'Alistair, old boy, this had better not be–'

'Actually, this is more of a family matter, Duffer,' said

Alistair. 'It concerns your lad.'

'What the devil has — ?'

'That old tradition our families share. Passing on the father's Christian name as the son's middle name. I've been so damnably slow. Blame it on the bomb blast, I suppose. Then I remembered.' Had he remembered exactly? Or had he benefited from future knowledge? That encounter at the graveside. 'Barnaby Frederick Hackett. How is he? What's he up to these days?'

'He's serving.' The words, like plucked nose hairs, came with some pain. 'Royal Navy.'

Just as Barney had said at the funeral, thirty years from now... 'Yes, I made some inquiries. He's currently attached to the US Sixth Fleet. And I think you need to speak to him.'

'Speak to him about what?'

'Come on, Freddie. Hasn't it occurred to you; if my target managed to get a hold of your boy's lighter, what might she have planted on him in return?'

A second ticked by. 'I'll see what I can do.'

'Speak to him. Before I do.'

Alistair put the phone down. He took no pleasure in being hard on a friend, but he wondered if he'd been hard enough.

Barney allowed Commander Perry to enter the CIC a full three strides ahead. He applied a brisk last-minute pat-down to his uniform and clutched his cap under his arm. Best foot forward.

Inside was a hive of chatter and shadows, partially illuminated by radar consoles, flashing communications lights and plotting tables. Officers and enlisted manned screens or talked incessantly into telephones and microphones. More roamed the aisles between stations, supervising, advising, gathering and relaying information. The place was as busy as a department store on day one of a January sale, and not altogether unfamiliar territory. Like 'home', only with a few telling differences and on a larger scale. Rather comparable, Barney fancied, to taking a trip from Britain to America.

Perry presented him to the captain. Salutes were exchanged, hands were pumped.

Captain Harlan J Birchdale combined a muscular build and muscular presence with an easy manner that made him seem like a friendly giant. Thinning slate-grey hair and well-seasoned features might've looked like old age on other men, but he wore his years like another set of ribbons. He measured Barney with a sideways smile like a bull shark with a sense of humour.

Forrestal could probably dispense with its ASW screen and rely instead on this man diving overboard and chewing the warheads off incoming torpedoes.

'Glad to have you aboard, Lieutenant Commander.' He opted for his native pronunciation. *Loo-tenant.* 'We'll spend most of our time up on the bridge, but I wanted you to have a look at our nerve centre.'

'I trust I'll learn a great deal.'

'Good to hear. But we're not having you just stand and watch. You're part of my crew, part of my command. You got things on your mind, son, bring them to me. I got ears and experience and you're cordially invited to use both.'

'Understood, sir. Thank you.'

'Good.' He drew Barney aside as a CIC officer moved around the plotting table. 'Now for the real news. Change of orders. You heard about Chicago?'

'Yes, sir. Dreadful business.

'We're not talking about the British weather, son.'

'No, I meant—'

'Relax.' The shark-smile made a brief reappearance. 'But ready your A-game. Intelligence has identified several targets; training camps and chemical munitions factories in Libya. We're going to teach those sons of bitches some hard lessons.'

Barney nodded. 'Yes, sir.'

There it was again. Power projection. That supremely American trait. Who would choose to be on the wrong side of that?

CHAPTER FOURTEEN
Whop Whop Whop

1971. NEW MEXICO.

Kneeling in the dirt, hands clasped behind her head, Sophia distracted herself with prophetic visions of a future archaeologist unearthing the skeletons of two females in the Chihuahuan desert. The holes in the skulls would tell how they died, but nothing of how they lived or what they had been doing here.

It was a morbid diversion. But it carried a degree of absurdity that made it unreal. Therefore, it wouldn't come to that.

She badly wanted to look to see how Anne was holding up beside her. But if she turned her head, she knew she'd feel the press of the gun muzzle in her hair again. This was not the scenario she'd envisaged when she'd suggested surrender.

'I'm sorry, Anne,' she murmured.

'It's all right. Not your fault,' came Anne's answer.

'Yo! The ladies are getting talkative!' Sophia's maybe-executioner called out.

'Be right there!' the leader of the mob called back.

He was over by the big truck, supervising the packing and loading. Looted relics were crated up and, before she had been forced to kneel, she had seen two bodies being zipped into bags. It wasn't the activity that troubled her: it was the stillness closer by. The men standing over her and Anne. She was sure their leader had just left them here as a scare tactic. A dangerous dose of uncertainty, intended to feel like waiting on news from your doctor. Would the test results come back positive or negative?

At last the light crunch of footsteps announced his return.

'So,' he said. 'I have a serious confidentiality issue here.

My burning question is, can I trust you ladies to keep a secret?'

'We won't say a word,' said Anne.

He strode past behind Sophia. 'Really? See now, you have *connections*, Miss Travers, and I have no idea whether we might want to share this particular intel with our British allies. I'd hate to think of them getting wind of this before we were ready to share. And you, Miss Montilla–'

'Señora.'

'Señora.' The guy wandered back in her direction. 'You're an out and out freelancer. I have no idea who you'd go running to. The press? And much as you'd have trouble producing corroborating evidence, I'd rather not have a bunch of journos getting themselves worked up over conspiracy theories.'

'Even when the theories are true?'

'Irrespective, Señora, I don't want the media-storm. So, you can appreciate my dilemma. It's not like I can get you ladies to sign a non-disclosure. But what's my alternative? I got to dig a couple of holes out here in the desert. Maybe just the one. Save myself some time and you'll be cosy.'

There it was: Sophia's morbid scenario.

'Execution?' Anne asked. 'I'd believe your government capable of many things, but they would not sanction murder.'

'Who's to know? Take a look around. When an archaeologist and a scientist die in a desert and there's nobody around to hear them, do their deaths make a sound? Maybe a few column-inches of mystery in the papers back home. Then how long before it slips to page four? Five? Six? You know how it goes. Even you, Miss Travers, with your high-level friends. A word to the right department and an investigation gets killed, stone dead.'

Clearly he has no idea of the tenacity of Alistair Lethbridge-Stewart, thought Sophia. *Not to mention Anne's fiancé.*

At the far end of the camp, two agents – a man and a woman, both sporting sunglasses – stood in the headlight beams of one of the cars. The man lit up a cigarette.

Sophia sighed. She would murder for a smoke.

'But hey, relax,' said their head captor. 'I'm not saying I'm going to whack you like some gangster. I'm saying I *could*. But I'd much rather come to an agreement like civilised people.' He touched a finger to his lips and shushed. 'Mom's the word. Right?'

Sophia finally felt free to move her head. She exchanged looks with Anne. They nodded in synch.

'All right, let's get this packed up. Get our show on the road. I presume you ladies can take care of your own transport. I'm a gentleman, but I'm not really in any position to offer you a ride.' He strode to the truck and gestured vaguely east. 'Airport's that way.'

Sat in a cell, cold metal chair under him. Hard steel table cooling his calloused hands. A single bulb glaring down. His spotlight. This was his stage.

Vasily smiled at the glass, at the audience hiding behind their mirror. Then slowly emptied the smile of everything. He closed his eyes and blew the four walls away.

There was no flight like a migrating bird, no homing in on his prey like a hawk. He was simply *there*. Welcome to the other side of the world. A ghost riding in a rumbling container with the cargo, he felt the shake of the truck's engine in his bones even though he had left his skeleton 'at home'.

He drifted forwards, invisible smoke seeping into the cab. He lurked between the shoulders of the two occupants. One driver, one guard. He looked out on the highway stretching away into night. He watched the tail lights of the two escort cars and glimpsed a single pair of headlights in his mirror. Gradually, he retouched the picture in the driver's mind, adjusting the view. To all intents and purposes, he was the driver now.

And he didn't need any company on the road.

Agent Parker Theroux's mind was on the stereo, thinking about scanning for some tunes. Long drives needed a soundtrack. He glanced at his partner. Behind her sunglasses, Agent Melody Quartararo was hands on the wheel and strictly eyes front, like the convoy was an engrossing movie with a hard-to-follow-plot. She would probably have a thing or two to say about his music choices.

Parker wondered how far he could recline his seat without looking bored.

Melody frowned, like the movie had taken a bad turn. 'What the hell is he doing?'

Ahead, the eighteen-wheeler slid across lanes. Snaking

towards the exit ramp.

Parker sat up. He snatched up the radio mic. 'Uh, Carnival King, there a problem? Some detour we should know about? Over.'

The radio shushed, as though urging him to keep a secret. The rig slow-dived down the ramp, dragging its load with it, as though the vehicle had developed a mind of its own. The rest of the convoy was visible, forging ahead, steadfast on the scheduled course and escorting nothing.

Melody let go of the wheel to throw a shrug. Basic body-semaphore for *What-the-hell?* She threw the car into a chasing curve after the truck.

'What are you doing?'

'We're the following car,' she said. 'So, we're following.'

Parker nodded. Fair enough. He clicked the mic. 'Yo, Carnival King, care to take a look in the mirror? We have a stray. Over.'

Even with this unexpected twist, the convoy wasn't the most exciting movie, but surely somebody up front was paying attention.

Director Bryant swore and checked his wing-mirror. The truck loomed large, right on their tail, right where it was meant to be. What was Theroux talking about? 'Carnival Three, what have you been drinking? The package is still with us. Stick with the delivery route. Over.'

Agent Sisco, driving, double-checked his rear-view. His face was an echo of Bryant's thoughts: What was Theroux on?

'Negative,' Theroux answered. 'We are sticking with the package. And the package has taken Exit Eight-One. Over.'

Bryant raised the mic, ready to swear some more. He hesitated, distracted by the shot of the truck in the mirror. A bit more than right on course. If anything, closer than it had been. Practically bearing down on their fender. 'Carnival Two, you want to ease off some? Leave a little air between vehicles. Over.'

The radio hissed and the rig continued to fill the mirror with its headlights and grill. Bryant felt obliged to turn in his seat. Confirmation, in case he needed any, that the mirror and the rear windshield told the same story.

Unless there were two trucks?

Surely to God another all-black eighteen-wheeler couldn't have slotted in between the following car and the target vehicle? Bryant could believe Theroux might've dozed off and missed that kind of action, but not Quartararo. Never mind noticing it, she wouldn't have allowed some decoy to muscle in on their convoy.

'Carnival Three, you'd better be sure you're following the correct package.'

'Carnival King, there is only one package. We're on it. I have no idea what you think is following you.' Theroux's smartass tone came over loud and clear. 'With respect, you need to get back here. We are going to need backup when the package gets wherever it's going. Over.'

That did it. He was going to haul Theroux over the coals when they reached their objective. Maybe send him for a drugs test too.

'Listen up—' Bryant choked. The wing-mirror showed empty asphalt.

Agent Sisco searched the rear-view and the road, his face now like that of a panicked parent whose child had wandered off. Bryant turned in his seat again.

Yep. The truck was gone.

'We're all ears back here,' said Theroux. 'Over.'

Bryant checked the mic was off then swore up a storm.

They hit the 122 maybe a couple of hundred yards behind the truck, racing past an iHop, a Sonic and a gas station. The rig accelerated.

The cab flapped a door open. Ejected a passenger. The body smacked asphalt and tumbled towards the roadside. Agent Priest hopped up, one leg hanging limp as a dish rag, and whipped out his sidearm. He cracked off three shots at the trailer.

Melody slowed. Agent Priest waved her on. He hobbled away to the gas station forecourt, swapping out his sidearm for his walkie-talkie.

'Go. Go!' urged Parker.

Melody floored it.

'We got this, baby.'

'Don't call me baby.'

Headlights flashed in the corner of Parker's eye. A white pick-up charged out from the intersection and rammed into their flank.

'Get us turned around!' Bryant yelled. The next exit wasn't for a mile, but the niceties of highway etiquette could go to hell. 'Now!'

Sisco stamped the brakes, threw them into a full U-ey. The lead car, Carnival One, now behind them, screeched to its own halt, taking its cue from them. They sped back to the exit, with the ex-lead car trailing very much in last place.

The driver pulled the cab door closed. Then settled back into steering.

Vasily watched the white pick-up with the crunched-up front closing in the wing-mirror. Only another half-mile of highway to the rendezvous.

Sisco slowed as they came up on the wrecked Agency car. The vehicle was skewed across the middle of the road, totalled. Theroux and Quartararo stood in a litter of shattered glass and busted chrome. They looked like a couple of beat-up hitchhikers. Not to mention looking like idiots, wearing sunglasses this time of night.

Goddamn eccentrics. The Company didn't need that kind of thing in its ranks. Eccentricity was a British flaw and should stay across the Pond, far as Bryant was concerned.

'Keep going,' he ordered. He rolled his window down and directed the pair to the trailing car. Stroud and Ross in Carnival One could pick up the strays.

Sisco stepped on the gas. Bryant scanned the road ahead, checking the terrain either side. Mostly farmland, low hills rolling away into shadowy treelines under a lot of stars. How hard could it be to find a damned eighteen-wheeler?

There! A trashed fence and a trail of ploughed-up grass.

Bryant slapped Sisco's forearm. Pointed. 'Take a right!'

Sisco swerved them off-road. They bumped through the field. Nestled close under the front ranks of Douglas Firs, the truck was parked tail-to-tail with a blunted white pick-up. Two Tangos were transferring crates from the truck's container to the pick-up. They looked like Allegheny Hill-Billies, in check shirts and windcheaters and baseball caps over Grizzly Adams hair. Two more Tangos were on guard duty, armed with–

'Down!' yelled Bryant.

Sisco threw the wheel hard over as the guards opened up. Automatic fire pelted the driver's side like badass hailstones. The car jerked to a halt. Bryant shoved his door open and bailed. Sisco crawled across the passenger seat and followed Bryant. The assault rifles cracked off again, raking the car. It was less a car now, more a wheeled barricade.

Bryant pulled his automatic and moved to the front of the car, Sisco pulled his Uzi and headed aft. Together they returned fire.

Beams flooded the field behind Bryant. Carnival One bringing backup.

The loaders ditched their current crate and piled into the pick-up. Gunman One hopped in with the cargo. The other let rip with a wild spray of bullets. Then dived in after his buddy, while his buddy strafed. The pick-up reversed, turfing up ground. The two gunmen rocked about in the back, laying down a lot of even wilder fire.

The Agency car pulled up and unloaded Theroux, Quartararo, Stroud and Ross. They chased the pick-up with pistol fire. Bryant stood and sent a half-dozen rounds after the vehicle as it turned and aimed straight for the new arrivals. Obliging the four of them to hurl themselves out of its path.

The gunmen covered the retreat. One rifle chewed a line in the grass alongside the Agency car, until Bryant caught the distinctive hiss of expiring tyres. And the pick-up bounced away across the field to meet the road.

'Damnit damnit damnit.' He shoved his pistol in its holster. Strode to the truck. Took one look in the container and hung his head, hands on hips.

'How much they get?' Theroux asked.

'Roughly, I'd say half.'

'Half seems fair, don't you think?'

Wise-ass.

'Shut up, Theroux.'

Bryant walked to the cab to check on the driver. Hudson was slumped over. A nasty close-quarters GSW to the side of the skull. Damn. Hudson had been a good Agency man.

Russians. Had to be the Russians. Bryant hated to think the damage the Sovs could do with this kind of hardware. He guessed his people would have to do more.

CHAPTER FIFTEEN
This is Not America

JULY 1981. SOMEWHERE OVER AMERICA.

The single-aisle passenger jet was a far cry from Air Force One, but the seats were comfortable and spaced for ample leg room. There was also no danger of confusing it with an IL-86, but still the memories resurfaced.

Bugayev's last two commercial flights – Budapest to Vienna, Vienna to Geneva – had involved the same baggage. He had probably exceeded carry-on limits with thoughts of that sweep through the plane.

Seated across the aisle from Alistair, he estimated at least an hour could be well-spent briefing his friend on the Soviet fugitives still at large. It was his feeling they were working their way west, ultimately to rendezvous with the American cell. The files were safe on Air Force One, but the information could be recounted easily enough from memory. It might help Alistair to know the essentials. It might not. Knowing the facts and encountering the reality were an ocean apart.

'Can I get you gentlemen anything?' The stewardess leaned between them.

'One can't hurt,' said Alistair, sounding grateful to be rescued from his own reverie. 'Scotch, please. Neat.'

Bugayev gave the matter due consideration. 'Vodka. And make his a double. Thank you, ma'am.'

The stewardess departed.

Alistair stared across the aisle. 'What was that?' he asked.

'It's a distilled spirit—'

'You know what I'm referring to. That accent.'

'It's authentic Virginian. That's where Bob comes from.' Bugayev flashed his United States passport.

Alistair did his inherited arched-eyebrow trick. 'I can't speak to its authenticity. I suppose it… just sounds strange coming out of your mouth. Could you, perhaps, keep it to a minimum?'

'I'll let you do most of the talking.'

'Right. Probably for the best. Why did you have to be American anyway? Why couldn't you pretend to be British?'

'You wouldn't have liked the competition,' said Bugayev. 'Besides, this spares me having to fill out a Visa waiver form. "Are you now or have you ever been a member of the Communist Party?"' He switched back to his usual accent and supplied the answer. *'Nyet.'*

'Yes, well, we wouldn't want you having to lie.'

The stewardess returned, delivering their drinks. Bugayev pulled down the little folding table and she placed the glass, wrapped in its serviette like it was tucked up in bed. 'Enjoy,' she said and was gone.

Alistair raised his glass. Bugayev left his in its bed. Alistair set his down. 'Well, are you going to drink that?'

'I believe I am.'

'You know, if you're worried about the Señora, she'll be safe. I've assigned her a discreet protection detail. Without her knowledge. And you said yourself, you believe these terrorists have moved on. Frankly, it's something of a miracle she agreed to stay behind.'

Bugayev laughed. At the truth of Alistair's assessment and at the idea that he was worried about her.

Alistair cleared his throat. A very British preface. 'Is there… something I should know about? Between you

162

two?'

'Tell me, if there were anything "between us", what makes you think you should know about it?'

'Fair point.'

'But no. The world is not Verona.'

'No future in it, eh?'

'Not enough for one. Too much for the other.'

'Well, forgive my intrusion. I rather felt I might've walked in on something. At the café.'

'We were discussing reasons. And actions.'

'I see. Your *methods,* I take it?'

'You're very astute, my friend.' Bugayev teased the serviette loose and laid it next to the glass. 'Torture and breaking the concentration of a dangerous illusionist. They look the same to the squeamish. On that plane in Moscow...' He glanced to see that Alistair knew exactly which plane. '...my actions were sound. Militarily; assuming I could replay it for you, you would agree. The "right" response. People died.'

'These people mess with our heads. Faulty intel. You can't hold yourself responsible.'

'I don't. Not exactly. It's a question of trust. We trust our instincts and our training. We trust ourselves. That becomes...' Bugayev sniffed. '...challenging when we can't trust the evidence of our own eyes.'

'Judgement calls. When the evidence is a lie. Yes, I've wondered myself what I'm doing on this mad chase. Am I doing the right thing? Am I doing it for the wrong reasons?' Alistair gazed into his Scotch with a look Bugayev knew well. 'Am I hunting her because she's a terrorist? Or because I was there when the...Well, when the bomb appeared to go off.'

'It did more than appear, I am sure.' Bugayev relived the airliner assault one more time.

'It's not about right and wrong. We can't tie ourselves up with some notion of an objective morality. We have to be our own judges. There is your own sense of what is right and what you can live with.'

Alistair nodded, mulling over the words or his Scotch, or both.

'You and I,' said Bugayev, 'we don't have to see eye to eye to understand one another.'

'*Na zdaroviye,*' said Alistair.

'Bottoms up,' said Bugayev.

DENVER, CO.

Welcome to paradise, Earl. Make yourself at home.

The whole stadium to himself.

Earl kicked back in his seat, spreading out and taking up as much space as one man could. Well, any man that wasn't Rufus maybe. Man, that kid had piled on the pounds since the old days. Like he had some kind of dog-years metabolism thing going on, but with weight. *Dog-pounds*, figured Earl. And laughed. Yeah, that had to be it.

He plucked a beer from his bag, snapped the cap with his bottle-opener and promised himself that'd be his last physical exertion for the day.

He raised the bottle in a toast to the empty field. Knocked one back.

The ball park was closed, but Earl had learned real young that he had free entry anywhere. B and E could drop the B when you could toss a dream or two around for everybody else.

What the hell. It was a nice afternoon.

He set the teams out on the field. Then populated the stands – for atmosphere, not company – and left a big circle of vacant seats around him for plenty of elbow room.

'*Here we are, ladies and gentlemen. Bottom of the tenth, one out...*'

Seth was all 'get this done now, get that done then.'

Like there was a set time or deadline for everything. Earl only knew there was time. No rush for much at all. He let Seth worry about which attitude was smarter.

'*Bases are loaded and it's zero-zero game. . .*'

Second best thing to fooling everybody, was being able to amuse yourself.

The Winnebago hadn't moved for an age. Anne had managed to doze off for a spell and, as she rubbed the last of her nap from her eyes, her window showed the same Denver parking lot.

Still waiting on Slow Earl to return from his 'errand'. She had seen him – a tall, rangy American man of African descent with a slovenly swagger – leave several hours ago. This was part of the routine. Wherever they stopped, one of the group would pull a holdall from the overhead rack. This was the same holdall from which Rufus had fished the 'hotel chocolate' in Chicago, so Anne knew what was being left at each location. Up on the rack there was a red Adidas sports bag and a big brown suitcase, neither of which were dipped into for these errands. The waits were usually shorter than the current one.

Being stuck in one place was one way to drive her more stir-crazy.

If Bill ever proposed they take a road-trip together, she might have to divorce him on the spot. Being cooped up in another vehicle was a prospect she wouldn't want to face again for at least five years.

Even with Earl absent, the Winnebago wasn't nearly as spacious, with the added passenger they had picked up in Edmond, Oklahoma.

Florence La Beau was at the kitchenette making herself a cup of tea. Dressed for mourning, her concession to decoration was a broad necklace of whelk shells, turquoise and what had to be bear teeth. Comet-tails of white streaked her midnight hair. A hawkish nose and high cheekbones gave her a regal bearing, striking Anne as an American Indian Cleopatra. Her cities and pyramids had crumbled and now here she was, reduced to making her own cuppa.

She prodded the teabag with a spoon, encouraging it to stew faster. A powerful herbal aroma wafted as far as Anne. Bonnie, roosting on the seat by the tiny table, looked up from her pad. She had been sketching, but with a light touch and a relaxed unhurried air that suggested this was recreational art.

'If you're gonna make some of that perfume broth, why don't you whip some up for our guest here.'

'She's a white woman. Neither of us should be serving her.'

'Making somebody tea ain't slavery. Besides, she's British and it's the afternoon. Making tea in front of her, that's gotta be like torture.'

'I'm fine, thank you,' said Anne. She didn't especially wish to put Florence's regal nose out of joint. Or be the cause of friction between the two women. Making connections and winning 'allies' might serve her at some point. She felt that Bonnie quite liked her, but she had some way to go with the others.

Most were suspicious of her slightest move. Every time she stood to stretch her legs or go to the bathroom someone looked at her like she was making an escape bid. Sadly, she'd concluded escape wasn't an option. The Winnebago wasn't a maximum-security prison, but even if she managed to slip out without being noticed, she evaluated her chances of evading recapture as microscopic. She would be on foot. Hunted by remote-viewers in an RV.

'I'll make myself endless cups of tea at home when you let me go,' she added by way of a little levity.

Seth squeezed past Florence, provoking an irritated look from her. He appeared apologetic for the brief contact, but also grimaced as though he had touched something slimy and unpleasant. Which was a bit rich, coming from him.

'Believe me, Mrs Bishop,' he said, 'I am as keen to secure your release as you are to receive it.' He moved to block much of the light reaching Bonnie's page. 'Since Earl is dragging his heels, now would be a good time to gather some intelligence on our enemies. Bonnie, perhaps you would do the honours.'

Bonnie waggled her pencil. 'I told you. I ain't looking at that man again.'

'Bonnie, he cannot see you. He can have no idea of your eavesdropping.'

'Nah-ah. Get Florence to do it. Or Rufus. He ain't busy.'

'Florence?' Seth prompted. 'Would you be so kind?'

Florence pretended not to hear, long enough to take her first sip of her tea. Then she downed her cup.

She faced Anne, eyes closed. Held her hands apart, as though cradling an invisible balloon, and began to chant. Her singing voice was a haunting, husky sound with an incredible vibrato drawn from the depths of her throat. Slowly, she compressed the space between her palms. Until her hands met in a mime of prayer.

'The British officer and the Russian are together,' she declared. 'Charter Flight TVC One-Five. Due in at Dallas Fort Worth, seven hours.'

'Guess we ought to be sending somebody to Texas,' Bonnie said.

'I think not,' said Seth. 'Allow them to collect our package on our behalf. Then we will make contact. We have something of theirs. Well, something of value to Lethbridge-Stewart at least. We stick to our itinerary.'

Anne almost let out a cry and a laugh at the same time. Alistair! Coming to her rescue? Did he know she was a captive?

'The Russian?' Bonnie fretted. 'He's coming here?'

'Dear Bonnie.' Seth's condescension earned an ugly look from Bonnie. 'He is not going to kill you.'

'Maybe not. But he's coming in range. And he ain't gonna stop at me.'

Seth swallowed what appeared to be a bad taste. Anne savoured the sight. That was more invigorating than any herbal tea.

DALLAS FORT WORTH, TX.

Bugayev returned from the Hertz office, the keys to their shiny new Toyota Land Cruiser in hand.

Alistair stood ready to take driving duties. 'No problems with the paperwork, I take it?'

Bugayev shrugged. 'He wished me to have a nice day. Is that normal?' He tossed the keys in the air, caught them and flipped them over onto the back of his hand. 'Shame. Keys don't have heads or tails. Looks like I'm driving.'

Alistair sighed. 'All right. That leaves me as navigator. And no satnav.'

They climbed into their respective positions. Alistair adjusted the seat for leg room.

'Sat what?'

'Never mind.'

'Okay, time to open *Nota Numero Uno*,' Bugayev said.

Alistair fished in his pockets. He double-checked he had Number 1. 'Really, Major, an American accent and now Spanish. Are there any more hidden talents I should know about?'

'Biathlon?'

Alistair rewarded that with a wry smile. Considering that he was already melting, the opportunities for skiing would be limited. Shooting, on the other hand... Well, that remained to be seen. He had arranged for a diplomatic bag to take care of the basic tools for that eventuality. Sidearms only.

Alistair slid his thumb under the flap of *Nota Numero Uno*. Hesitated. 'When I open this, it could lead our psi-spies straight to the location...'

Bugayev adjusted the mirror. 'Depends what Sophia wrote. I expect she's played it smart and expects us to do the same. These people are clairvoyant but not prescient. As far as we know. It's possible they are looking in on us and we will be in a race to reach the location first. If it were me, I would have someone in place to tail us from the airport.'

Of course. Alistair glanced at the mirror. He fancied any ordinary tail would struggle to escape Bugayev's notice. But people who could make a VW camper look like an Audi might easily cloak a following vehicle.

'Also,' continued Bugayev, 'there's the possibility that folds are no defence. They've already visualised what's inside, deciphered Sophia's message and they'll be waiting for us when we get there.'

'Cheery thought.'

'Open it.'

Alistair unfolded the note and read. 'I think the Señora means for us to check the phonebook.'

He showed Bugayev. Just the one word in legible and rather fluid script: *Blacksnake*.

'She thinks of everything. 'Bugayev keyed the ignition and started them rolling.

COLORADO SPRINGS.

It was like walking into *Star Wars*. All the gunfire and explosions, the lasers pew-pewing and triumphal fanfares drew Rufus into the Colorado Springs' arcade.

A half-lit world with a lot of heads bent towards glowing and flashing screens, it might have been a Death Star control room, with dedicated Empire crew firing up the planet-killer for the big one. Imperial dress code had slipped: it was all t-shirts and vests. Maybe Moff Tarkin had introduced Casual Fridays.

Defender, Berzerk, Battlezone. Violence distilled to colour and noise. Beeps, whistles and klaxons. Hypnotic. Heaven.

Rufus stopped by the *Galaxian* machine. He dug a fistful of quarters from his pocket – and dropped a couple. One rolled between the machines. One bounced behind him and a player stooped to collect it and return it to him.

'There you go, man.'

Rufus palmed the coin. Then bent to retrieve the other rogue one. He picked it up and deposited a small bone in its place.

Job done, he rose and pumped the slot full of quarters. Then settled in to play. He was out to record a high score. See his name in lights.

HARTSFIELD-JACKSON AIRPORT, ATLANTA.

Vasily hated airports.

They were processing plants, where travellers rode conveyor belts to be stamped and processed then ferried on to other cities. Seated in the departure lounge, he watched the boards and the bored. He prayed that their transfer flight would not be delayed.

Better that than waste a good prayer on Ekel. May he rest in…Peace? Hardly. No peace for the damned.

There was no picture in the paper and he had not been publicly identified, but Vasily knew. Austrian police had found the body of a man in a Viennese market and were investigating the possibility of a connection with the terror attack on the Hotel Ruby-Gisele.

No, he was innocent of any involvement, Vasily could've told them. But Ekel had done a masterful job on the Shemyatovo hijack. The thought of Major Bugayev shooting innocents acted as mild anaesthetic to Vasily's pain.

Of course, the effects were countered by the company of the damsel who had come to his rescue in Vienna. Romola. His debt to her was almost as aggravating as his wounds.

He studied her, two seats along from him.

'What's wrong?' she asked, without bothering to return his attention. 'Need your dressings changed?'

Dressings. She was masking his wounds and bruises, making him and the world see an uninjured man. The placebo was working, to some extent. All without sign of effort.

'Who are you?' he said. 'What is your story?'

'Mine. My story is mine.'

'You know what I mean.'

Now she looked at him. 'What's yours?'

So, a trade then. 'Mine? Terror is an old friend. From childhood. Christopher Robin, he had Winnie the Pooh and friends, yes? Mine were the dead and the lonely and the terrified.'

'And how did that begin?'

'Nightmares, you would call them. My mama, she told me stories of my papa…Away fighting in the Great Patriotic War. But I didn't need her words to paint the pictures. Stalingrad. That was where the nightmares became something more. I searched for Papa many times. Even in my waking hours. I walked among them. Nazis. Russians. Terrified young men. Aged by winter and fear. They all belonged to the same country in that city. Good men, bad men, no difference. Every man went to Hell.'

'And when did Stalingrad begin?' she fired back.

'What?'

'Wherever you think your story begins, there's always another beginning before that. And another and another. We all have our stories and there's always a battle. The world tries to make something of you; you fight, try to make something of yourself. At some point before you

171

die, you get to see who wins. Who cares what made any of us?'

She was right. His past had started him on a road, but he had fought to take the wheel. Who he was now… For that he should credit himself, not blame events from a childhood no longer relevant.

He watched the constant murmuration of passengers. Flightless starlings, without orchestration or symphony. He fancied seeing them scatter in terror.

'We should leave this airport a token,' he said.

'We could do more. Slip a few gifts into different bags. Look at this place. It's a distribution centre.'

'No. These people might find them in their belongings before we are ready. Then they will end up in the hands of authorities.' At last a mistake from her: an opportunity to teach her. 'If you wish to be a part of this, you will need to *think*. Exercise your mind for more than imagination.'

'Thanks for the advice. Try lecturing me again and I'll take the damn plane down around us. And trust me, I'll be the only one to not feel the crash.'

He wondered what she had done with Ekel's luggage. The contents were probably mystifying the Austrian authorities right now. Never mind, they could still be used to make an impact. They needn't go to waste.

Yes. Vasily did not doubt that this woman had finished Ekel. He could not see into the past and she would not answer if he asked, would offer no defence if accused. But she made no special effort to conceal it.

Life was skin deep, she had said. Murder also. He read it in her face.

NW TEXAS.

As they pulled in at the ranch house, they were met by a Native American gentleman posted in the doorway. He was armed with a hunting rifle, but it wasn't raised to his shoulder. Not actively hostile; not exactly an

172

invitation either.

Alistair was first out, with hands at half-mast and what he hoped was a disarming smile. Bugayev emerged with hands down, but he had the benefit of an entire car between himself and the potential shooter.

'Mr Blacksnake? I'm Alistair Lethbridge-Stewart. My friend here is… Gregory. We're friends of the Señora–'

'There's a lot of *señoras* in these parts.'

Apart from the silver-grey hair, rugged complexion and a budding paunch, Blacksnake was in comparable shape to Alistair. The life of a rancher no doubt kept the man fit. The house presided over a considerable acreage with a corral, sizeable stables and a fair number of horses grazing in the surrounding fields. They did not appear to have come at a busy time. But Blacksnake struck Alistair as one of those chaps who, while never in any hurry, did not warm to time-wasters.

Alistair raised one hand higher and used the other to carefully slide the second note from his pocket. 'Sophia Montilla. Archaeologist. Likes cats.'

Mister Blacksnake didn't move. He allowed Alistair to approach as far as the porch. '*The* Señora. I don't know about any cats.'

'Really?' It struck Alistair as odd that Sophia wouldn't have discussed her precious strays.

'Kidding. She never stopped talking about them. Showed me pictures.'

Blacksnake let the rifle point to the deck. 'Guess you'd best come inside.'

Alistair lowered his hand, but waggled the slip of paper. 'There's still the matter of our letter of introduction.'

'It's all right, I believe you. I don't need a note.'

'All the same, she insisted we hand it to you… And I make a habit of following her instructions.'

'Smart,' said Blacksnake. He came forward and

plucked the note from Alistair's fingers. Flipped it open and scanned with barely an eye movement. Then turned and headed into the house. 'Come on in. You too, *Gregory*.'

Alistair glanced over his shoulder. The major rounded the front of their car and gave an 'after you' gesture.

They entered a relatively open-plan space with immaculate dark wood flooring, a rug here and there, and a staircase dividing living room from the dining area. Blacksnake pointed them in the direction of the sturdy frontier dining table and headed for the cased opening, which afforded a view through into a large kitchen.

'Get you guys a beer?'

'Water?' Bugayev asked. He and Alistair took seats at the table.

The rancher set the rifle down by the kitchen opening. 'Suit yourselves.'

'No offence intended, Mister Blacksnake. We need to stay sharp for the time being,' Alistair said. 'Once all this is over, we will be happy to come back and break open a few beers with you.'

'That assumes you'll be welcome back,' said Blacksnake, currently out of sight. There was a degree of pottering, the light thunk of a fridge door and the rattle and hum of an ice dispenser. 'For that, you'll have to lay off calling me Mister Blacksnake.'

'Deal.'

'Chess will do.' He returned with a pitcher of water, enough ice to form a polar cap, plus a couple of glasses and a perspiring bottle of Lone Star. 'Help yourselves. I'll go fetch what you came for.'

He burrowed in the cupboard under the stairs, but returned shortly bearing an old toolbox. He planted it in the middle of the table then snapped the cap off his beer bottle and drank. He pulled out a chair for himself. 'Well, go on. Take a look.'

Alistair did the honours.

The contents were much as Sophia had described in her account of events at the New Mexico site. Pearlescent bones and strange banded armour pieces, complete with tiny legs that made them resemble very rectangular centipedes. Prize of the lot: the skull with its undeniably extra-terrestrial – and not a little demonic – physiognomy.

The contours invited touch, but at the same time something stayed his hand. Perhaps some foolish and borderline superstitious notions seeded by Sophia's insistence on referring to this as 'the Child'. Or perhaps there was some alien energy running through the filaments that laced the remains, like a current coursing through an electrified fence.

'Careful handling those,' Chess warned. 'There's a reason they've stayed safe.'

'Yes, I admit I've been curious about that...' Bugayev helped himself to one of the armour sections, examining it from every angle. 'Whatever has kept these artefacts hidden for all this time, I'm afraid we may have bad news.'

Alistair cleared his throat. 'What my partner means to say is, there is some risk that the people who want these have tracked us. We're deeply sorry, of course, but given their *abilities* it's unavoidable.'

'Abilities?' Chess set down his beer as though swearing off drink for good.

'Vision quest,' said Bugayev. 'That kind of thing.'

'These people can see from afar; a manner of clairvoyance, as it were,' Alistair added. 'And they can project illusions. Hallucinations.'

Chess did not appear entertained. He stood and strode to the window. 'Looks like you're right.'

Alistair jumped up and hurried over. A single black SUV stirred a train of dust, coming up the track. Bugayev joined them at the window. He gestured at the rifle.

'You have any more of those?'

Chess nodded, warily. 'A Remington.'

The man's reluctance to go handing out weapons was entirely understandable, but Alistair and Bugayev had left their sidearms in the car. It would be good if at least one of them could aid Chess in defending his home from people that they had brought there.

'These people have a friend of the Señora's,' said Alistair.

'Take it. I'll go get the shotgun.'

Bugayev went for the rifle.

The SUV trundled to a halt a few yards behind the Toyota. The dust settled. The shooting match was about to begin. And Alistair was unarmed.

CHAPTER SIXTEEN
Loving the Alien

JULY 1981. CHICAGO.

Reporters and cameramen flocked around him in a half-circle, filling the forecourt of the Imperial Hotel. Not so much a captive audience as one that had him cornered. But the truth was, he had them right where he wanted.

He put all trace of a smile in park. Pitched his speech between heavy-heart and steel *cojones*.

'You know, folks sitting at home watching their TVs might look at the footage of this fine city – the same scenes that have played time and again on news bulletins, on every channel. And they will have seen the swift response and the courageous efforts of the men and women of our law enforcement and emergency services. And they will have seen the faces of the victims. The suffering in every one of those faces, I do not mind telling you, is engraved on my mind. And I have met and spoken with every one of those souls and I don't think my memory of their pain will ever be erased.

'But some people might watch those pictures and they will see no smoke and imagine that to mean there was no fire. And they will see no blood and imagine there are no injuries, no wounds.

'Allow me to assure you all, those assumptions – as understandable as they may be, because we have never suffered an attack of this insidious nature before – those assumptions are mistaken. They are wrong.

'They might assume this city is undamaged. Well, let me tell you now, I've done plenty of soul-searching and I have thought long and hard about that one. And that one is a bit more complicated. Because yes, this city is damaged. It has been the target of a vile and cowardly attack, the likes of which the free world has never seen. Chemical weapons that tear at the very fabric of our hold on reality. Chemical weapons that shred the nerves and strike at the very heart of our sense of personal security and our ability to feel safe. So, yes, this city – its sons and daughters – have been damaged. But understand this one crucial thing. This fine city has not been broken. Not by any measure. This great nation of ours will never bow to terrorism.

'Enemies who attack from hiding will be rooted out, they will be found, and they will reap the consequences of their crimes. Justice will deal the hardest blow that can be meted out by our law enforcement agencies and by our military. The same retribution awaits those who choose to harbour or supply these basest of criminals.

'You know who you are. Mark my words: you will be damaged. You will be broken. And you will be buried in the dust.

'While America will heal and stand strong. Stronger and more united than ever. And this fair city and its people will be avenged.'

The closing syllable was barely rounded off before the barrage opened up. Raised hands and shouts fighting for his attention.

'Mister Vice President. Mister Vice President.'

He pointed.

'June Salisbury. CNN. Does the Pentagon already have intelligence on the perpetrators? Is there already a target in mind?'

Vice President Bryant weighed his words and then served up the answer he had prepared earlier.

'Hello! We're the Central Intelligence Agency. Maybe you've heard of us?'

A man and a woman had stepped from the SUV, placement and dispositions not unlike Alistair's and Bugayev's on their arrival. Alistair had to press close to the glass for a less than satisfactory view of the pair. He soon gave that up and relocated to the living room end of the house. The window there offered the best figurative seats in the house.

'I'm Special Agent Parker Theroux,' the man continued his introduction. 'This is my partner, Melody Quartararo.' The woman shot him a look. He answered with a look. Both looks were guarded by designer sunglasses. 'Sorry, Special Agent Melody Quartararo. She gets cross when I forget that part.'

They raised their hands, letting ID wallets fall open.

Even from his vantage point, Alistair would struggle to read let alone authenticate them. The badges looked the genuine article. And, for government agents who were undoubtedly armed, they appeared harmless enough. The woman: heart-shaped face, a softer shade of pale, and lustrous dark hair in a shoulder-length bob. The man: tall with slicked-back hair and a dimpled smile – and a head that liked to be on the move, tipping in unexpected directions as if to appraise the world from fresh angles.

Of course, there remained the possibility that this was all an elaborate deception. Powerful illusionists could certainly rustle up a pair of Agency IDs and sunglasses. But neither he nor Bugayev – or Chess, presumably – knew anything of the American cell. So how elaborate did a deception need to be?

'Guns in the dirt,' ordered Chess, from the doorway. His firm instruction was backed up by the substantial presence of the pump-action shotgun in his hands.

Bugayev had posted himself upstairs and doubtless had the rifle trained on them.

'All right,' said Theroux. 'But can I have a cloth to clean the dust off when we're done here, or am I going to need a warrant for that?'

Quartararo sighed. 'Just do what the man says.' She drew her sidearm, advertising every motion and tossed it to the foot of the porch.

Her partner strolled around the SUV and followed her example. The pistols lay side by side on the ground and yet somehow the tension in Alistair's stomach notched upwards.

'State your business,' said Chess.

Theroux opened his mouth to speak, but Quartararo stepped forward and stole his lines. 'We're here to see Brigadier Lethbridge-Stewart and his partner. In the spirit of international co-operation.'

'How do we know they're not projections?' Alistair cautioned.

'Lethbridge-Stewart wants to know if you're illusions,' said Chess.

'Offer us lemonade?' suggested Theroux. 'If it pours out of us we're not real?'

Surely, Alistair thought, *no illusionist could make up this character.*

LITTLE ROCK, AR.

America was truly a land of opportunity. Abdulin knew he had found the right store for his needs as soon as he spotted the leg of a swastika tattoo, protruding below the proprietor's t-shirt sleeve. A skull in a spiked Kaiser helmet also adorned his flabby biceps and the shirt bore a chaotic design that shouted of some heavy-metal band.

After a short and quiet negotiation, the proprietor led him through to a private viewing of the goods in the back room.

There, Abdulin found quite the museum celebrating the Great Patriotic War. The exhibits were predominantly German and there was a shelf or two dedicated to the American Civil War. A German naval flag hung on one wall, a Dixie flag on another. Abdulin wondered at this American patriot's obsession with the paraphernalia of an enemy. On one level he supposed they counted as trophies – scalps of Nazi braves – but there was more to the man's pride as his customer browsed.

Abdulin had what he called tangential military experience. As a conscript in his home country, he had seen no combat. But he had served in his special capacity up until very recently, scouting the Afghan mountains for Mujahadin from the safety of a KGB bunker in Moscow. In that capacity, he had sometimes roamed – remotely – among the soldiers who had to do all the hard climbing and trekking, and he had enjoyed a measure of their camaraderie – vicariously.

He passed on to the second table. Towards one end, the merchandise left world wars behind and moved on to the Vietnam War. A less auspicious conflict for the Americans.

Abdulin picked up an AK-47. He had no love of home, but this… this was a souvenir of that time he had lived, if only in his mind, among true soldiers. Far better than the weapon of an enemy.

'This,' he notified the proprietor.

'I should tell you, I only got the one mag's worth of ammo for that baby, but that being the case, friend, I can let you have her for a good price. Cash.'

Abdulin tossed a bound stack of ten-dollar bills on the table. The proprietor's eyes lit up at all the green.

Abdulin examined his purchase, while the proprietor went to fetch the ammunition. He stroked the wood of the stock and underbarrel grip. He could kill the proprietor. No witnesses. But in all probability the man would not invite police attention, even when all those dollars vanished in his hand.

Anyway, what would he tell them?

'Yes, officers, I sold a Kalashnikov to a white man in a blue windbreaker with a Dixie flag on the back. He looked like a patriot.'

NYC.

Irena twirled and imagined herself in a Broadway musical. Times Square was a kaleidoscope of possibilities. Signs and hoardings called to her in Hollywood Technicolor. Pedestrians and traffic rushed around her in a dazzling whirl of vibrant fashions and sparkling lights.

Too soon, the weight of her bags – one hanging from each hand – began to drag her wings down. She halted her spin and set her luggage down.

She became a statue. To what? Liberty?

Freedom was the grandest illusion of all. Americans had to erect a giant statue to celebrate it, and yet here they were running through warrens. Still, they could claim greater freedom than her.

Vasily expected to tear all this down. And she was his lucky rabbit. His guarantor of success. A pet, a good luck charm and a prisoner to someone else's ambitions. What of her own?

She picked up just one bag and sashayed – almost a dance move – towards the heart of this open-air palace.

WALK. DON'T WALK. The crossings flashed their message.

Choice.

Maybe Liberty was the grandest illusion, but it was not the best. Some deceptions did not require special powers.

I am no rabbit, Vasily. If anything, I am a bird. But not the shy little sparrow you see. That was all a show. Only acting.

Vasily and the others could still exploit the contents of the abandoned bag, wreak their terror on this city. But that would be their doing, not hers.

For her own plan, for her own freedom, she would need to be free of Vasily.

She walked out into the X that marked the very centre of this stage. And she sat where the streets met. Cars trumpeted their anger.

Irena smiled. It was an ugly soundtrack, but she revelled in it.

Soon a nice policeman would come and arrest her and give her a place to stay for a while. That detention would be the beginning of her freedom.

NEW MEXICO.

Memory lane was a steep hand-cut staircase in blistering heat. Nothing much had changed, except ten summers had baked the land a little harder – and robbed Anne of a little stamina.

On this occasion there would be no sun-cream or a borrowed hat waiting at the summit.

Bonnie had a purple headscarf. Seth appeared unfazed – the benefits of lizard blood – although the sheen of sweat made him slimier. Florence was similarly unflustered, even dressed in sun-swallowing black. Rufus would suffer the worst, but he was below with Slow Earl, working Sophia's old baggage elevator to hoist the group's supplies to the top.

Amongst the luggage, there was a pack loaded with bottle water, so that was something to look forward to. Then there was the red Adidas bag, its contents still a mystery. And there was the big brown suitcase, which Anne had finally seen the inside of when Seth had opened it to pick out a pistol from among a range of firearms. For reasons of his own, he had chosen a chrome revolver; the one he now used to prod her up the final few steps and onto the site of Sophia's old camp.

The area was cleared, and Anne wondered about the fate of her equipment. The tools, well, she had long ago forgiven Sophia for their loss. And in all honesty her equipment would be severely outmoded. One of the earliest CCD video cameras might have some antique value. Maybe she would get to learn its fate if these people intended to venture underground. She entertained an idea of breaking away in the tunnels. Maybe whatever they planned here would be a higher priority than chasing her down.

On the other hand, she was still their bargaining chip.

'Keep going,' said Seth. Anne trudged on towards the pueblo. 'Bonnie. Florence. If you would.'

Bonnie and Florence peeled away to the A-frame and the bags waiting on the cargo pallet. Anne led the way through the dusty streets, obeying the occasional verbal direction from Seth. Every doorway was a temptation, not for escape but for the respite from the sadistic heat. Soon they reached the kiva and Anne climbed the short flight of steps to the roof. She missed Sophia's guided tour. She had explained the roofs of some kivas were flush with the ground, but this was raised.

This, apparently, was to be their stage. Complete with an open trap door for unwitting actors to fall through if they missed their mark.

'Whatever we're doing here, can't we do it inside?' Anne pointed down. 'The heat is killing me.'

'Alternatives are available.' Seth waggled the gun, spelling out the joke.

'I seem to recall you saying you needed me alive. And presumably not burned to a frazzle.'

'Need would be overstating the case. I daresay we could find a workaround in the event of your death. But yes, for convenience, I would prefer you alive for now.

We have a trade to transact – I hope. Speaking of…' He searched about. And smiled as Bonnie and Florence made their entrance on stage.

They deposited the bags near the steps. Florence wandered the rooftop, surveying the rest of the pueblo.

'Florence,' Seth called. 'Perhaps it would be a good time to check on progress?'

'What'd your last slave die of?' she answered.

'Bonnie, meanwhile, I am sure your creative talents will be just the thing for arranging what we have so far.'

'We haven't even got half—'

'I am well aware of our stock levels, yes. But we can make a start. Mrs Bishop will be happy to assist.'

She will, will I? Anne glanced over at Florence who had walked to the far edge and launched into her chanting routine.

Bonnie picked up the red Adidas and wandered over. She dropped the hold-all by Anne's feet. The other bags remained by the steps. Anne couldn't help thinking about the guns in the case. And the water in the pack. She wondered, if she made a run for it now, which would she run for first?

Bonnie unzipped the Adidas bag and knelt to take out bones one or two at a time. She set them in the sand. The size of the individual pieces confirmed these were the bones of the 'Child'. Somehow, without the aid of an anatomical diagram, Bonnie was laying them out in positions to assemble the skeleton.

There were plenty of gaps. But Anne finally understood what they wanted with the missing pieces. That still left the question of why.

Chess did not serve the new guests lemonade. Or anything else. He leaned by the kitchen opening, arms folded, as though guarding against anyone trying to help themselves to refreshments or provisions. The pair took the lack of hospitality in their stride and made themselves right at home around the dining table.

Agent Quartararo opened proceedings by laying out five passport-sized photos, one by one, as though dealing a slow hand of poker. 'First of all, these are who you'll want to be looking out for. They need to be shut down.'

Alistair glanced them over. Quite the eclectic rogues' gallery. 'These would be your homegrown psychic terrorists, I take it?' he asked.

Theroux threw in a round of mock applause. 'Hey, I love it when we get to brief folks in the know. Saves a bunch of preamble.'

'We've pieced together some of the picture,' said Alistair. 'But what I don't understand is why you're sitting here in a Texas ranch house talking to us, instead of mobilising the entire Agency to hunt these people down.'

'Ah, now there's a story behind that...'

Quartararo waved her partner quiet. 'Technically, we're not here on official Agency business. This is strictly off the books. I'm sure that's a situation you can appreciate, Brigadier. Officially you're a serving officer, but you're on your way out and you're here in an extracurricular capacity.

'And we don't know who this guy is,' said Theroux, shaping his hand like a six-shooter and pointing at Bugayev. 'But we're not stupid. You have a fair touch of Virginia going on, mister, but I'm betting there's a faint trace of Moskva under there.'

'You want to see my passport?' Bugayev dared him.

'Funny. No, I expect it'd stand up to a litmus test. And I expect you'd stand up to interrogation. But we're not here to have you arrested.'

'The point is...' Quartararo barged her way back into the exchange. 'You two are Stateside to get things done. And our boss–'

'Technically ex-boss,' Theroux amended.

'He's still our superior.'

'Speak for yourself.'

She shot her partner a look that, even behind the sunglasses, packed some heat. 'Our ex-boss – but I'm going to abbreviate that to just "boss" from herein – he wants those same things done that you do.'

'So we can work together?' Alistair asked.

'Together is a stretch,' said Theroux. 'You two are on your own.'

'Wait a minute,' said Bugayev. 'Your superior has a personal interest, but he's counting you out?'

'You don't get it,' Theroux said. 'The man has a family. A career. *High profile*. These people know his face. All they have to do is close their eyes, do their freaky voodoo and home in on him. See him coming a mile, or a thousand miles away. Us too, probably. Maybe they're eavesdropping on us right now.'

'Unlikely,' said Quartararo. She nodded to the open toolbox.

'Oh, right. Yeah. Well, anyway, you two are Butch and Sundance on this. You can fight about who gets to be whom.'

Bugayev sniffed. 'What does that make you two? Lucille and Desi?' That prompted a glare from Quartararo – and a salute from Theroux, who clearly relished a good fencing opponent. 'Fact of the matter is, we'd rather do this on our own. No offence. But we're going to need equipment.

'We can put you in touch with a supplier. He operates out of Albuquerque. He'll see you right.' Agent Quartararo pulled a pen and card, and quickly scrawled across the back. She slid the card over to join the photos. 'Call that number. The Company will cover it.'

Alistair drew a sharp breath. He didn't especially welcome the idea of cleaning house for the Americans.

But he supposed it was something to know they would be issued with the right brushes for the job.

Anne knelt close to Bonnie. The kiva roof cooked her knees through her trousers.

'It's okay,' said Bonnie. 'You don't gotta do nothing you don't want.'

'I can try. It'll be guesswork, mind. And some memory, I suppose. After all, I did once see this laid out before.'

'I know you did.'

Anne didn't know quite what to think about that. It had been unnerving enough to have armed CIA agents hunting them. Add in a host of remote spectators and the whole experience took on fresh dimensions of discomfort.

'But I'm sure you can point out where I go wrong,' Anne added cheerily.

Yes, she thought. *This will be just like sitting down to complete a jigsaw on a Sunday afternoon.* With missing pieces and no box lid to guide her. And she was the Sunday roast.

Florence broke off her chant.

'Nothing.' The woman threw Seth a shrug. 'A ranch. Somewhere. Vague impressions. No context. Too hazy.'

'To be expected. It tells us they are close to our missing pieces.'

'That's great. But how are we going to send them a message?'

'That presents a minor hurdle. We may be able to rely on a little amplification using our youngster here.' He moved to stand over the bones, inspecting progress on the macabre exhibit.

'Uh, again, not even half,' Bonnie reminded him.

'Nonetheless.'

Anne frowned, trying to read between the lines of conversation. She wondered how tolerant Seth would be if she interrupted with questions.

'Why don't I take care of that?' offered someone.

The newcomer appeared near the bags and dropped her burden. A backpack patched with denim.

Seth aimed his pistol. 'Who might you be?'

His face was a hive of tics. This intrusion had knocked him for six, like a bomb dropped smack in the middle of his precious equations. Bonnie and Florence appeared guarded, but a good deal calmer.

The new woman had the most incredible cascade of red hair and a pale complexion that ought to suffer worse than Anne in the heat. The look in her eyes, though, was a cold that wasn't about to melt any time soon.

'I brought Vasily for you,' she said. 'You're welcome. Rufus and Earl are helping him up the stairs right now. He's been through the wars.'

'I don't—' Seth began, but the rest of his sentence was a formula that went unsolved.

'Now,' said the woman, 'would you like me to take care of your communications problems or not?'

Seth lowered the gun. The terror club had gained another member.

The ghost of Anne Bishop intruded on their conference.

Alistair and Bugayev jumped up from their chairs. Chess stood straight and reached for the shotgun propped beside him. The two CIA agents remained seated, but a measure of surprise spilled from behind their sunglasses.

Alistair missed his sidearm. Bullets were generally of little use against phantoms, but it never hurt to take a pop. The rippling apparition lurking in the doorway was a rejuvenated Anne, of course, with unlined complexion and black hair, like a long-lost version of her, returned. But the figure shimmered and flickered like a television picture in need of tuning. And when it spoke its voice was familiar for all the wrong reasons.

'Brigadier. Can we take it you have our items?'

'Can't you tell?' he challenged.

'The question was rhetorical,' said the ghost.

'Can I take it I'm not talking to Anne?'

It was *her*. Romola. The same voice with which she had addressed him in Paris, at any rate.

'Naturally not, Brigadier. But you will have every opportunity to catch up with her once we receive our property. So, let's have a get-together, shall we? Let's say Harts Cross. Noon tomorrow.'

'We want proof of life,' said Bugayev.

As though in direct defiance, 'Anne' winked out of existence.

'Miss Travers,' murmured Chess. He searched for answers in every other face in the room. 'What the hell was that about?'

'We told you,' said Bugayev. 'These people can project hallucinations. And they have her.'

'But don't worry,' Alistair added. 'We're going to make an exchange.'

'Harts Cross.' Chess nodded. 'South East of Albuquerque. I can point it out on the map.'

Agents Theroux and Quartararo finally decided to rise from their chairs.

'Ah, yeah,' said Theroux. 'An exchange. Great idea to draw them out. No two ways about that. But an actual exchange; not an option, I'm afraid.'

Alistair and Bugayev turned to face the two agents. 'Really? Care to explain why?' Alistair asked.

'Listen,' said Quartararo, with a delicate note of regret. She pointed to the toolbox. 'What's in there can't be allowed into their hands. Under any circumstances. Those "infant" bones share a special connection – call it a bond – with the bones of the adults. If they assemble the whole skeleton they'll be able to access every bone they've hidden who knows where.'

Alistair frowned. 'From what I've seen they're able to do that already.'

'Every bone. Simultaneously,' said Theroux. 'They'll have a sort of network. They'll be able to trigger them all.' He made a show of his hands blowing apart. 'Who knows where they've deposited them.'

'Or how many,' appended his partner.

That did paint quite a different picture.

'How do you know all this?' asked Chess.

'The Company conducted extensive experiments.' Theroux scratched at the back of his neck. 'We're not proud of it.'

'In any case,' said Quartararo, 'you're going to have to renege on your end of the exchange and take them down.'

'That was what we intended anyway,' said Bugayev. 'There is no way we can allow these artefacts into the hands of terrorists.'

'Good for you. Happy to have you on the team.' Theroux extended a hand. Which Bugayev neglected to accept. 'Well, one thing: you can take this ghostly visitation as an encouraging sign.'

'We can?' Alistair was all ears.

'Yeah, you noticed her picture was wonky, right? Ever wondered why a group of remote-viewers couldn't find these things remotely?'

'I'm guessing the armour pieces have something to do with it,' said Bugayev.

'Exactly.' Quartararo nodded. 'Those plates provide a measure of ballistic protection. Their primary function is psychic shielding. I'm not saying they'll be a hundred percent effective. But they might filter out the worst of the rays.' She gave a wry smile and tapped the rim of her sunglasses. 'Like shades.'

'Call them dreamcatchers,' Theroux said, clearly

enjoying his joke. He looked to Chess for appreciation. Which he didn't get.

'I'd like to know,' said Chess, 'how you CIA people found your way here.'

'Detective work, Mr Blacksnake.'

Quartararo sighed. 'Rest assured, it's nothing sinister. The Brigadier's enquiries through channels set off some alarm bells, flagged for the attention of our boss. He supplied us with a list of the volunteers attached to Montilla's dig. As well as vehicle registrations noted at the site. The smart money said the Brigadier would head here. Proximity to the site, plus you were the only volunteer Miss Montilla kept in touch with.'

'Señora,' Bugayev corrected her. 'While we're filling in gaps, how did our people get their hands on their share of the artefacts?'

Theroux grimaced, as though reminded of a bad tooth that needed extraction. 'They hit our convoy, post-operation. We imagine they used one of their remote projectors, plus a small crew of sleeper agents physically situated in the States.'

'There's something else,' said Alistair.

'Isn't there always? Let's hear it.'

'Not a question. A concern.' Alistair took a breath. 'Sir Frederick Hackett. His son is assigned to *Forrestal*. Now, I gave him an ultimatum. But I'm not sure he can be trusted to deliver the message. You need to get a warning to the Sixth Fleet.' Alistair outlined his concerns about the lighter and Romola's potential substitution of some other focusing object. 'It might be one of those "adult bones", if she managed to get a hold of one. But my feeling is, the lighter served as her focus at the pub. So, it could be anything.'

'Think of it as a target designator,' Bugayev added.

'Okay. That is serious.' Quartararo looked at her partner. 'We had better move.'

'And you're sure you don't wish to tag along with us?' Alistair asked.

'No. We're out.' Theroux made a toy six-shooter of his hand again. 'Butch and Sundance, remember.'

Yes, thought Alistair, acutely conscious of how that film ended.

CHAPTER SEVENTEEN
Let's Dance

JULY 1981. ALBUQUERQUE, NM.

If there was a fine line between clandestine and sordid, Alistair and Bugayev had found the border.

It was marked by a rather desolate-looking lane behind a strip mall. Dustbins – or trash cans, to use the vernacular – guarded the tradesmen's entrances, attracting flies and giving off smells that ought to be banned under the Geneva Convention. Thanks to their precautionary recce, he could be sure they were conducting business at the back door of a store proudly bearing signage that boasted of VIDEOS of XXXX variety stocked within.

The neighbouring shop was a nail salon. Their contact had chosen to park alongside its rear. The tan station wagon was not quite nose-to-nose with their rental car. The driver – balding, with a tanned and heavily liver-spotted face – had traded handshakes, but no names. After a cursory inspection of his clients, he led them to the goods.

On their right, the lane was lined with ramshackle sheds and the odd span of chicken-wire fence. Across dusty yards, Alistair caught a view of the back end of a motel and he briefly wondered why they couldn't have met there.

The merchant unlocked the boot – or trunk – and

raised the door. He ushered his customers forward, like a manager declaring his store open. Standing back to avoid the rush.

'Feast your eyes, gentlemen.'

Alistair appraised the impressive arsenal on offer. Probably surplus to mission requirements. Somewhat alarming, if truth be told, considering the firepower that could find its way into civilian hands. If the dealer anticipated seeing his eyes light up, he was going to be disappointed.

Bugayev adopted a more active approach, reaching for different weapons, one at a time, to try them on for size. Weighing them, turning them over, testing the fit against his shoulder, checking their condition with near-scientific interest. This was no over-excited bride trying on gowns.

The dealer opened his mouth, but whatever sales patter he had rehearsed, he shelved. He could plainly tell there was no need for infomercials. 'The Company is bankrolling you,' he said instead. 'So take what you need.'

Bugayev tapped, or pointed, at his selections. A Remington M40 sniper rifle with a decent-sized scope. A Colt CAR-15, a shorter cousin of the American M16. A rather brutal-looking Italian SPAS-12 combat shotgun with a folded stock. A Heckler & Koch MP5 with its distinctive curved, slimline magazine.

He ended on a box containing a small variety of grenades. Four 'pineapples', plus two pairs of colour-coded cylindrical grenades: red for incendiary, and light grey with a yellow band for white phosphorous.

'You got your Mark Two frags, your M-Fourteen thermites and your M-Thirty-Four Willie Petes,' said the dealer, perhaps surplus to requirement but he seemed proud of his wares and happy to have two such discerning clients.

'You have more?' Bugayev asked.

'Not on this trip. I can get you more in two days. Three, tops.'

'Then I guess we'll take these.'

Hands were shaken. Goods and ammunition were transferred. They had enough materiel to deal with a small army. All the same, Alistair hoped they didn't run into one.

HARTS CROSS, NM.

Except for wide open space on all sides, the place boasted all the properties of a dead-end town. Something of a blip on the desert highway, where a dozen buildings had fallen from the back of passing lorries and clustered around a single intersection. The approach road's modest elevation allowed Alistair to look down on not much at all.

A corner store, a garage, and, rather astonishingly, a chapel. Alistair wondered what sort of congregation the reverend could muster, unless he threw open the doors on Sundays and waited for tumbleweeds to gather.

Bugayev pulled over a good two hundred yards from what might be termed the outskirts of town, although more accurately amounted to a shed.

'One hour early. We have time to kill.' Bugayev popped the door and climbed out. 'Or to prepare anyway.'

Alistair stepped out and took another brief sweep of the town. Not a soul in the streets. He imagined he could hear cicadas roasting on the tarmac. He turned. Bugayev delved in the car boot. A mere twenty yards back up the incline, a water tower dominated what passed for the rise. Bugayev proffered the sniper rifle. His plan did not need outlining.

Alistair declined. 'I'll be the goat staked out in the sun. Besides, we agreed I should do most of the talking. Spare everyone that American accent.'

'I think I might use my honest voice with these

people. Assuming I have any words to say to them at all.'

'Remember, we're here to retrieve Anne first and foremost.'

'I won't jeopardise that. Trust me.'

Alistair's mind flashed back to forty-two years ago – only eleven for Bugayev; a small boat in the Aegean, a Soviet chopper covering their approach on a rig. A Russian officer with all that firepower at his back, and the question of trust keenly felt like a red dot with an unnerving degree of tangibility. They had come a long way since then, and had further to go.

'Just watch yourself down there,' Bugayev cautioned. 'We don't know how effective these totems of ours will prove. You're going to be in handshake range. Their powers may be greater.'

'Noted. If they pull their trickery, how will you know?'

'If I observe any un-Brigadier behaviour, I will take them down.'

'Splendid.'

Open, empty streets. For a marksman of Bugayev's skills, it ought to be like shooting fish in a barrel. While he, Alistair, tread water amongst the fish.

He slid into the driver's seat and drove the car at a cautious pace down the gentle slope.

Alistair planted himself slap-dab in the middle of the intersection.

He checked his watch: ten to noon. No sign of shooters lying in ambush on the rooftops or in upstairs windows. Which might well mean nothing when arranging to meet illusionists.

It occurred to him that this entire town, such as it was, could be a mirage manufactured by the enemy. Now wouldn't that be quite the trick? And here he was standing at the centre of the trap. But then – wouldn't they go to the extra little trouble to complete the illusion with a dash of population?

Movement caught his eye. A bearded fellow peered out from the corner store. The storekeeper, by the looks of his apron. After prolonged study, he shook his head and retreated from the window. Disappointed that this visitor was not a prospective customer, no doubt. Or perhaps relieved, given the stranger's behaviour.

Alistair glanced to the car. He'd parked it a short sprint away, next to the church, keeping Bugayev's field of fire as clear as possible. The stage was set.

He paced and scanned. Paced and scanned. Two vehicles surfed the heat-haze on the West highway.

Alistair stopped his pacing and straightened his jacket to hide the lines of the pistol in his belt. A mere formality: even if the 'dreamcatcher' interfered with the clarity of their viewing, surely these people couldn't be so naive as to imagine he would come unarmed.

Showtime, as the Americans said.

Bugayev tracked the cars through the scope. Two unremarkable sedans: a grey Ford and a metallic blue Lincoln. Twelve by fifty magnification was a little overpowered for this range, but the town would box them in to a certain extent. For now, the Ford crawled to within five or six metres of Alistair at the crossroads and stopped. The following Lincoln loitered nearer the far end of town. There was a lot of glare off the windshield so that vehicle presented no soft targets yet. The lead car was a different matter.

Tango One stepped out. Immediately recognisable from the CIA-supplied photos. Glasses and a raincoat – unbuttoned, but still, he looked dressed for a rainy-day commute to the office.

Tango Two was a large silhouette, seated in the back of the car. Too big to be the hostage.

Which meant Anne Bishop would be held back in the

second car. Assuming they had brought her at all. If not, that second car was strictly backup and would need to be taken out. He sighted the driver's side: still no figure he could discern, but a fair probability of a hit if he fired through the glare.

He switched back to cover Alistair and his new acquaintance. Negotiations had begun.

'I did not come to banter, Brigadier. Shall we proceed to business?'

The man had introduced himself as Seth. The chap looked decidedly overdressed for the climate. Alistair wondered if he should brace himself for an illusory thunderstorm. He glanced down the street to the second car, speculating on the various plays these people might have in mind.

'Where is Doctor Travers?' he demanded.

'Where is our property?'

'Still can't see them, eh? Even when they're practically under your nose. Interesting.'

'Fetch them, please.' Seth gestured towards the Toyota. He glanced about as a playful mime. 'Unless you have secreted them elsewhere about this wonderful town. But please, fetch them.'

'Doctor Travers first.'

'*Au contraire*, Brigadier. You may believe you call the shots – with your friend up there on the water tower.' The fellow oozed as much smugness as perspiration. 'Oh, I can't *see* him, but it's where I would be if I wanted to be on overwatch.'

'Then you know you're a target.'

'Entirely to be expected. But if we are to discuss targets, let's talk cities. Let's say every minute you delay, one major incident hits one major city. Don't for a second doubt our capabilities or our resolve.'

'I don't doubt you're a monster,' retorted Alistair. But

he knew – and Seth plainly knew – there was no bluff to be called. He had no choice but to fold. He walked to the Toyota and fetched the toolbox from the back seat.

Round one to the monsters.

Bugayev felt a jolt. The water tower creaked and groaned under him.

Metal buckled and snapped. The tower lurched forward, threatening to topple. He lay flat, fastened to the surface like a magnet. None of this was real. As long as he didn't budge, there was no way he was sliding off. He would just have to ride out the attack. Rock beat scissors, rationality beat false gravity.

Rationality also told him there was someone powerful down there in the town.

Anne sat trapped in the back of the Lincoln. She had the redhead, Romola, for company, with a large automatic aimed in her general direction. Romola appeared to be concentrating on something for a while, but she never once looked like she was lost in the sort of trance that might have allowed Anne to make a break for it.

She returned, fully present, and none too pleased.

Earl, up front at the wheel, glanced in the rear-view mirror. 'What's up, lady? Not getting any joy?'

'Not without losing our decoy.'

Up the street, the Brigadier and Seth were engaged in discussions. She wondered what decoy this woman had in mind, but she had her suspicions.

'Something tells me I'm going to need all my concentration just to maintain her.'

Her, thought Anne. Yes, she rather felt she knew the 'her' in question.

Alistair placed the toolbox on the ground. He opened it for Seth's inspection of the contents – all present and correct, save for a couple of armour pieces. He stood over it, maintaining a close guard.

'Rufus!' Seth beckoned to the lead car.

A fat fellow in a baseball cap struggled out of the back. Anne emerged halfway, then the rotund chap grabbed her and tugged her out. He sweated profusely, but didn't shirk from the manual labour. He held her in place.

'How do I know she's real?'

'Really, Brigadier. I know you have a shield segment about your person. And you have clearly deduced its purpose. The strongest of us would struggle to produce a convincing simulacrum of Mrs Bishop to deceive you.'

'I'm real, Brigadier. And in a foul mood,' Anne assured him.

It sounded like Anne. 'Glad to hear it. Step over here.'

'Good to see you.'

'Likewise.'

'How's Sophia?'

'She's very much her old self. Step over here.'

Seth wagged his finger, as though chiding a child for stealing candy. 'Now, Brigadier. Our *bones*, if you would be so kind.'

Alistair stiffened. 'What do you intend to do with them?'

'What do you imagine we will do?'

'To be frank, it's what you lot imagine that concerns me. More terrorist attacks, I suppose? You and the Russians planning to seed more cities with focusing objects.'

'Sterling detective work, Brigadier.' He awarded Alistair a solitary hand-clap. 'But what do you care? Nobody gets hurt. A few nightmares. A few cold sweats. Fear. Our terror attacks don't actually happen, there's no physical damage, no harm done.'

'Really? Some were injured in Chicago. Traffic

accidents and the like. People reacting to what they believed they saw.' Alistair still carried everything he believed he saw in the pub blast. The image of that girl: the blood-streaked face, locked in a scream. He didn't take kindly to this man trivialising any of it. 'Besides, people have a right to live in safety. Free from fear.'

'Do they? Then why are they never permitted to? The world thrives on it; governments demand we be afraid of something. If it wasn't us calling the shots, it would be governments. Yours included.'

'Listen, you're not here to banter, and I'm not here to debate. Least of all with a monster. Return Doctor Travers. Now.'

'Monsters.' Seth sighed and smiled. 'Listen to yourself. Utterly oblivious to your own cruelties and atrocities. You rarely shy from a kill. Neither does your Russian friend. He does not blink.'

'When necessary.'

'Protecting the innocent, of course. You're a guardian, Brigadier. A shield-bearer for us all. With that role in mind, I think you – and *Doctor Travers* too – will enjoy a slice of the truth.'

'What truth would that be?'

Seth took a step closer. 'That to keep us from reuniting these bones would be the truly monstrous act.'

Alistair arched his eyebrow. *Reuniting?* Putting the skeleton back together?

'You imagine we are here to trade a life for bones,' Seth continued. He advanced another step. 'But this is a hostage exchange. One prisoner for another, like they do at Checkpoint Charlie. It is the skeleton of a child. You look on them as remains; as did your archaeologist friend. But they are so much more.'

'More how?' Alistair glanced at the pieces in the toolbox.

'They are *alive*. The Child remains aware. It was aware

when Doctor Travers and Señora Montilla disturbed its sleep and stole pieces of it. It was aware when agents of East and West stole the remainder and carried them to opposite sides of the world for experiment and study.'

'How could you know any of this? Have you talked to the little chap?'

'*Idiot!*' Seth dispensed with his smugness and fake smiles, lashing out with real venom. 'We were subjects of those same experiments. We were the laboratory rats and the bones were our toys. But any attempt to channel the energies within the Child's bones merely unleashed its screams trapped inside. Screams to be made whole. Must I describe them? Or are your powers of empathy sufficient to imagine yourself in the position of such a child?'

Alistair preferred a scientific opinion. 'What's your assessment, Anne?'

'Her assessment is immaterial,' Seth interrupted before Anne could say a word. 'How can there even be a question?'

He was right. There was no question. 'Irrespective of this…*creature's* state of awareness, these remains can be used as weapons. We can't hand you the means of perpetrating countless further terror attacks.'

'Terror attacks with no deaths versus the healing of a child. How does the guardian feel about that, Brigadier? You, a protector of innocents.'

'My guardianship extends to preserving peace and security for human beings. Not the life of some alien offspring. Least of all a threat.' Alistair dropped a hand close to his sidearm. 'Guilt or otherwise, I am not about to sanction the arming of a terrorist cell.'

'We have a deal, Brigadier. And I assume you have your honour.'

'The deal is off.'

'What?'

'You're right about one thing, of course. My Russian friend doesn't blink. He's also a sharp sort of fellow. For example, if I were to turn my gun on myself...' Slowly Alistair raised his arm, turning his pistol gradually, painstakingly inward. Making it appear quite the desperate struggle. 'What do you suppose he would make of that?'

'Stop!' Seth lifted a hand.

The shot hit the back of his skull and blew out the right lens of his glasses.

Anne vanished. Just like her ghost had done at the ranch house.

The big fellow – Rufus – charged at Alistair like a bull.

A second shot rang out. Rufus threw himself to the ground. Blood sprayed from a hole in his Led Zep t-shirt, but he was still breathing – in loud, ragged gasps. And he had landed almost where he wanted to be: arms laid across the toolbox. Alistair knelt and had a go at wrestling the box free. But the man had some fight in him.

A tyre-screech turned Alistair's head. The Lincoln had skidded to a stop, mere yards away. The rear passenger door pushed open. Alistair swung his pistol to bear.

Anne stumbled out. With someone tucked in tight behind her. He saw a wash of red hair – and an automatic aimed over Anne's right shoulder.

He dived towards the Toyota, seeking swift cover. Pistol shots chipped the tarmac behind him.

'Grab it! Grab it now! Let it go, Rufus!'

Alistair came up, pressed himself against the Toyota's side. He looked for a line of sight to Romola's flank. She sent another two rounds in his direction. Forced him to duck.

He popped up again.

Anne was backing up, still serving as a shield, carrying the toolbox in both arms. Romola reversed to the open car door. Then they were both gone.

Bundled into the Lincoln, of course. But also swallowed in a giant dust-storm that blew up from the street. As though the entire road had disintegrated and been churned up into a granular tornado.

Alistair shielded his eyes. But felt no sting of particles. The grains ghosted through his hand. Intangible. But visible enough to cover her escape. He heard the car screech away.

Whoever the woman was, she had the better of them. Round two to the monsters.

CHAPTER EIGHTEEN
Rebel Rebel

1967. ENGLAND.

POLICE.

White letters on a blue lamp above the door.

She ran in out of the rain, brought some of it with her. She dripped on the counter and shouted for the desk sergeant's attention.

'Hey! Hey!' Ring for attention, said the notice. She rang the life out of the bell. 'Hey!'

The sergeant marched over and clamped a muffling hand over the bell. 'Settle down there, miss!'

'There's a woman…She's… she's going to die if you don't do something!'

'All right now, let's have some calm, shall we?'

She dug hands in her hair, wanting to tear it out. 'He's not there with her right now, but he'll be coming back; she's so alone. He has to be someone you've interviewed already and if I tell you what he looks like you can go pick him up and he'll tell you where he's got her.'

'Pardon. You've lost me, miss.'

Why couldn't she get through? Tears threatened. She pressed palms to her head, wished she could claw out the pictures and scratch them in the desk for the sergeant. He had to see.

'If you know someone's in trouble, I'll need to take some particulars.'

She searched the hall, walked left and right, craning to peer into the back offices. 'You must have some sort of incident room, an inspector whatever I can talk to. He could be back any minute!'

'Now wait up, miss. If you're talking about the Riverside murderer, well, there's an incident room but it's not at this station.' The sergeant lifted the counter and came on through. 'When you say you've seen this woman…'

She backed up. Slapped her head. 'In here. In here! That's where it all happens! Stay back! Don't you touch me!'

The sergeant stopped. 'It's all right, miss. I'm not going to touch you. But you need to calm down. I'm beginning to get the picture.'

She could hardly breathe. 'You are?'

'Yes, miss. I daresay you've had a few. Taken something you shouldn't have. Now, it may be your friends put you up to this. A dare, maybe?'

'What? No! You don't get it! She's going to die!' she yelled into his face. 'And you could stop it!'

'Miss. I won't tell you again. Calm yourself. And listen. The best I can do…The best I can do is sit you down in an interview room, get you a cup of tea and take a statement.'

'And you'll tell them? Tell the detectives?'

'I'll pass it up the line, miss. Now I can't say fairer than that, can I?'

The sergeant extended a guiding hand, but he didn't touch her. The hall wouldn't stop spinning. She let him show her into the room. It was going to be all right. He promised.

The rest was a blur: a cold hard table, a mug of tea, the sergeant taking notes as she spilled her words. A constable stood by. They took her name and address. She signed. And then they gave her a lift home. It was going to be all right. They promised.

That night, she shut herself in her room. Sitting up in bed, she hugged herself and tried to shut out the nightmares by listening to the rain against the window and music. Loud music. Mum hammered on the door again and again.

But Romola was with the girl. Shut in the damp and dark, while rain drummed on a tin roof. She was there when he came back. Breath froze in her throat at the rattle of the padlock. She shivered in a coat of sweat and shrank into the corner, coarse rusty pipe pressed against her shoulder blades. The figure stomped towards her. His boots squeaked, air escaping from tiny punctures in rubber soles. There were no sirens heralding a last-minute rescue. The police were nowhere. And Romola could only be there and watch, and couldn't change a thing.

That was the last night Romola spent at home.

1968.

Cold night.

The car crept close to the curb, slow like a predator. Police probably, come to shift her on from her porch.

She'd spent most of her day here, apart from trips to the café to visit the lav, and spend some of the coins pedestrians had chucked her way. Around eleven, she'd had the idea of making the punters see a dog – a black lab, a few ribs showing – curled up with her. That had earned her enough loose change for a decent lunch. Nothing for the dog. Imaginary companions were incredibly low maintenance.

'Time to relocate, Buster,' she murmured to the dog that wasn't there. She'd decided he was called Buster. A name to give the punters who stopped to pet him.

Her stomach growled and then came the shivers. She stretched, working slow life back into frozen muscles. The car door popped, shoes tapped the pavement. She poked her head above the blanket for a look.

Not police. At least, not the uniformed kind.

He was mostly silhouette, features blanked, but there was no hiding the Colonel Blimp moustache. She thought only old guys and walruses went in for that kind of facial hair. The streetlamp behind him crowned him with an artificial halo that wasn't fooling anyone. The car was a navy blue Rover. Another man – a shadowy driver – lurked inside.

It wasn't the first time she'd had cars pull up. But the men usually stayed inside their vehicles, rolled down their windows to call out. And they didn't usually have drivers. They prowled solo.

'If you and your friend are window shopping, you want the next street.'

'Yes. We showed your picture to some of those ladies. They directed us here. I'll say this much for them, they know their neighbours.' He flashed her a photo.

Stupid school portrait: her, parcelled up in a uniform, done up with a tie and forced to sit in front of a blue screen. There was only one place he could've got that. 'My mum offering a reward, is she? You should know, she's broke.'

'Yes, we saw. Not exactly prospering. Not like you, eh,

sweetheart? Poor Mrs Tulliver doesn't have the foggiest where you are or what you're up to. I bet she went out of her wits when you first went missing. I daresay she's still distraught, but she hides it well. Trust me, darling, we're the only ones who care enough to look for you.'

Those 'darlings' and 'sweethearts' were going down like day-old blancmange. 'What do you want?'

'We want to take you somewhere warm. Give you a bed–'

'Yeah, I've heard that song before.'

'No, love.'

'Love' now, was it?

'We want to give you a place to stay. Roof over your head. Three square meals. Nice hot cuppas.' He puffed up his moustache. 'Bathroom privileges.'

'You make it sound like prison.'

'You'll be taken good care of.'

'You haven't answered my question. What do you want?'

'We'll get to that. Something to talk about after a good night's sleep.'

Bed and board sounded good. This guy's demeanour screamed officer. Didn't make him an automatic threat. Didn't make him not one. But whatever rent he expected her to pay she reckoned it would be something she could handle.

'Come on, there's a train waiting. Ever been to Scotland? Sleeper compartment all to yourself, we can talk more over breakfast.'

Scotland? Bloody hell.

She stood, gathered up her blanket. The man reached for her bag, but she warned him off with a glare. 'All right. But if I hear anyone at my door before breakfast I'll kill them.'

He backed off, miming surrender. 'Fair enough, love. Where's your dog?'

'What?'

'The ladies round the corner said you had a dog. Sometimes. I don't know.'

'He's not mine.' She fake-smiled to stop herself laughing. 'Just some stray.'

SOMEWHERE IN SCOTLAND.

'Now, we're going to try a little experiment. That gentleman in the other room is going to hold up some cards. What I want you to do is concentrate on each card and tell

209

me what you see. Do you understand?'

'Of course.' What did he think? She was twelve?

The officer gave a nod. The 'gentleman' in the window slid a card off his oversized deck and held it up. His eyes were fixed on the card, and she stared into them. She barely had to visualise anything. The man was concentrating so hard on the picture in front of him, he'd turned it into a word, repeated over and over in his head.

Circle. Circle. Circle. Circle. She saw the perfect circle, thick black line on white. Clear as day. If days were made of ink.

'Square?' she offered.

The man set his card aside. He dealt himself a replacement card. Same routine. A black cross. Like an enormous plus.

'Circle?' she guessed.

The man picked another card. Square. Like an empty box.

'Wavy lines?' she said.

Next card. Waves. Like a child's drawing of the sea. She imagined it stuck to some parent's fridge door. *Mum, Mum, look what I drew in school today. And I've never been to the seaside.*

She pretend-frowned. 'Cross?'

Quarter of an hour of this and the dealer had been through his deck three times, lots of awkward shuffling in between. The cards were too unwieldy for a magician's touch and she doubted the man would ever get work in a casino. She smiled. She buried the smile quickly, but the officer studied her long seconds after. That moustache really did look ridiculous on him. Maybe he expected to grow into it.

'Can I get a cup of tea?'

The officer rose, sighing like he was using the air for propulsion. He rested his fingertips on the table as though set to play piano standing up. About to go full Jerry Lee Lewis. 'I have this feeling you're playing games with us. You wouldn't be playing games with us, would you, sweetheart?'

'Games? What else d'you play with cards?'

He laughed without an ounce of humour. His teeth minced, chewing nothing. 'Well, I suppose you could look upon it as a game. So… why don't we give it another go, and this time play to win.'

He strode to her end of the table and stood guard, folding his arms. Then gave a nod to the man behind the glass. The man rearranged his deck with the patience of a jig-saw enthusiast. Then started another round.

Cross. She shut her eyes, making a show of effort.

'Umm... circle?'

The officer looked to the dealer. 'Try harder, sweetheart.'

Square.

'Umm...'

The fist knocked her head sideways. Her cheek burned. The officer folded his arms again, tucking the offending fist away.

'S–square,' she said.

Tears welled. But she saw that damned square bold and sharp. Oh yeah, clear as day. She smiled behind a veil of tumbled hair. Imagined using her tears like watercolours, making the ink run. She changed that square to a circle in the man's vision. He blinked at that card like it was lying to him. But he couldn't see through the forgery. How could he? She'd drawn it in his head. He set the card down. Uneasy, but unable to argue with his own eyesight.

The officer looked for a signal. The dealer didn't even bother to disguise it: he gave a single, short shake of the head.

She brushed the hair out of her face. Showed off her stinging cheek like a medal.

The man held up another card. He peered at it a shade nervously. Waves.

'Square?' said Romola.

Playing to win.

She sat on her bunk, picking at her toenails. She'd tease a crack in one side of the nail then rip it all the way across. Then toss it in the wastepaper bin at the end of the bed. Shedding one more useless piece of her, leaving another rough edge.

The door opened to admit the officer. He watched another nail torn off and flicked to the bin. 'We can get you nail-clippers.'

No scissors though? She laughed silently. 'All the comforts of home. I'll want for nothing, right?'

'Well.' He closed the door. Parked himself in the chair against the opposite wall. 'Unfortunately, a lot of the comforts here are performance-related.'

'Not very scientific. Where's the objectivity? Lab rat only gets the cheese if she gives you the results you want.' At best

211

their experiments would be skewed. At worst, the rat would really start to resent the cheese. 'Maybe I can't do the things you think I can do. Five-star luxury's not going to make me.'

'The thing is, I leave the objectivity to the scientists. I'm a military man.' No, really? The smart suit might as well have been decked in buttons and gold braid. 'There are limits to the things I believe. I rely on the evidence of my own eyes. What I'm seeing here is a girl who sees herself as a prisoner, so she's refusing to co-operate. All we want to do is help you discover your true worth. And you're doing your damnedest to hide your gifts. Trouble is, you're such a habitual liar, you're telling too many lies and you're not helping anyone.'

'That's how you see it, huh? My worth equates to my so-called gifts?'

'That's not what I meant. Clearly, you have worth beyond what you can do.'

'Everyone does.' *But not to you*, she thought.

'The fact is, nobody – *nobody* – would get the negative results you do. If you were guessing, plucking random answers out of thin air, you would guess some correctly. Law of averages. That many, they're false positives. My suspicions? If you're going to such misguided efforts to conceal them, then your powers must be impressive indeed.'

'So, you believe in God?'

'I'm not sure I follow, but–'

'I'm saying, you look around at the world, see no evidence of any divine power in any of this mess, so by your logic He must be really powerful. He just goes to a lot of trouble to hide it well.'

'I see your point. But my point is, I know you're hiding something. And unless you co-operate we have no way of knowing the extent of your gift.' The officer leaned forward. 'And I'm beginning to feel alone in my belief in you. I'm under pressure from my superiors to cut our losses and let you go.'

She knew. She'd been a fly on the wall at enough heated discussions in the upstairs offices. This guy fighting her corner, but like the owner of a prize pitbull he wanted to keep in the ring.

'So, let me go.'

'You don't understand.'

'What? You're going to take me out to the woods and shoot me?'

After the train, they had blindfolded her for the car journey. Grade-A dumbness. These people who believed in her clairvoyant powers tried to shut her eyes with a blindfold.

'Nothing so melodramatic. But understand, if we let you go, that's it. You don't get to come back home. Not to this house.' He smiled like every bristle of his stupid moustache was tipped with poison. 'Of course, you could always go back to your mother, but I've a feeling if you wanted to do that you would've done so before we scraped you up off the streets. So, I'm thinking that's where you'll end up. Right back on those streets, begging, fending for yourself day after day, out in the cold and the wet.'

'You don't have to paint the picture.'

'Right. In which case, might we have a little more honesty in our dealings?'

Sure. They could have a little more. Enough for a month or so, maybe. Until she was ready to be moving on. One more month, tops. Then she would be gone.

Romola chucked the book. She hadn't been reading it anyway.

It had been another tough day. Giving them enough to keep her in accommodation for another week. She flopped back onto the bed and stared at the ceiling.

Then went for a wander. Through the halls. She found the officer. Followed him out through the gate to the car park. Rode with him on the lonely drive home. Walked with him from the garage into the house.

A voice floated out from the kitchen. 'Is that you, dear?'

'Yes, dear. Only me.'

That's what you think.

He shucked his coat and hung it on a hook. Coughed to clear the smell of cigarettes from his moustache – he'd smoked two in the car – then brushed the lip-ferret back into place. Ready to kiss his wife as she fluttered into the hall. A dutiful little butterfly in her floral apron.

'Something smells good.' The officer rubbed his hands. Headed right, into a high-ceilinged living room. Beelined for the sideboard and fixed himself a Scotch from the decanter.

Mrs Officer waited in the doorway. 'I'm glad you're home in good time for a change. I'm cooking up a special dinner.'

'Oh? What's the occasion?'

'Our son is home.'

'Eh? Is he now? Thought he was supposed to be knuckling down at college.'

'Keep up, dear. It's a study week. You remember he wasn't sure if he could make it. Was going to take a sailing trip down around the Solent.'

'Oh yes. I do recall something of that sort. Boat didn't sink, did it?'

'No, I believe they cancelled before any water was involved.'

'Ha. Where is he then?'

'Up in his room. His friends only just dropped him off.'

'Well let's have him down here. Family toast before dinner.'

'Well, go easy. There's wine with dinner.'

'I should jolly well think so.'

It was a regular picture postcard of domestic bliss. Romola felt like chucking up. If only she could be sick there, and not pay the price for it back in her cell.

Wife leaned into the hall and called up the stairs. 'Barney! Your father's home.'

Down came the son, answering the call like a pet. Everyone was so dutiful in this house. In he came. His mum laid proud hands on her boy's shoulders. He would look all right in a few years, once he'd filled out a bit, shed the boyish looks and the Hitler Youth haircut.

'All right, Mum.' The boy wriggled from her affectionate restraint. 'Welcome home, sir.'

Romola thought he was about to salute.

'Welcome home, yourself.' Daddy Officer raised a glass, an invite.

'I wouldn't say no.'

The mum excused herself and retreated to the kitchen. 'Remember what I said, Freddie, darling.'

The officer, the family man. Freddie had the perfect home life. A handsome son. Such a lot to lose.

1981. ENGLAND.

The Old Fusilier buzzed tonight. Not with excitement about anything special. Only with lots of inane but animated chatter. Romola queued up a playlist of tracks from *The Clash* on the jukebox and watched the older regulars twitch with annoyance. Petty. Childish. But fun. And bloody good music. So – bonus.

She meandered back to the bar and hopped onto a stool. Ordered a refill. Even with her hair screening her view, she'd caught the sidelong glance from the guy propped next to her. He enjoyed what he saw so naturally he immediately pretended he hadn't seen anything. The mirror behind the bar was giving him difficulties.

She'd been right about him though. The boy hadn't turned out too shabby. For all his coyness, he was almost a man. He made for entertaining viewing, glancing every way but her, busy laundering his thoughts behind random smiles. Finally, his idle hands reached for the pack of John Players in front of him and produced a fancy silver lighter from his jacket pocket.

Romola thanked the barman for her pint, then drew a ciggie from her own pack. 'Got a light?' she said. 'I can see you have. Got one for me?'

He smiled, a bashful shade of red to his cheeks. He seemed to appreciate a woman with plenty of front. She leaned in, so he could light her up.

'Nice,' she observed. 'From a girlfriend?'

'No. Father.' He handed her the lighter for inspection. She turned it over.

'Father?'

'Yes.' Another smile, this one with less blush and more confidence. 'You know what one of those is, right?'

'Not really,' she said. 'I know the theory, not so much the practical. But I meant, father? Not dad?'

'Oh, I see. No, he's definitely more of a father. Not too much the dad type.' He sipped his pint and rolled his eyes.

'Old-fashioned, uh?'

'You could call it that. Might be the military upbringing.'

'What's the F stand for?'

'Frederick. My father's name. It's a family tradition.'

'Quaint. You'd best not to have a daughter.'

Smile. Not a trace of blush. 'Ah, well, I don't plan on having a family any time soon. Wouldn't be fair to them. Navy. Away too much.'

She plopped the lighter in his hand. Held his gaze while her fingers skated across his palm. 'Now that's a shame. Handsome fella like you, wasted away on the ocean.'

The Clash pounded out another beat to upset the older punters. *London Calling.*

'Well, thank you.' The blush made a brief comeback. 'I'm Barney, by the way.'

He extended a hand. She took it, introducing a touch of shyness of her own to seal the deal.

'Romola.'

CHAPTER NINETEEN
Scary Monsters

JULY 1981. WHITEHALL.

Secrets were like caged animals. They paced around and around the confines of their enclosure. And God help you if they ever got out. They quickly became wild and uncontrollable. Most of all, they turned on their keeper.

In his office, Freddie Hackett reached for the decanter, thirsting for a swift shot of Royal Lochnagar to wash away such thoughts. Alcohol was a damned good disinfectant, after all.

The photograph, just beyond the decanter, stopped his arm in mid-reach and his hand hovered there, shaking. Ridiculous.

Lynne, Barney and him. Beaming pride in triplicate. His son's inaugural family photo as a commissioned officer. Royal Navy, but still, a father couldn't win every battle on the home front. There had been so much going on outside the frame that day; that whole year, in fact. Freddie wondered if he could count the lies behind those smiles.

He could almost see the secrets. The ones he knew about, at least. Caged.

Lynne had always known there were secrets. *Secrets are part of your job, dear.* He suspected she knew something of the ones that weren't work-related. And she pranced happily along with her home life and her wives' club.

Even her understanding was a pretence.

She was good to him. Too good.

As for his boy…

Freddie turned his attention to the other items dominating his desk. The file; TOP SECRET, CONFIDENTIAL et cetera. And the lighter. Silver, elegant lines and the initials that meant more than any other trio of letters. These two belonged together.

He picked them both up and fed a corner of the document to the lighter. He watched the flames lap up the paper before dumping it in the wastepaper bin. The fire burned itself out, safely contained.

He slid open the lower right-hand drawer. Where his old revolver lay waiting.

GULF OF SIDRE.

Barney hastened from the radio room to his quarters. He had been assigned a cabin in what was referred to as the 'high-rent district' and encountered a good many senior officers en route. To all of whom he did his best to appear less hurried and more affable than he felt.

His face burned. What was he… fifteen? His old man putting through a private call to harangue him about a date.

'Lethbridge-Stewart has it in his bonnet there's this woman involved. Whoever she is, she had your lighter. How that lighter came to be in her possession; you need to tell me.'

Lethbridge-Stewart. The name rang a bell: one of Dad's old chums.

'There's been no woman. And I have my lighter, sir,' he had answered.

There was a woman. But it was nothing. One of those chance encounters in a pub. Harmless chat over a drink or two. One thing led to another led to a B&B. She was gone before breakfast. He had no idea if he would ever see her again, although he had quite fancied looking her up on his next stay in London. And he distinctly remembered taking his lighter from the bedside table. Indeed, he lit up with it outside after polishing off a Full English and a hearty cuppa.

Honestly, it was a nuisance to be pulled away from duty for such nonsense. To say nothing of embarrassing. He hoped the Yanks would attribute the redness to a touch of Mediterranean sunburn.

'I suggest you had best make certain. Either you are mistaken, son, or I am looking at an exceptional forgery. And if she gave you some token in return, it could be dangerous.'

Rubbish. His old man was losing his marbles. Urgent private call, indeed. But now it was a matter of personal urgency to search his cabin. If only to prove to himself – and his father, whenever he got the opportunity – that it was all, at best, a misunderstanding or, at worst, time for his old man to think about retirement.

Barney slipped into his quarters, grateful to be shut away for the time being. A chance for his face to cool off.

He set about a brisk search. He had managed to unpack some of his belongings, so postponed the rummage through the kit bag until last. As luck would have it, the search required only the opening of a few drawers.

And halle-bloody-luljah. There it was: his silver lighter.

He collected it from the drawer and flicked it on for a test. Even read his own initials, imagining he was reading them aloud for his old man.

B. F. H.

Crisis averted. A knock at his door jumped him out of his skin.

He took a moment to recover and to berate himself for being so on edge. He popped the lighter in his pocket, patted it for good measure. Then answered the door.

Commander Perry was there, accompanied by two marines. Not the same pair that had formed his welcoming escort. 'Lieutenant Commander Hackett. The captain would like to see you in his ward room. Right away.'

The immediacy, combined with Perry's apologetic look, did not hint at reason to celebrate.

Alistair rose from exchanging a final few words with Rufus. When pressed, the big fellow had wheezed something about 'the pueblo' as the place to find Anne. He spent his final breaths on assurances his friends had 'treated her okay'. Blood puddled the road around him.

Bugayev jogged down to meet Alistair and wasted little time surveying the mess. He returned the M40 to the Toyota's trunk.

'The pueblo,' Alistair informed him. 'I imagine there's only one place he can be talking about.'

'Let's get going.' Bugayev hopped in the driver's side.

Alistair took a last look around the small town. No sign of the locals, not even the storekeeper in his window. Sensible fellow had to be keeping his head down. Or calling the police. Alistair trotted to the car and climbed in.

They weren't too far behind their prey.

The climb to the top of the mesa was even more punishing the third time. Shoved and herded up the long staircase and through the pueblo streets, Anne felt the blood in her legs turn to lead while the heat continued to dry-roast her lungs. When she finally reached the kiva roof, she collapsed on her knees and almost fell to tears.

Bonnie was soon by her side with a bottle of water. Anne snatched it gratefully and drank.

The gathering had grown since she was last here.

Although these people didn't yet know about their losses in the town, there were two members to replace the two lost. She had known to expect somebody, since both Romola and Earl had remarked on an additional vehicle parked beside the Winnebago. A yellow car with twin black stripes from bonnet to boot was hard to miss.

There was a dusky guy with a goatee and a Kalashnikov rifle. And there was a blonde in a ludicrously over-frilled blouse and split skirt, attire she had at least coupled with a sensible pair of plimsolls. A pink suitcase on little wheels stood by her side, as though she were waiting for the next train out of the desert. Both regarded Romola warily, but presumably Vasily or one of the others had briefed them about her. The blonde visibly stiffened though.

'What happened?' Florence asked. 'Where's Seth?' No mention of Rufus. Perhaps she assumed he was still struggling up the staircase.

Slowly Earl set the toolbox down. Romola put a boot on it and propelled it across to the other woman's feet. 'We got what we needed.' She eyed the blonde and the pink suitcase. 'You must be Valentina, yeah? With the rest of what we need.'

Valentina nodded.

'Well, since we've got everything, we might as well put it all together,' Romola said.

'And who put you in charge?' the gunman asked.

'That would be the Russian. When he blew Seth's head off.'

Earl shuffled awkwardly from foot to foot, and turned from the gunman. 'It's true, Florence. Rufus caught a bullet too. Bam. To the chest. Bleeding out or bled out by now.'

Bonnie's eyes widened mournfully. 'The Russian done that?'

'Hey, just 'cos you predict something don't make you

responsible,' Earl reassured her.

Vasily, seated on the big brown suitcase, his wounded leg extended, pitched his voice at a volume to secure everyone's attention. 'I have a prediction,' he declared. 'One for which I will feel responsible if I do not share it.' He paused. Then launched himself up to hobble aside from the suitcase. He rested a hand on Florence's shoulder, for balance. 'They will be coming here. Major Bugayev will want to finish me, if nothing else.'

'Right.' Romola moved in to take the centre of the stage. 'So, do we want a leadership election, or do we want to get on with it? Let's vote.'

Nobody said a word. A great many looks were thrown around the group.

'Okay then.' Romola gesticulated, the automatic pistol in her hand coincidentally backing up her case. 'So, everybody needs to grab a gun. Somebody needs to volunteer for lookout. And we need to get this skeleton put back together.'

The Russian may have put this woman in charge, but it chilled Anne to see how she was taking to it like a natural born dictator.

'There's the Lincoln,' Bugayev pointed out as he headed the Toyota off-road and along the dirt track.

Alistair noted the metallic-blue sedan, as well as a Winnebago and a yellow-and-black Camaro parked in a patch of cleared ground below the mesa. He scanned the row of buildings lining the cliff-top, but spotted nobody. All the same, an enemy would have to be worse than amateur to neglect the advantage of such high ground.

'There goes our element of surprise, I expect.'

'We would never have had it anyway. Unless we waited until nightfall and made our way in on foot.'

Bugayev steered them away from the improvised car park and homed in on the base of the mesa, where a cleft in the rock slowly revealed itself, cutting a lengthy curve from foot to top. The staircase Sophia had described.

'High road or low road?' Bugayev asked.

'I suppose I'll take the stairs,' Alistair volunteered. The heat would be murderous, but he could afford to take his time if Bugayev planned to move up through the tunnels. 'And I may be in Scotland afore ye. Or I may not. We won't be able to co-ordinate.'

'If I hear gunfire before I'm in position, I'll hurry.'

Alistair inhaled. Yes, that ought to work. He would have preferred radios. But beggars could not be choosers. And at least he and his team-mate were not impoverished in the firepower department.

Captain Birchdale did not trouble himself to rise from the leather-bound sofa. He acknowledged Barney's arrival by gesturing to the identical sofa on the opposite side of the cabin.

Somehow, the invitation seemed more like an order.

Barney dutifully took his appointed spot. A rather ornate coffee table stood between them, on a rug emblazoned with *Forrestal*'s seal. *First in Defence*, it proclaimed. *Power for Peace*, declared the Sixth Fleet's eagle-and-anchor emblem, hanging on the wall above the captain's head.

'Son, I understand you had a private call from home. I'm going to need to hear a précis of what was discussed. Just for my peace of mind.'

Barney dug at his collar. It was hot in here. 'Some foolish notion my father had lodged in his head. Honestly nothing.'

Birchdale shifted to the edge of the sofa. He rubbed his hands. 'So, nothing to do with a communication I've received from Langley about a dangerous "artefact" that could threaten the safety of my crew and my ship?'

Barney swallowed on a lump in his throat. It refused

to go down. He feigned confusion and mystification. Was that why the marines had not accompanied them when Commander Perry had delivered him here? Could they be turfing over his cabin?

'Nothing like that, sir. My father works for the Ministry, so I can only imagine he rang the wrong people and managed to spread his foolish notions.' He shrugged, as much to say that was the best he had to offer.

Why was he lying? Covering for his old man? It was so stupid. Over a whole lot of not much. The last thing he wanted was to trouble the Americans about a lighter on a ship known as the Zippo. Sailors were notoriously superstitious sorts.

'Captain to the bridge. Captain to the bridge.'

The squawk almost made Barney jump. Birchdale leaped up. Barney rose immediately, making his 'jump' look like anticipation. On his way to the door, the captain pointed a finger at Barney.

'To be continued,' he said.

Jigsaws didn't usually require an audience. Everyone was gathered in a loose circle while Anne and Bonnie approached the end of their task.

Only Abdulin, the man with the Kalashnikov, was absent. On lookout duty. Anne wondered if he would see her rescue coming.

She lifted the final piece from the toolbox. The skull. Her arms trembled as she handed it to Bonnie. It wasn't heavy, but there was a different kind of weight to it: a fear or dread that dragged at her heart. A leadenness in her head too, that forced tears into her eyes. She was glad to be relieved of the artefact, although the emotions seemed to have taken up residence. Like the impressions Sophia had talked about; the idea of bloody history staining a place.

And now the relic passed a measure of that stain to

224

her.

Bonnie set the skull in position with a reverence usually reserved for the coronation of kings and queens. The figure laid out on the kiva roof was complete. Was it a him or her? Anne was sure even an archaeologist would be obliged to shrug in answer. It seemed imbued with that same tragic air Anne had felt when she had first laid eyes on it, resting in its coffin.

Bonnie rose and dusted off her knees. Anne did likewise and mopped her brow with her sleeve. With the assembly work done, what were the chances her captors would let her rest in the shade underground?

Slowly, they drew closer around the Child.

Threads of lightning flashed through the filaments, like neurons firing deep within the pearl bones. The milk-and-rainbow surface became more fluid. A trick of the eye? Anne didn't know what to believe.

The Child raised its skull like a weak hospital patient trying to lift its head off the pillow. It screamed. Or Anne screamed. Or everyone did.

CHAPTER TWENTY
Supercreeps

JULY 1981. NEW MEXICO.

A scream of centuries tore through Anne's brain. It was a sound she remembered: the same scream that had erupted from her detector array and practically deafened her and Sophia ten years ago. Worse, she recognised the raw emotion ripping through her on that blast of sound.

She had felt a fraction of it in her Chicago hotel room, when she had looked down on amputated legs. Paralysing dread. The life-stopping chill that struck with evil news. The death of a loved one. The death of all your loved ones and the certainty you were next.

Around her, the loosely arranged ring of people weathered the storm with unnatural stillness. But she could almost see a myriad of terrors buried like fossils beneath their faces. Horrors she could scarcely guess at. Except... Surely the tears looming so large in Bonnie's eyes had to be for her boy.

From its prone position at Anne's feet, the Child flexed bone-fingers, fighting to lift its skeletal wings from the dust. Anne couldn't tell if it was reaching for help or straining to take flight and claw them to death.

Abdulin ran into their midst, waving his rifle. Getting in front of all their faces. 'Break out of it! We don't have time!'

His shouts were muffled, as though Anne's ears were

heavily water-logged. But she knew his voice was drowned out by the raging scream. He kicked sand over the Child. Stamped on one of its legs. Its head dropped to rest on the ground. Its hands fell still. The writhing energies within the bones dimmed. The scream died. Cut off by a guillotine of silence.

Abdulin killed that silence with another yell: 'They're here!'

Everyone pulled guns. Mostly pistols, but Florence had availed herself of the sole shotgun in the group's suitcase armoury.

Romola took charge. 'You and you,' she picked Slow Earl and Abdulin with the point of her gun, 'go defend that staircase. The rest of us, let's get this done. Except you.' She aimed at Valentina. 'You keep *that* from interfering.'

Anne was 'that'.

Valentina stationed herself behind Anne. Ensuring she was a captive audience.

Alistair clutched the Colt CAR-15, ascending the staircase in brief sprints. Cut from the rock, it afforded ample cover from everywhere but up or down. With no cause to believe anyone was chasing up behind him, he could concentrate his wariness in one direction.

He rushed up another few steps and pasted himself to the inside wall, watching for targets, the Colt ready and keen. The carbine would pack a punch and he had his trusty sidearm for backup. The grenades…Well, overcooked was preferable to underdone, as a rule. The enemy probably had other weapons besides their hallucinogenic talents.

He felt prepared for anything. The unexpected was where experience and instinct came to the fore, after all.

There was only the single expected that troubled him. And her name was Romola. Too powerful for anyone's good.

'*Gracias, Señora.*'

Bugayev shone his flashlight into the vault, sweeping the beam over vacant grooves where the bones of the adult creatures had been embedded. Around the chamber, most of the lighting rigs lay toppled – and dead, of course – and the main cable trailed from the inert generator to the exit passage.

Progress had been swift and smooth through the caverns and up into the undercity, aided by his innate sense of direction and by Sophia's descriptions. He could afford to move fast, confident that these tunnels would be unpatrolled. The added insurance of a combat shotgun didn't hurt.

He carried the H&K, slung over his shoulder, and his fair share of the grenades. Anything that crossed his path would not remain in his way for long. Anything physical and real, at least.

Proceeding to the passage, he encountered the shallow crater from the grenade blast. He took a knee and felt around in the dirt. Found a couple of discarded armour segments. He shone his flashlight at the electronic tower in its corner. Anne's machine, all the wire spaghetti spilling from the back.

All the essentials for a quick spot of improvisation.

Two steps from the top, Alistair popped his head above the wall and sighted along the Colt.

Bullets rushed to welcome him.

At the shots, Bugayev jumped up. That was his starting pistol. Plus, a starting AK by the sound of it. No time to stand back and admire his handiwork.

He hopped over the wire he'd stretched across the passage and ran the maze, following the cable to the action.

A single bullet chipped at the wall above Alistair: the pistol recommending he keep his head down. Nothing from the assault rifle this time. Someone was trying to conserve ammunition.

He pictured his targets, visualised their positions: pistol firing from a roof, rifleman tucked against a corner of the same building.

Time to risk a severe haircut.

Sure as hell wasn't baseball, but this was kind of fun. Slow Earl felt the adrenalin high kicking in, making him pretty quick off the mark as soon as the Brit showed his moustache.

From his rooftop roost, he squeezed off two rounds. Both went wide of the mark, but they cut short the man's firing time.

Anyway, figured Earl, what should he care? The Brit did all his shooting at the corner. Probably nothing personal against Muslims, but Abdulin made himself a priority target with that Soviet hardware.

The Brit popped up again, a little ways to the left. Earl switched aim, playing Whack-A-Mole. An auto burst came his way this time.

Hell, this wasn't so much fun after all.

Alistair surfaced a foot or so to the right and fired at the building corner. The rifleman ducked back as the impacts obliterated a wedge of adobe.

He returned fire, but not before Alistair had dipped back down. Probably time to change things up a little. He plucked the WP smoke grenade from his belt. Pulled the ring and lobbed.

The gunfire had rattled more than a few nerves. Even

Romola was a fit of frustration every time concentration broke, and, despite all the meditative efforts, the Child hadn't stirred. The explosion, although not a loud one, broke the circle.

Bonnie and Florence stepped out. 'This ain't gonna work.'

Anne watched the white cloud swelling upwards, blotting out the western end of the pueblo. Bonnie made a valid point.

'We have to keep trying!' Vasily snarled. He was having trouble standing steady and that was doing nothing to improving his temper.

'We do,' agreed Romola. 'But maybe not here.'

That provoked a lot of uncertain faces. More shots rang out from inside the wall of smoke. That seemed to decide Valentina. Behind Anne, she sounded a hundred percent in favour.

'Absolutely. I'm a thinker, not a fighter. These people have shields, so what use am I if I can't use my mind?'

'A very pertinent question, Valentina,' said Vasily, like he was coughing up sour apples. 'Perhaps you had best run.'

'Fine, I will. Nobody needs this anymore, do they?' Anne turned her head, wondering what she was talking about. 'Good. I'll take a shield of my own.'

Valentina seized Anne by both arms and shoved her at the trap.

Whoa! Not fun! Not fun!

Earl rolled on the roof, beating at his sleeve. Damn grenade had thrown burning gobs everywhere, like dragon spit. White smoke poured up over his end of the pueblo and his damn shirt was on fire!

The rolling wasn't doing squat. He tore his shirt off, even as the unholy-hot flame started to barbecue his arm.

'Motherfu–!'

230

He rolled off the roof.

Alistair ducked and zig-zagged through the phosphor smoke, all the way to the building corner. He swung around, weapon aimed —

At nothing. Gun leading the way, he proceeded up the street. He swept left and looked in on the first doorway. Clear. Swept right to check the next hovel. Clear.

He came up on the first junction. A lane to the left.

Earl swore a couple more times under his breath. He hopped to his feet and tested his legs. Nothing broke. Maybe the bruises would distract him from the damn burn.

He grinned. You are one lucky son of a —

A shadow leaped into the thinning white fog at the end of the lane.

Earl brought his pistol up. Fast.

Alistair fired a burst of three.

The chap with the pistol fell in a rolling stagger along the house wall. Then pitched face down in the dust. One down.

Valentina landed inside the kiva. She hauled her hostage onto her feet. The woman complained a lot. Maybe her winces and moans were real; she seemed to have some trouble putting weight on her right leg and yelled 'ow!' a lot more when Valentina gripped her upper arm and marched her forward.

'Let her go.'

Valentina spun, pulling her shield firmly in front of her.

A man advanced from the shadows into the square of daylight. He had a persuasive-looking shotgun pointed at Valentina's shield.

'Let her go and you can walk out of here,' Bugayev promised Valentina.

'Liar,' she said.

She circled slowly towards the shaft, towing her human shield with her. He tracked her with the shotgun. The SPAS was not the ideal weapon for precision. Anne's expression suggested she understood that.

'Last chance,' he offered. 'I'm here for Vasily. I've no interest in you.'

Valentina stopped at the lip of the shaft. Her dilemma appeared to pain her. She shoved her hostage towards him. Bugayev single-handed the shotgun and caught Anne. Valentina dropped out of sight below.

Bugayev helped Anne to the wall and lowered her to sit against it.

'Thanks. I take it you're Major Bugayev? The terrorists talked about you.'

'All good, I trust. And you are Anne Bishop. I've met your ghost-double.'

'Ohh-kay.'

'Stay put.' He handed her his torch. And the shotgun. 'In case Valentina comes back this way.'

She looked to the shaft opening. 'Did you mean to let her go?'

A blast reverberated from the depths.

Miss Travers wouldn't need the shotgun, after all. But she could keep it, for comfort.

He un-slung the submachine gun and headed for the ladder. 'Stay put. I mean it. Anything above that isn't Alistair, is getting shot.'

Alistair dashed from house to house, corner to corner. Searching, aiming, searching. Many of the pueblo dwellings were small, ripe for the most cursory of checks from the doorway. The larger buildings required him to burst in for a proper sweep of the interior.

The street corners and lanes presented the greatest danger. Often, he had two directions to cover in a rapid one-two.

He poked his rifle in another doorway. Clear.

He backed out–

A figure leaned out from a doorway four houses along. Alistair dived back inside. A brief hail of bullets peppered the sandy street outside.

You got such pretty eyes, you should look up more. Quit looking at the ground, girl. Back in the day, folks were always telling Bonnie she had pretty eyes. Bonnie would roll them, just to show what she thought of their nonsense.

But the advice was sure handy now.

She nudged out onto the ledge and sidled along with her back to the house, nothing but a long drop a few inches past the tips of her shoes.

'Your people didn't leave a lot of space between the buildings and the edge,' said Romola. The fiery-haired, mean-ass Brit was ahead of her, defying death with a whole lot more confidence. And she had the bag, with the Child all packed up inside.

Florence followed on after Bonnie. 'Not my people. This is Hopi.'

There was a real thorn of contempt on the end of that. Romola had a temper on her, she might've sent Florence flying for less. Bad way to go. But had to be better than facing the Russian. And the ledge would slip them past the attacking soldiers to the staircase. Off the mesa and high-tailing it away across this desert.

Bonnie just had to not look at the ground until she was safely down there.

*

Vasily knew he was bait. Romola had at least returned his Tokarev, as if by way of paying him for his services.

However, he was determined to show Major Bugayev that the fishing line was baited with a shark. He had heard the blast rumble from below and took that as his signal to depart the kiva roof. He waited in the street for the major to show. And fired two shots at the head that peered over the roof edge.

He turned and fled. A fraction ahead of the answering burst. Managing a hobbling run, he turned and led his hunter on a chase.

Alistair traded shots with the gunman further up the street.

The Kalashnikov rattled off again. Alistair broke from cover and emptied his magazine at the target's hiding spot. He raced up to the next doorway and ducked inside. Reloaded.

The gunman shouted. Something in Arabic? He followed it up with two angry bursts in rapid succession.

Alistair stepped into the street and fired. His target was already back indoors. Alistair dashed forward.

Abdulin waited in the shadowy interior of the pueblo hovel. Who knew what manner of people lived here? Who cared? They were long dead.

He levelled his AK at the doorway and listened. Boots pounded the street dust. The British officer was close. He had perhaps three rounds in the magazine.

Movement under the window. Abdulin switched his aim to the small square cut in the wall. A small rock sailed through and clattered on the floor. Rounded and ridged, like a pineapple.

He—

Bugayev hurdled from roof to roof on an intercept course.

He pounced down to street level, missing Vasily by a handful of seconds. But soon enough to see him disappear around the nearest corner.

Bugayev chased. He leaned into the lane. Vasily fired wildly behind him as he limped along. Back in cover, Bugayev heard two closely paired shots and three clicks.

He resumed pursuit.

Vasily broke left. Bugayev followed in a flat-out run, dispensing with corner cover. At the end of the lane, Vasily slowed. A yard or two past him the mesa ended abruptly, giving way to a commanding view of the desert. Vasily hopped in an awkward turn, dropped to his knees and raised the Tokarev. Training the empty threat on Bugayev's centre mass.

Bugayev approached at a walk. He lowered the H&K.

'My friend,' he said. 'Alistair Lethbridge-Stewart – you've met – he's been puzzling over the why. Why you people have been doing what you do. Me, I'm less curious.'

'You can tell your friend,' said Vasily, showing teeth, 'he can go to hell still asking that question.'

'But ever since I found out that infant skeleton was alive and aware, I've been thinking…'Bugayev released the clip for a quick check, snapped it back in place. 'Your connection with this Child; is it two-way?'

Vasily's nose was badly swollen, decorated with blacks and purples. Maybe it was the hurt that set his face twitching a little.

'Because if it is, I have this interesting theory that, as much as you and your comrades were hoping to exploit its terror as a weapon, maybe the Child's terror was using you.' Bugayev slung the submachine gun from his shoulder. 'I'll give you an extra second or two to think that over.'

'What? said Vasily.

Bugayev picked the man up and threw him off the

cliff.

Announcing his approach so as not to get his head blown off, Alistair jogged up behind Bugayev. 'Are you all done here? Did you find Anne?'

'She is safe.' Bugayev nodded; but gestured at the desert below. 'But we're not all done.'

Alistair moved close to the edge. 'Damn and blast.'

Down in the makeshift vehicle park, three fugitives were boarding the Winnebago. The last one chucked a sports bag aboard and turned her head for a farewell glance at the mesa.

Intended for him? He couldn't say.

But even at this range her firebrand-red hair was unmistakable.

CHAPTER TWENTY-ONE

Heroes

JULY 1981. NEW MEXICO.

'Express elevator,' said Bugayev. 'Come on.' He led a full-pelt dash through the pueblo. Alistair's mind raced, but he was obliged to direct most of his energies into keeping up. He only cottoned on when they made a sharp turn —

Straight at the A-frame jutting from the cliff-edge.

Bugayev hurled himself at the rope. Grabbed. Swinging outward, he dropped from sight.

'I'm too old for this,' muttered Alistair.

That goes double for me. A thought from the back of his mind.

But then he enjoyed the rush of adrenalin through his younger body as he ran and threw himself off the cliff, regardless.

Taking it slow and telling her bruises to quit complaining, Anne negotiated her way through the tunnels. The shotgun was four more kilos than she felt like carrying, but she kept it. Just in case.

When her torch beam found Valentina in the petroglyph chamber, she was glad to have it. But before she brought the gun to bear, she realised it was redundant.

Anne crept close.

The Russian woman was a gory mess, propped by the entrance. She cradled fragments of alien carapace in blood-caked hands. Anne stepped over the body, noticing other components of the major's booby trap: wire and chunks of sensor equipment. It had found another application after all this time.

'Virgin... Mother.'

Anne yelped and backed up from the corpse. Valentina opened her eyes to a feeble squint. Did she want confession? Absolution?

'Child.' Her voice was a choked rasp. 'You and... Señora. Mothers. Gave birth to... feelings of division. And separation. Torment... of a... dismembered... Child. Worst... kind of... terrorists.'

Empathy and imagination conspired against her, replaying what she'd done... through the eyes of the Child.

'We didn't know,' she protested.

But her accuser was dead, and Anne's defence was a hollow echo.

Florence called to the land. The Child cried out to its parents. To bones that circled the world. Scattered scenes bled together: a New York precinct evidence locker, a Denver stadium, a Colorado Springs arcade, Los Angeles, OKC, Paris, Milan, Madrid, Rome. A world of worlds. Energy burned along threads between them.

Boom! The bang was too soon, too close – and came with a screech of tyres. Florence slammed into a cabinet as the Winnebago was thrown into a violent swerve.

Romola, sprawled on the vehicle floor, held the Adidas bag in place. 'What was that? Drive straight, for crying out loud!'

'Ain't me!' Bonnie hollered back from the driver's seat.

Florence staggered to her feet.

The yellow Camaro with the black stripes was coming up to sting them again.

Alistair accelerated, stealing up on the outside. He jerked the Camaro left and bumped the Winnebago's rear wheel. The RV side-slipped, but recovered. Alistair drafted in the big vehicle's slipstream. Bugayev sat ready with the submachine gun.

An oncoming car shot past. There was nothing following; and at those speeds they would see nothing behind for a while. That stretch of desert highway was pretty much their private arena for now.

Bugayev waved left. 'Move!'

The Winnebago's rear window blew out. The Native American woman stood in the frame, pointing a smoking shotgun.

Going with his football-pitch comparison, Barney equated *Forrestal*'s bridge with a VIP box – minus the luxury fixtures – with a tremendous grandstand view. Forward of the ever-busy flight-deck, escorts were visible, drawing choppy white lines across an impressive expanse of the Gulf of Sidra. There was *Broadsword*, out on right field, but very much onside.

Birchdale perched on his raised chair, overseeing everything. Commander Perry was on the phone to the CIC. 'Multiple bandits. Six *Étendards*. Twelve Fitters in the following group. Bearing ten degrees, one-one-zero miles. Low and fast.'

'Clear CAP to engage. Scramble more Phantoms. I want clear skies for those airstrikes.'

Perry relayed the commands.

Barney visualised the enemy aircraft racing low above the sea, spearing straight at the fleet's defence screen. Unbidden, his imagination flashed forward: missiles streaking inward, striking the flight-deck. Explosions.

Men and aircraft engulfed in an inferno.

'Everything all right, Hackett?'

'Sir. Yes, sir.'

Barney resisted a shake of the head, even though he needed one. Heat crept up his neck.

Alistair swung the car left and nudged the brake. The shotgun blast perforated the bonnet. The engine growled back with a lot of angry horsepower as Alistair stepped on the accelerator and played catch-up again.

Bugayev opened up through the windshield, strafing the Winnebago's rear. The RV's tail-gunner ducked. Wind rushed in and slapped Alistair's face. The woman popped up. Bugayev hit her with a controlled burst. She reeled, squeezed off a wild shot, then toppled inside.

Bugayev ditched the H&K and pulled his pistol. 'Get us closer.' He gestured at the ladder fixed to the Winnebago's stern.

'Are you mad?' said Alistair.

But he upped the speed and aligned the Camaro for a docking manoeuvre.

A marine sergeant entered. Saluted. He directed a glance at Barney.

'Anything?' Birchdale asked.

'Nothing out of the ordinary, sir.'

Surely the marine was one of the pair from outside his cabin. So, they had conducted a search. Barney's hand shot to his pocket.

'No bones?'

'No, sir.'

'Bones? Why would—?' Barney shut himself up. He closed his hand around the lighter in his pocket. It didn't fit as snugly as usual. It felt… odd.

'And if she gave you some token in return, it could be dangerous.'

He fished it out. Familiar silver, initialled. His vision flickered like a guttering flame. Silver melted into gaudy purple: a Playboy cover-girl design, in a chrome border.

He bolted from the bridge, chased by incendiary visions.

Bugayev made the leap. Alistair held the car steady long enough to see him safely clinging to the ladder. Glad not to have his Russian as a hood ornament or roadkill, Alistair nipped left and applied the accelerator.

Bugayev climbed a couple of rungs. He fired blind into the Winnebago. Then leaned in for a quick scout through the window.

The redhead poked out from cover and let loose with a pistol.

Bonnie looked at the punctured windshield. Hands glued to the wheel, she stole a glance over her shoulder. Romola was tucked inside the john, shooting it out with somebody back where Florence La Beau rested in not a hell of a lot of peace.

Bonnie caught a ghost of a face at the busted rear window and that was all she needed. The Russian pounced at her out of that damn vision. Panic pumped her heart fit to burst.

Yellow and black flashed in her wing-mirror. The Camaro raced up on the inside. She slammed the RV sideways, trying to ram that sucker off the road.

Alistair accelerated, trying to zip out in front. The Winnebago fetched the Camaro's tail a nasty thump and sent him spinning to a standstill.

The RV ploughed past and up the embankment.

He craned around for a view. In time to watch the Winnebago tumble back down the slope and crash onto its flank. But he'd missed what happened to Bugayev.

Barney ran through a blur of grey bulkheads and stairwells. He barged past uniforms, ignoring shouts that pursued him. He broke out into salty winds and the roar of engines.

A Phantom jet rocketed by, a black devil mocking him from the tailfin.

He dodged past a flight crew wheeling bomb-laden trolleys under the wings of a Corsair. A sun-bright arrowhead blazed on its tailfin. The men gestured and yelled. Barney's mind flashed again: on fighter jets, on missiles. On an inferno raging across the carrier, consuming the entire flight-deck.

Alistair hopped out of the car and searched. Bugayev was on his feet, ten metres back along the embankment and limping his way. A dragging sound turned his attention to the Winnebago.

Romola hauled herself out of the rear. A battered and bedraggled figure, she had amassed quite the collection of grazes. She tugged a red Adidas bag out of the vehicle and staggered clear of the wreck.

Alistair drew his sidearm and went over for a chat.

Nothing broken, Bugayev assessed, working through the pain. He had rolled with the landing, but the rough ground and his knee hadn't hit it off too well when they met. Alistair was moving to intercept one fugitive, so he figured he'd check on the other.

Rounding the front of the Winnebago, he looked in through a shattered windshield. The cracks spider-webbed over the portrait of a dead black woman. Face bashed in, neck probably broken.

Nothing more to be done here.

Alistair had his gun on the other woman. She had

dropped a red bag at her feet. Her hands were down at her side and the desert heat was nothing to the hate in her gaze. Not exactly a surrender then.

He walked over to join the tête-à-tête. Stopping by the car en route.

Alistair's aim didn't waver. He looked Romola in the eye, along the barrel of his pistol. 'Give me a reason,' he said.

'Now why should I do that?'

'A reason not to,' he clarified.

'Want me to do it?' offered Bugayev. Generous to a fault.

'She has answers to provide.'

'Now why should I give you that?' she said, mimicking her earlier answer.

'Well, I suppose you have a right to remain silent,' Alistair reasoned. 'However, the slightest ripple in reality, the tiniest thing out of place and I will fire. There's a good chance I'll hit you before you've had time to move.'

Bugayev crouched beside the red bag. He unzipped it for a brisk inspection. Then zipped it up three-quarters of the way. 'This is your precious Child, yes?'

He produced two thermite grenades. Pulled the pins. Dropped the lot into the bag. Then stood and flung the bag in the direction of the Winnebago.

Before it landed, the bag was consumed in a ferocious furnace.

Romola's hands tensed into claws and she looked set to pounce on Bugayev and tear him to shreds. Instead, she clutched at her head and dropped onto her knees. She looked to be pushing pain back inside her skull.

Her agonies subsided into shakes.

'You haven't won,' she said. 'I'll still get the cherry on the cake.'

'What are you talking about?' Alistair asked.

She aimed a smile up at him. It was one of the most

frightening things he had ever seen. 'Look at your face. I can scare you with a few words. Cherries and cakes.'

'I've no idea what she's talking about,' said Bugayev, 'but she's making a convincing case for you to kill her.'

'No. I don't think so. No, I think she's playing for time.' Alistair flashed back to *The Old Fusilier*. The lighter. 'What did you do to Freddie's lad? You slipped some sort of focusing object to him, didn't you?'

She made her face a blank page. 'Did I?'

'That's as good as a confession.'

'I don't need trinkets.' The hate returned with a vengeance. 'I left the lighter for dear old Duffer. And as for the Navy boy, you only need to sow a seed. Plant an idea. And that arms the device.'

'What device?'

Romola sealed her lips.

The only place ideas were planted, thought Alistair, was people's minds.

Barney!

Barney ran to the port edge. Vertigo threatened to pull him into the drink. Marines and other crewmen invaded his peripheral vision. Fires leaped up in their path. Barney thrust out a hand as a stop sign.

'Wait! Stay back! Keep back!'

The lighter in his other hand flickered: silver to purple, elegant initials to cover-girl. Heat washed over him, battling the breeze sweeping over the flight deck. He hurled the lighter as far as he could. Out over the waves.

A marine fell to the deck and rolled, screaming as he burned alive.

'Terror is contagious,' said Romola. 'Especially when five thousand men have the same idea planted in the back of their heads.'

Five thousand men, Alistair thought.

Was that reason enough? Would it make any difference? There he stood, watching for the faintest shift in reality – and this woman could be affecting things halfway around the world.

'You can't do it, Brigadier,' she said.

No. You can't, said a voice at the back of his mind. *This isn't like burying a lot of lizard people in their caves.*

'Want me to do it?'

Bugayev... Had he repeated his offer, or was Alistair merely remembering? Damned heat was getting to him. Delirium. He held the gun rock steady and fired.

Romola hit the ground. The shot seemed to ring out from an impossible distance away.

Barney collapsed to his knees.

The flames died. The marine lay still. Flight crew and other marines crowded around. A couple helped him to stand. He was okay. Unscathed and un-charred. Just shaky on his legs.

Everybody looked at Barney, but he was shaky even down on his knees.

'Hey, man. You did it!' cheered somebody. 'I don't know what you did, but you sure as hell did it!'

Commander Perry forged his way through the wall of crewmen. 'Well done, Lieutenant Commander. Let's get you to sick bay. Everybody else, break it up and back to work. We have airstrikes to launch.'

TRIPOLI.

The bomb ripped through the market.

Hassan Maghur staggered in a sea of screams. The explosion rumbled on in his ears, but he heard American jets sawing across the skies. He was caught in a cross-current: people fleeing the blast, blinded by dust and blood and tears, arms outstretched to him or to heaven;

and others pushing their way towards that hell.

He joined the latter tide. Running, fumbling, pleading and shoving.

Searching for a face. *Nesreen!*

Hope and prayer clashed with a growing dread in his heart. With every second, every step, love gave way to crushing uncertainty.

And terror.

Freddie hit the intercom. 'Get me Lethbridge-Stewart would you, Janet?'

Funny, how he'd sworn at her when she'd buzzed the other day. Relaying a message from his wife; don't forget dinner at the Pembertons, Sunday. A trivial interruption at the worst time. Which turned out to be entirely the right time. She had his eternal gratitude, which she would take to be his clumsy attempt to make up for his brashness.

Today the picture on his desk filled him with pride, and an inability to quite look his photographic family in the eyes. Odd sort of mix.

But that would change. They would send David and Emma their apologies for Sunday, and all go out for a big slap-up meal. Together. Everything would be different from now on.

The intercom buzzed.

'Brigadier Lethbridge-Stewart for you, sir.'

'Thank you, Janet,' said Freddie sweetly.

GENEVA.
Alistair set his newspaper on his lap and accepted the phone. He was sitting comfortably in the bar of the *Hôtel des Rois,* the rather fine hotel the UN had put him up in, when the phone had been brought over. He'd considered refusing the call. But any claims he was busy might have fooled Duffer, but would've sounded hollow to him.

'Alistair, old boy, I, ah, wanted to thank you. My lad's coming home. Had a rough time of it by all accounts, but the Yanks looked after him. They're saying he's a hero. Imagine. My Barney.'

'Always knew the boy had it in him, Freddie,' said Alistair. 'Chip off the old block, eh?'

Freddie laughed. Or coughed. Or both. 'Don't know about that, old boy. But anyway; all's well that ends well. And... and I owe you an apology. An explanation, at any rate.'

'Never mind all that.'

'Well, I owe you the lowdown on that school post. Let me do that, at least.'

'We'll set that up,' Alistair agreed. 'Thank you, Freddie.'

All's well that ends well.

With the psychic terrorists out of the picture, they were left to deceive themselves. The news, for one, was weaving its own brand of illusion: TERROR CAMPS DESTROYED. Embedded in the multiple pages of coverage, a couple of paragraphs acknowledged Libyan protests that there were no terror camps and claims of civilian casualties from American bombs striking a market place.

There was no other way.

Alistair replayed the same argument he'd had with himself for thirty years. The argument he had lost over and over again, until he had decided that the only way to win was not to listen.

Of course there were other ways. Other ways might've led to other outcomes. You made judgement calls, based on available intelligence. *'There's your own sense of right and wrong and what you can live with.'* And you only get one go. Barney was – will be? – there in 2011 to salute him. For what?

Revenge? No, not that. Her getting under his skin?

Perhaps. Preventing a terror attack? Surely that. Murder? That was not his intent, but as Bugayev might point out, it would look like that to bystanders. And if he had let Bugayev do the honours, that might've been as bad as pulling the trigger himself. Perhaps worse. There were a hundred reasons to shoot, and a hundred reasons to refrain.

Alistair!

He might never be a hundred percent certain of his reasons. But he had lived with his choice. Twice now.

Alistair!

And at least, this time, he could forgive himself.

Alistair!

He looked up. A familiar female voice calling and, finally, with a smile, Sir Alistair felt himself being pulled away from 1981...

EPILOGUE

NOVEMBER 2011.

Alistair! Alistair!

'Alistair!'

Hands grasped his shoulders. Then a soft palm pressed against his cheek, lifted his head.

'Alistair! Oh god, please–'

Alistair blinked. 'Mmm?'

He awoke to Fiona's terrified gaze. 'Oh, thank God. Alistair, you scared me half to... Are you all right? What happened?'

'What happened? I must've nodded off is what happened.' Alistair feigned a laugh, but was conscious of Fiona's ability to see through such deceptions. Breezes rustled the branches of the sycamores. The sun didn't appear any lower in the sky than before. Alistair pretended to rearrange the blanket over his knees. A stone weight rolled in his lap. The gnome rested there. At least its laughter was silenced. 'How long was I out?'

'I've no idea. I was off looking for –' She gestured at the stone figure. 'Looking for more things like that. Remember?'

'Of course I remember.'

'But I came back and you were –'

Alistair laid a reassuring hand on Fiona's arm. 'Asleep. That's all.'

'Well, clearly. I can see that now. But you were out, so... cold.' She had a go at playing the stern school teacher. 'I was about to slap you.'

'Really now? All this fuss about forty winks.' Alistair straightened in his chair. Still, he smiled at the picture of her slapping him awake. He was grateful for the humour. Something genuine to mask troubled thoughts. The gnome pulled at his attention even now, as though possessed of its own gravity.

'Forty? We'll never know how many.' Fiona manoeuvred around behind the chair and started pushing. 'We should get you to the home.'

'No argument from me there. It's getting chillier.'

'Brr. Yes, it is.'

Alistair's gaze fell to the gnome. It lay face-down in the blanket. He was glad not to have it leering back at him. Laughing. 'What are we going to do about this thing?'

'We can leave it on the church porch. Or here at the side of the path. Someone will find it. They'll put it back wherever it came from.'

'Hmm. I'd —' Alistair could scarcely believe the words rolling around on his tongue. 'I'd quite like to take it home.'

'What? Why on earth would you?'

'I don't know. Memento of today.' Alistair shrugged. He was glad Fiona couldn't see his face. 'I don't know.'

Hahahahaha!

The laughter was only a faint echo from earlier.

'I spotted the verger. Round by the entrance. I was going to ask her.'

Fiona sighed. 'Well, all right. I'll go find her. But if she says it belongs here, then here it stays.'

Fiona parked Alistair by the church porch and snatched up the gnome. She pulled the door, calling a tentative, 'Hallo?' The door swung open on a squeaking hinge. 'Oh, hello there,' said Fiona. And she marched in to accost whoever she had greeted.

Alistair nudged himself a foot or so further, for a better view. There in the aisle, Fiona and the verger conferred in low voices, shadowed by the church interior. Fiona presented the gnome, the verger looked it over, Fiona pointed roughly in the direction of where they had found it, the verger threw a glance through the doorway. Then threw him another look, one that lingered for all of a second. Before the woman returned her full attention to Fiona and, finally, shook her head.

Fiona said her farewells and thank-yous. She made her way back with the gnome in hand, her expression less than elated. She set the ugly figure back down on Alistair's lap. He steered his eyes clear of it. For now.

'So, we get to keep it?'

'It's not any part of the church or the gravestones. She seemed very sure. So, yes. I'm afraid *you* get to keep it.'

Alistair had known somehow. As they passed down the path, he tried to turn to offer the verger a grateful wave, but there was no seeing past Fiona.

He took another look at his 'prize'. And mulled over everything he had relived in the past. Maybe it wasn't a question of what he made of it. But what it made of him.

Home. *The* home, anyway.

All the comforts. Bed, armchair, desk, wash basin. Four walls, pale beige wallpaper patterned with a selection of intricate botanical studies, complete with the Latin names next to each plant. Even if he had never developed an interest in gardening during his retirement, he felt confident he could identify *hepatica nobilis* and *fragariavesca* if pushed.

Fiona wheeled Alistair into position in front of his desk. She fished the gnome from his lap. 'So… Where do you want this?'

'Bedside table?' Alistair suggested.

Fiona made a face. 'Nonsense. Windowsill, I should think.' She set it approximately in the middle, then made a show of turning it around. 'Facing out. That way it has a lovely view of the garden and I don't have to look at it when I visit. Everybody wins.'

Alistair nodded. He could always reposition it later.

Fiona checked her watch. 'Now, are we sure you still want to see Dame Anne and Brigadier Bishop this afternoon?'

'Of course I want to see them.'

'I know that. Naturally you want to see them. I'm just worried whether you should be trying to do too much in one day. Doris will be by tomorrow and she won't thank me for tiring you out.'

'Tiring me out? We'll only be chatting over a cup of tea. Hardly running a marathon. Besides, they'll be here any minute. I'm not having them show up just to be sent packing.'

Fiona sighed. 'Very well. I'll go have a word with catering, see about arranging that tea. And maybe fetch the doctor.'

'What?'

'Doctor Sombroek. Have her come round and give you a check-up. There can't be any harm in that.' Fiona ducked out before Alistair could argue.

She left him alone with the gnome.

A knock at the door announced Alistair's guests. He half-shut the laptop, putting the Googled images of vintage garden gnomes to rest. He had barely begun.

'Come in!'

Brigadier William Bishop and his wife breezed in, bringing warm smiles and a flood of memories. Bill shucked his coat and helped Anne off with hers. Good old Bill would keep chivalry alive well into the twenty-first century. While Bill laid the coats on the bed, Anne

252

leaned in and gave Alistair a peck on the cheek.

'Are you all right? Fiona was out there at the front desk. On the phone to the doctor, she said.'

'A lot of fuss over nothing. I fell asleep at the church.'

'You nodded off at the funeral?' Bill feigned horror.

'Not actually at the funeral, no. Afterwards.'

Bill stationed himself in front of Alistair. They exchanged smiles, enjoying the familiar routine. 'On three then?'

'One. Two. Three.'

They raced to be first to salute each other. It was a close-run thing, but Alistair was sure Bill pipped him at the post. By a whisker.

Anne shook her head. 'Now you two old soldiers are done playing, are you sure you're all right, Alistair? Fiona was very worried about you.'

'Naturally. She's very good at it.'

'Alistair...' When it came to it, Anne could give Fiona a run for her money when adopting school teacher mode. It was a role she had a gift for, even as a young scientific consultant.

'Well, I mean...' Alistair began. 'It was probably nothing. In any case, we're all too old for mysteries.'

'Mysteries?' Bill's ears perked up. 'What's that? Do we have another case?' He searched about like an eager detective.

Alistair gestured to the gnome on the windowsill. 'Only that. There's something... odd about it. Hardly warrants a full-scale investigation, but... well, no need to beat about the bush with you two. I think it had something to do with my "falling asleep".'

'A garden gnome? How?' Anne made a face like she'd tasted week-old custard. She picked it up and examined it. 'Well, it stands a decent chance of frightening the birds. Probably keep cats out of your flower beds too.' She handed it to Bill.

'I can see how it could give you nightmares,' he said. 'Not sure how it could send a chap to sleep.'

'That's the thing. There's something strange about it.'

Anne gave him a guarded look. 'Strange? Well, it's a good job we're all done with strange.' She glanced to the desk. Eyed the laptop with the screen not quite closed. 'Fiona won't thank you for poking into more mysteries.'

'I know that much. Still, there's something... to do with the past. I'm sure it sent me back to–'

Hahahahahahahaha...

Alistair sat up. 'There! There it is again.'

'There's what?' Bill cast glances in ten different directions.

'Didn't you hear that?'

'Hear what?' Anne shrugged. That answered that question. Bill's expression was a similar blank. But their blank looks folded steadily into concern.

Alistair sighed. 'Fiona didn't hear it either.'

HahahahahahaHaHaHaHaHaHAHAHAHAHA!

Alistair stared at the gnome. Looking slightly unnerved, Bill moved to set the figure back in its place at the window. Alistair followed the motion, fixed on the gnome. Time slowed. Bill's hands turned the figure, facing it inward; whether inadvertently or because the gnome wanted to stare at the room. At them. Laughter echoed from the gnome's gaping mouth. Growing louder.

HAHAHAHAHAHAHAHAHAHAHAHAHAHAHAHA!

The shadows at the back of its cavernous throat tugged at his vision. Drawing Alistair in between the stone teeth. This time, he felt Anne and Bill being pulled in with him...

Into the black.

*To be continued... in **Fear of the Web***

254